THE
GOLDEN
DRAGON'S
Surrogate

T.R DURANT

_____

Editors: Kemely Parfrey, Zita Louw,
Renae Ballantyne, Matthew Spades
Cover Design: Getcovers
Formatting: Ctrl Alt Publish

_____

WARNING
This book contains sexually explicit scenes, violence, light kink
and adult language that may be offensive to some readers. It is
intended for adults 18 and over.

To all daydreamers and those brave enough to chase, chant, and write dreams.

GLOSSARY

* Indicating

Agapiti (Ancient Greek): Dear, beloved.
Masc Iomlán (Irish): Absolute Mask
Fanny (Irish slang): for vagina
Langer (Irish slang): Penis
Agapiti mou Eos (Greek): My dear, my beloved
Eos

CHAPTER 1

Alev

My dragon, Horus, roared in protest within me. Horus was sick of these nights roaming clubs and parties. Yet, I needed the diversion; I needed interesting conversations and to get lost in the arms of a beautiful and smart woman, otherwise, I would lose my mind.

I caught her dark brown gaze, and she beamed. Instead of pouting or looking away like every other woman in the club, she gave me a genuine smile. That was what I was looking for, something genuine, even if only for one night. I was sick of lies and games, except for the exciting game of a good hunt. Thinking about my past only brought me pain and sorrow, and so did any thoughts of my future. I had already given up on love, yet having a family, and a child, was something I could never give up on.

My gaze shifted back to the sweet eyes of the brunette, and she smiled again as if she had nothing to hide. Good, she was indeed the kind of girl I liked. I closed the distance between us with firm and slow steps, without breaking eye contact.

After introductions and a little chat, I bought her a drink and got straight to the point.

"Pri, I'll be honest. You are a fascinating woman, but all I am after is a night of passion. A night to remember," I told her, tucking a lock of her smooth hair behind her ear.

The last thing I was looking for was a relationship. All I needed was for this passion to burn for one night. I wouldn't cheat, lie, and leave. I wouldn't be sneaky like my ex, Niki, had been with me. My head shook at the thought. Loneliness came over me as the corners of my soul became jagged and tainted, but I was above games and tricks. No one deserved to have their hopes crushed.

"Alev, I've never had a one-night stand, but I am new to this city and I want an adventurous life. So, I will give it a try," she replied with a shy smile, sipping her margarita. My lips twitched at her sweet accent.

"Are you sure? You can always change your mind, but I want you both sure and willing for when I set all your senses on fire." Her body trembled slightly at my husky voice.

"I am sure," she murmured in my ear. My heightened shifter senses went to a sweet alert as the tangy scent of her arousal perfumed the air. My hand wrapped around hers as I took her already empty glass and put it on the table; I brought her body closer to mine and sealed her lips with a kiss. My fingers traced her back, down to the generous curve of her ass, and I cupped it. I was a hungry beast, insatiable, and Pri was a great feast.

As we parted, she panted for air. Yet without stopping to catch her breath, she took a step further, aiming for the dance floor. A grin formed on my lips. Taking her hand in mine, I led the way. My hands reached her waist, and I squeezed her petite frame against mine as we moved to the rhythm of typical Latin music, reggaeton.

I'd already won my little prey. After dancing, talking, and exchanging kisses and caresses, I took Pri to my hotel room.

We strolled down the hotel hall with her hand in mine until she stopped in her tracks, smiling. Holding on to my arm, she lifted a dainty foot and in one swift movement; she took off her high heel, and then she did the same to the other. It only made her look remarkably more petite. A grin formed on my lips. Pri was tempting me! I was more than ready to devour her.

"This way will be much faster!" She chuckled, her voice filled with eagerness.

After dancing all night, she was still filled with something that resembled supernatural stamina. Her liveliness and the solar energy in her smile were what attracted me. She was the opposite of me lately, as I felt only half alive.

"We don't have to wait a minute longer," I said, lifting her by her waist and caging her against the wall as our lips crashed in a passionate kiss. Her legs wrapped around me, and she rubbed herself against my hard-on, moans filling our kiss. Her shoes fell from her hands and she got lost in the moment, as did I.

To lose my mind in that moment was all I needed, all I craved. No thoughts, no emotions, only sinking into the sweet and fleeting oblivion that pleasure could bring. Mindless passion, skin against skin. My arms tightened around her as I reached down and grabbed her shoes, taking her down the long hall, never breaking the kiss.

Soon, we found the room, and I opened the door without letting her go. Urgency flared in my blood. My dragon and I needed this brief reprieve, or else we would burn, and the world would turn grey and empty.

Gently, I lay her on the bed, my body hovering over hers. My lips caressed her jawline and neck as my frantic hands freed her from her tight dress. She was a pretty human, with tanned skin and voluptuous curves. As I feasted on each curve, I got rid of my clothes. Soon we were naked and entangled in each other.

My palms played with her breasts until her buds were impossibly tight and swollen; she threw her head back and let out a groan, aching delight clear in her expression.

She wrapped her hand around my shaft, a mischievous smile on her face.

"That's quite a — I wonder how it will fit. I am willing to try, even if you wreck me," she laughed. She didn't want to wait.

"I won't wreck you. I will get you ready, and wet enough to take every inch of me, Pri. We have time and should savour everything. I just need to have you drenched with desire before I enter you," I whispered in her ear, and she shivered, her back arching.

A wicked smile formed on my face. I wouldn't just have sex with her, but steer her towards ecstasy. I would give her all the attention and caresses a woman deserves. I would take my time awakening and overwhelming all of her senses, submerging her in thick, hot pleasure before seeking my own satisfaction. It was only for a night, so I would make it a night that she would remember forever.

"You remember my name," she moaned, her eyes filled with surprise and delight. Of course, I did. Even for a one-night stand, I would call my partner by her name as she screamed mine. It was only proper and chivalrous.

"Alev!" she cried as my face dove between her thighs, and I kissed her slowly, teasing her folds, giving her body only an ounce of the pleasure I intended. Circling her entrance, I sucked her nub of pleasure faster, and she tangled her fingers in my dark hair, pushing my head down, yearning for more.

My tongue worked her up, thrusting into her until her inner walls clenched and her whole body trembled. She sang my name in the language of moans, coming undone in my mouth. Kissing her mound, I crawled upwards, sinking my tongue into her parted lips and letting her try her most intimate flavour.

4

"That's how good you taste, beautiful," I murmured. Every woman deserved to be worshipped, even if only for a night.

"I need…" she squirmed. I didn't give her time to calm down; her pleasure shouldn't stop but rather grow in an endless crescendo until her consciousness drifted off, and she was completely sated.

Pulling her legs over my shoulders, I entered her inch by inch. She gasped at the stretching. It was a tight fit, but I would be gentle and give her all the time she needed to adjust.

As soon as I felt her relax, I started thrusting, angling my hips to touch all her sensitive spots and drive her crazy. Her warm brown eyes drew me in, and she bit her lip as her nails scratched burning trails down my back. For a split second, the thought of my ex, Niki, surged in my mind; she used to do that, too. I looked back at her pretty eyes, reminding my body and my torturous mind that it wasn't Niki but Pri. I wouldn't think of another woman as I slid my shaft in and out of her. No one deserved that.

Adjusting her legs, I thrust deeper, faster, wildly while Pri screamed.

"Yes, Alev! Yes!"

"I can give you more, Pri. Tonight I can give you whatever you want," I groaned, and she rocked her hips against mine, taking all I gave her. Soon, my dragon, Horus, flared to the surface, wanting more, wanting it all, enough to forget Niki's face and all the emptiness she left behind.

"Faster?" I asked her. Pri was only human and, regardless of Horus's feral desire, I wouldn't do anything to hurt her.

"Yes… Alev, I am coming. I am…" she cried out as her sex clenched around my length, taking me to the brink of my climax. Except I refused to finish before she climaxed at least twice. I wasn't a young dragon, and I would control myself even in my semi-feral and desperate state. I would reign over myself, her body, and her desire, and drown her with pleasure.

After she climaxed, I tugged her gently to the edge of the bed and stood up, entering her again immediately. Her body was still spasming with the aftershock, but I wanted to take her to the apex once again before losing myself in the peak of pleasure and diversion. Flicking the sensitive spot within her folds and sliding faster in and out of her, I coaxed her to come around my length in no time. This time, I let her take me with her to the heights of ecstasy, spurting deep within her.

After another round, I gave her some water and a soothing back rub, then wrapped her spent body in my arms. She told me her name, Pri, means earth; blossoming, gentle, nurturing. As her name indicated, she was a generous lover. My fingers ran over her velvety soft skin and I inhaled her unique smell. She had a powdery scent to her, a gentle mix of cinnamon and sandalwood. Her long black hair was now drenched, glued to her back, as her lips curled up into a relaxed smile.

She was a special woman, bold, brave and filled with life. Pri told me her story. I didn't sleep with any woman before knowing something about them, something that made them special and unique. I wasn't a young dragon to choose a woman based only on her looks. Instead, I needed something fascinating, the light of a smile, a beautiful story, a gaze filled with peace. Pri had travelled from faraway lands for a job and made a life in this city.

She fell asleep immediately, a satisfied expression on her face. I, on the other hand, fought against unwelcome thoughts. Since my ex, the woman I had chosen to be my mate, left me for a werewolf suddenly, my mind had been in chaos. A void had taken root in my soul and it was growing. It didn't matter what I did, I couldn't fill it; I couldn't find peace. Every Golden Dragon of my clan had found and claimed their mates and was enjoying the utmost happiness and joy with their new families and even welcoming kids. I was the only lost one, the only lonely Golden Dragon, but that would change very soon.

After a few hours, I finally fell asleep and into the recurring haunting dream of a woman with ebony hair and an ancient white tunic.

Her long, soft, and dark hair floated in the breeze. The sunlight filtered through the locks, giving them a magical glow. I looked at her, frozen, hypnotised. Then, without minding my ogling, she took a step towards me. The more she walked, the more distant she felt.

This time wasn't any different from the previous nights; I still couldn't see her face. However, the haunting and dreadful sensation that I had lost her was as clear as day and woke me with a racing pulse and a clenching chest.

Once again, I woke up with a start, the pain and loss flowing through my blood like wicked ice. I was a dragon-shifter, my blood wasn't supposed to feel cold, ever. However, that dream, that woman, liked to challenge logic.

Pri was resting in my arms. She stirred and spun around slowly, her half-open eyes meeting mine.

"Good morning, Alev… I thought you would have sneaked out and left me." The glowing and sated smile lit her face.

"Never. I still need my breakfast." I flashed her a half-smirk and her brows wrinkled in confusion.

"Are you leaving already?" she pouted a little.

"Not yet." I smiled, my brows arching with mischief as I brushed my lips on hers and then kissed my way down to her core. After making her climax twice more, I bid her goodbye.

As I walked down the hotel hall, my phone rang. A flutter of peace washed over me for the first time in weeks as I saw the caller, the Overnatural Surrogate Centre. I answered the call, praying to the Great Golden Fire that the Centre had finally found *her* and that she had said yes.

7

CHAPTER 2
Alev

Filled with excitement and anxiety, I greeted the warlock.

"Miss Rose, it's good to hear from you."

"Mr Alev Aureus, I have good news. We contacted the witch you chose, and she has agreed to become your surrogate. Since she wasn't in our system, we have to complete a background check and run some tests to see if she is fit to join our program. As you know, quality, discretion and trust are our top priorities. Assuming she passed the first round of tests, she will head to the Lisbon headquarters for her first interview with me," I could hardly hear what Miss Rose said after she told me that the woman I had chosen said yes — it was very unlikely, as Miss Rose had made clear many times over. My smile only grew; the euphoria spreading through my body was more substantial than the pleasure I had experienced the night before. Damn, it was stronger than anything! She said yes!

"Are you listening to me, Mr Aureus? Her first interview will take place in Lisbon. I will see to it myself," she said patiently.

I knew she didn't do this for all her clients; the fact that I was a Golden Dragon made my case exceptional. The warlocks and Golden Dragons had a good relationship, and my case was indeed special. There were only nine Golden Dragons in existence and a new child meant hope, not only for my shattered soul but also for my kind.

"When is this interview, Miss Rose? I will join you for it." I could skip a day or more of work. The other dragons would take care of our new cryptocurrency company. Nothing but my future child mattered.

"I am afraid according to our protocol, the client doesn't join the clearance interviews since the service provider hasn't been approved by the centre yet," Miss Rose explained.

"I am aware of that, but I want to speed up the process. *She* is the one I want." My voice carried determination.

A single look at her photo was enough to hear the call from a primal part of my soul, and I didn't know if it was instinct or part of the magic embedded in my DNA. However, I was sure that she was supposed to be the one carrying my child.

"I... I will review the result of her tests, which include fertility, general health and a final compatibility test. Then, if everything goes well, the interview should take place tomorrow. This is rather unconventional, but if you are certain, you can meet her after the interview." My smile widened at Rose's words. I could only hope to bring the witch to my clan's mansion very soon and start the sweet work of bringing my child into the world and creating a family.

Finding a surrogate wasn't an easy task, only a few females could conceive and carry a Golden Dragon's child. They were either Golden Dragon shifters like me, their fated mates, or a very special and rare kind of witch.

Among the witches with summoning powers, some could call the spirit of an animal. Only a few dozen of those witches could summon the spirit of a Golden Dragon. Because of this ability, these were the only kind of witches magically compatible with us.

There were precisely thirty-four Golden Dragon Spirit Summoner witches, twenty unmated and of appropriate age, but only one was her. As I opened the email app, my eyes scanned the twenty profiles Miss Rose had sent me and, once again, my eyes found her photo. She was beautiful, but that wasn't what attracted me to her like a magnet. I couldn't understand why, but her unique blue eyes held a hypnotic grasp on me. They were filled with the sweetest melancholy and deep mysteries.

My dragon roared his agreement in my mind, but I could see what was passing through his mind.

"No, Horus, I won't be with her. You know, the only thing we want is for her to bring our child into the world," I told him. That was the reason the Great Golden Fire guided me to her and made her cold gaze a beacon for my eyes; she was the one destined to help save the Golden Dragons breed.

There were some very odd and remarkable things in her file. Besides the fact that she was a witch without a coven, she had two abilities instead of one unlike any other witch. She wasn't only a Golden Dragon Summoner, but also a Water *Elemental.*

Stopping at the hotel reception desk, I paid for the night and made a special request, "Please send some breakfast to Miss Pri."

She had been riding the aftershock of her pleasure and almost dozing off when I left the room, and would indeed need some food to recover her energy. Leaving the hotel, I climbed on my red Harley Davidson and headed to the Clan's mansion where I lived with almost all the remaining Golden Dragons. I couldn't wait any longer and had to tell them all, especially our Duke and Duchess.

Thoughts and concerns popped into my head, but I let go of them. At full throttle, I sped, feeling the wind in my face, and leaning into it.

Entering the living room, my eyes were immediately attracted to the sweet faces of our Duke and Duchess's twins — a boy and a girl. Precious, perfect babies. Little Amaris stretched her tiny arms towards me even before I had time to greet her parents.

"She missed her favourite uncle! I carried you for six months in my womb, and as soon as Alev comes, you swap me for him?" Alma cooed at her baby, laughing as the almost four-month-old gave her mum the most delicious giggle.

"She has great taste!" I teased our Duchess, Alma, and took the tiny Princess in my arms. Her giggles grew in intensity and pitch as she rubbed her drool-covered hands on my face. "Aren't you making a mess, baby girl? But uncle Alev doesn't care, many girls drool over me. You are not the first, but you are surely the cutest and most loved!" I laughed softly as Alma shook her head at my joke.

Rocking Amaris back and forth, I made funny faces for her to laugh, and she couldn't stop, pulling at my hair softly and squirming her tiny body in joy. Being with the dragonlings was amazing and I couldn't even begin to imagine what I would feel when I finally had my own child in my arms. Horus roared his agreement within me — he, too, could hardly wait.

Our leader, Duke Egan, was on the sofa reading something with their baby boy sleeping in a bassinet beside him.

After I played with the little lady, she started yawning adorably.

"It's nap time," Alma told me, stretching her arms out to take Amaris.

"I can lull her to sleep," I assured Alma, and she smiled, nodding. A few minutes after I started rocking Amaris slowly and rhythmically, she was already asleep. With hesitation, I let Alma take Amaris in her arms to lay her in the bassinet. Her sweet, sleepy face filled my heart with peace.

Exhaling sharply, I cut to the chase. Now that the babies were fast asleep, the three of us could talk.

"I have received a call from the surrogacy centre; they found the perfect surrogate for me. I am flying to Lisbon tomorrow to meet her and see to the contract," I told them. Alma's jaw hung, and she took a step towards Egan, who stood immediately, wrapping two comforting arms around his wife.

Their behaviour confused me to no end; it wasn't like I had threatened her, so why were they reacting in such an extreme way?

"What did you say? I am not sure I heard it right: you hired a surrogate to carry *your* baby?" she asked, placing her hands on her head in exasperation, and looking between Egan and me as if she was expecting her husband to say something.

"Are you serious, Alev?" Egan asked. I nodded in response, and Egan's face contorted into a small frown. "Is this because of your breakup with Niki? Some sort of rebound? Alev, please… This is a very serious matter, a very important decision to take in such a rush, on impulse. You are being reckless," he spoke softly, mindful of his sleeping babies.

"A baby can't be a rebound! And you are paying someone to have your baby; that sounds wrong! And I thought that the noisy motorbike was your rebound! Please get something else, things normal people do after a bad break-up, like a weird haircut, a trip somewhere exotic, lots of one-night stands, a pet… just not a baby!" she exclaimed.

A small huff left my nostrils. It wasn't a bad break-up, for the sake of the Great Golden Fire! My chosen mate left me suddenly for another man; it goes much further than any fucking break-up. Besides, that wasn't the reason I contacted the surrogacy agency. It wasn't about Niki, not anymore. It was about me, my family, my clan.

"It's not a rebound, Alma. I only want to have what you and Egan have, what Marion and Adrian are about to have. Keep in mind that we need more babies to save our species," I told her, gazing at her green eyes and trying to make her see reason.

I wasn't only doing this for myself, but also for my clan. She and Egan had a pair of adorable twins that had me wrapped around their tiny little fingers. The other two couples in the house were either newly mated or expecting their first dragonling. *They* had it all while *I* had nothing. All I wanted was a taste of that love, and family, and connection — something that only having my baby in my arms could give me.

"Not like this, not with a stranger and for money. Who is this woman? Have you ever met her?" Alma furrowed a questioning brow at me.

"She is a Dragon Summoner like you, Alma. She doesn't have extensive powers like you and her Spirit Dragon isn't the Great Golden Dragon Spirit, only a regular Golden Dragon, but it's enough for her to be able to conceive and carry my child."

Besides being Egan's soulmate, Alma was a Dragon Summoner witch, and the most powerful one at that. The spirit she could summon was the Great Golden Dragon.

"If you want a child, we can find a way without having to pay someone. Having a family, bringing a baby into this world shouldn't be a matter that involves money," Alma sighed.

"Which other way?" I asked. There was no other way. The only three adult female Golden Dragons in existence were mated, so I had to choose the one to carry my future child among the few Dragon Summoners that existed.

13

They both exchanged a look, and Alma sighed, "You could wait for your mate or date a Dragon Summoner witch, see how things click between you both, fall in love and then make babies," she suggested.

"Alma, there aren't any Golden Dragon females available. I won't ever find my mate. I don't want to date or fall for anyone. I've *been there, done that*, and look where it got me! I know what I want," I told her firmly but not unkindly.

"I hope you know what you're doing, Alev." Egan's voice was filled with apprehension.

"Alev, I don't agree with what you are doing... I think things can go very wrong, and you can hurt yourself even further. I am so sorry about what happened with Niki, I... never mind, you are family, you are clan and a dear friend. I am here for you regardless of what you decide to do," she said, gazing at me with sympathy.

I knew she felt bad for how things had gone down with Niki. After all, she was Alma's best friend. It wasn't Alma's fault, and it shouldn't really matter now. I was over my ex, and I wanted to step forward to take control of my own destiny.

Before dawn, Horus would spread his wings and we would fly to Lisbon to meet my surrogate.

CHAPTER 3
Alev

At the first morning light, I cloaked myself with the rune of invisibility. Horus stretched his gigantic wings and took to the skies. The flight to Lisbon would take a while, and flying that high, soaring swiftly always gave me some clarity.

The rush of adrenaline in my blood and the feeling of challenging the wind with my speed would silence my unsettled thoughts. Strangely, everything disappeared from my mind, except the silhouette of the woman from my dreams. Her dark hair seemed to drift very close, almost in front of me.

It was only a dream. It didn't matter, yet it occupied every inch of my mind. I needed to forget the stupid dream and focus on my reality, which was getting closer with each flap of my golden wings.

Horus roared in contentment, pushing even faster. He and I couldn't wait to meet our surrogate, Nicole. Suddenly, Horus growled, and I could sense the disturbing thought surging through his mind.

"No, Horus! Her name is not similar to Niki's. It has nothing to do with her. Niki is in the past and Nicole will help us with our future!" I told my dragon.

He growled and shook his head, a thin trail of smoke leaving his snorting nostrils. He was judging me in the same fashion a cat would.

"More flying and less grumbling!" I told Horus. He grumbled in response, but flapped his wings faster.

As soon as we crossed the border between North Spain and Portugal, a familiar smell entered Horus' nose and he roared. This tainted stench was long-imprinted in my mind; the bloody and rotten scent of monsters: Scarlet Dragons.

The Scarlet Beasts were close, cloaked with a spell just like Horus, invisible to our eyes, yet their smell was subtle but there. Could they smell Horus as well? We Golden Dragons were much more powerful than the two other breeds, our senses more enhanced and our fire power incomparable. However, I wouldn't take any risks since these nasty beasts had ambushed and killed my people in a treacherous war. They were the reason that my kind was almost extinct.

A roar vibrated through Horus' body at the memory of the slaughter. First, the Scarlet Monsters killed our children and elders, placing the blame on the werewolf packs, which ignited our war against werewolves, while the real and sneakiest enemy was attacking us stealthily and killing us slowly but effectively. Our Dukedom crumbled, and only a few of us survived.

In their attempts to both steal our powers and wipe our breed from the face of the Earth, they never stopped hunting us. Even though we were only a little more than a handful, we were powerful and had been hiding for decades whilst fighting to survive and rebuild our clan, our family.

"They are too close to Marbella," I told Horus. Portugal wasn't far from our mansion in the South of Spain. Fuck, those beasts were too close to our clan, though they

16

couldn't spot me. Were they searching for our hideout? It didn't matter. I had to lose them, make sure that they didn't smell or follow me.

Their scent was getting close as Horus flew away. Damn! They could surely smell us, and they were down for the chase. My blood boiled and a torch of fire built up in Horus's chest.

Turning around, Horus flew back in an attempt to track our potential attackers' location by their smell. There were four of them, and two were dangerously close. I could even feel the warmth radiating from their bodies. Horus inhaled deeply and, opening his mouth, he breathed a bright and powerful burst of flame.

Sharp screeches of pain filled the air, and the wind moved around the large falling creature. One down, three to go. Without giving us a single breath of relief, the other Scarlet Beast spewed his fire in Horus's direction. He dodged abruptly, doing an upward spiral spin in mid-air with a grace no one would expect from such an enormous creature.

Horus held his flames in as he nose-dived, wings folded against his torso. The fire burning in his mouth seeped out through the side of his muzzle, coating his scales like a second skin, and in his rapid attack, he smashed into the Scarlet Dragon like a comet.

His body moved with the speed of a bullet until his fire-covered talons sank into the red back of our enemy, cracking his bones and charging the air with a thunderous thud.

Once Horus made contact with the monster's red back, the cloaking spell started to fade, exposing him to our gaze.

The beast blinked his red eyes. I could almost feel his agony as the air was knocked from him. More than anything, I had to protect my clan, to protect *her* — the one who would carry my future. Without a shadow of doubt, I would kill and die for them.

17

Before the red-coloured beasts could even try to move, my golden flames surrounded him. A crackling sound filled Horus's ears and the stench of burnt scales hit our nostrils. My victim's body, now covered with flames, was completely visible and lifeless. Two more to go, and they were close.

Using our gift, Horus shrank to his mini size; he was as big as a cat. The beasts didn't know about our special ability and certainly weren't expecting that. Taking advantage of their confusion as they searched for Horus, he stoked the flames inside of him and sprayed a huge stream that surrounded both attackers. He was small, but his flames were as big as they always were. Leaving the Scarlet Beasts either dead or seriously injured, we darted away even faster than before.

We had to meet Nicole and take her to the mansion with us immediately. There was no time to lose. If the Scarlet Clan found out about her and that she was to be my surrogate, her life and the lives of all those she cared about would be at risk. I couldn't let that happen. I had to protect her, keep her safe within the magical shield of our mansion. Maybe we would have to move and find another hideout for our clan.

Only one thing was clear: I wouldn't let Nicole out of my sight until she gave birth to my baby and her life wasn't in danger anymore.

Nicole

As I closed my eyes, I leaned into his touch and felt the warmth of his hand on my cold skin. His firm yet gentle touch roamed from my waist to my hips, branding my skin with desire.

"Vasilis." A breathless moan parted my lips, and I threw my head back at the insane pleasure seizing my lower stomach. He spun me around and soon my lips were one with his, melting in a passionate kiss.

"Are you sure about this?" he asked me, his hazel eyes hot, intense, lighting sparks of desire within my soul.

"I couldn't be more sure. Tomorrow doesn't matter; I just want tonight, this moment, you and me here!" It seemed like I couldn't say a word without moaning. Yet I didn't care and it seemed to please Vasilis so much that his lips curled into a mischievous smile. His big and warm hands moved down, cupping my butt and bringing me closer to him.

As thunder rumbled outside, a feeling of dread spread over my body, replacing his warmth and making my flesh tremble. He pulled me closer to him and drew soothing circles around my tense back.

"Don't worry, Agapiti*. You are safe," his voice, his words were all the reassurance my body and soul needed to relax immediately and, once again, I was lost in a thick haze of pleasure.

A quivering gasp left me, only this time it had nothing to do with fear. Desire, passion, and even tenderness swirled within my soul. Everything but hesitation. I trusted this man with my life and I would enjoy every second in his arms. Or so I thought until the bloody alarm rang, waking me from my sweet dream.

Damn! Sitting up, I rubbed my face in frustration. It was only a dream and reality was calling me. I couldn't even try to sleep and cast a good ol' spell to get back to my dream. Nope! I had to wake up and meet the staff member of the Surrogacy Society. They would arrive at any moment to transport me to Lisbon for my first interview.

Dragging myself from my bed, I crossed gazes with my familiar, Lucky. She was a grey slim cat who thought she was royalty. She narrowed her eyes at me and meowed in annoyance.

"Don't look at me like that… Oh, did I moan in my dream? Sorry if I woke you up, Your Feline Highness, but I can have some fun in my dreams, no?" I shook my head at her and she mimicked my movement.

"Come on, Lucky. You need to get up too; we have to go to Lisbon soon," I told her and after meowing her protest, she did what I said.

She wasn't a normal cat, but a familiar. Something the witches of the Purple House like me would have from childhood. Our familiars were supposed to assist us with spells, protect us and even give advice. They were powerful and wise, to the point that witches from other houses envied us for having them. Lucky didn't seem to get what her job description was. She rather thought she was here to reign and do a spell or two whenever she was bored, while my job was to serve her.

Well, she could be a handful, but she was all I had. I loved her, and not only as a familiar but as a family or something like that. Going to the small kitchen of my tiny one-bedroom rental apartment, I filled her bowl with milk and some of her favourite corn sparkle. Putting it down on the floor, I let Her Royal Highness help herself. Taking off my clothes, I headed to the shower to get ready to leave with the warlock. I knew they were quite powerful and considered some sort of royalty, so they wouldn't wait for a plain witch such as me.

Attracted by Lucky's grumbles, and the puddle of milk she'd spilt with her light-grey paws, my eyes met her jade-green ones. It was enough to know what she meant. She didn't like the cheap discount milk brand.

"Don't worry, Lady Lucky! We will soon solve our problems. In a few months, we both will have all we need,"

I smiled at her, coming closer and petting her head. Since our apartment was as small as they came, I could hop from the bathroom to the kitchen in a few steps.

She pulled her head away, and I laughed, knowing well that even though she played hard to get, she liked to be petted.

Leaving Lucky meowing over her spilt milk, I went to the shower. A sigh left my lips as I let the water wash away my dream and my doubts. Soon, things would be better.

CHAPTER 4
Nicole

I was almost ready when a purple light beamed into my bedsit. An austere-looking warlock woman in her mid-fifties stepped from it. She stood tall and impatient, giving me an annoyed look before saying anything. Warlocks thought, better said, were sure that they were much superior to witches and wizards. They were more powerful than us most of the time, but that didn't justify their bad attitude.

"Miss Nicole Clerigh? It's time," she said, as I put my jacket on. Glancing at my watch, I noticed she was a few minutes early, but decided against saying anything because I really needed this to work.

"I am ready now. I just have to get Lucky and her bag," I told the lady, nodding slightly.

"It's only an interview. You should be back in a few hours. Your cat doesn't have to come." She shook her head in irritation.

"She is not a cat, she is my familiar," I explained, looking between the annoyed warlock and an equally upset prideful Lucky.

"It looks like a cat to me," the lady said and Lucky meowed in protest, jumping from the table she was resting on and coming toward me. Shaking my head, I looked at Lucky's annoyed face. She hated to be called *'a cat'*. *Her Royal Feline Highness* was much more than that.

To my surprise, Lucky stood on her rear paws and nudged me. Crouching down, I took her in my arms, and I just knew what she wanted. She had to come as well.

"Sorry, Mrs, but Lucky has to come too," I told the warlock lady, whose name I didn't know. She didn't even make the effort to introduce herself.

She sighed deeply and nodded.

"Fine. You can leave *it* in the accommodations for candidates before you head to your interview. Now, hurry!" She waved her hands, opening a portal of purple light before she even finished her sentence. Grabbing Lucky's bag, I followed the grumpy warlock into the light. Within seconds, we arrived at a very fancy building, which had to be where the surrogates from Lisbon stayed during their tests and interviews.

"You can leave your cat in the first room on the left and then head to the building on the other side of the street, my colleague Rose will be waiting for you there," the warlock lady said shortly before disappearing through another portal of light.

"Such a nice lady," I muttered under my breath and followed her instructions. I put Lucky's carrier on the floor of the first room on the left and looked intently at her piercing green eyes. She must have had a reason to insist on coming with me. That cat never did anything without a reason.

"You know something that I don't, don't you?" I asked with a small smile.

Lucky meowed as if to say that it was a stupid question and, of course, she knew things I didn't. Our communication consisted of empathy, annoyed meows, and stares filled with judgement. Sometimes, I wished she was more like the TV witch-cats, or maybe even a dog.

However, my magic chose her, and she chose me too, even though she wouldn't ever admit it.

"Well, Lady Lucky, you will have to stay in your carrier until I am back," I told her and she narrowed her eyes at me, pretty much telling me that was stupid and she wasn't a pet cat, "I know, Lucky, but the warlock lady wasn't on the same page as me. They don't have familiars and don't seem to get the concept. There is nothing I can do. Remember, I am doing all of this for us. We both have to make sacrifices for our family. So, please be patient and don't cast any magic or turn anything into rats again. Not everyone appreciates your sense of humour."

I crouched down, motioning for her to enter her cat carrier. After rolling her eyes at me, something that normal cats couldn't do, she stepped into the carrier.

Inhaling deeply, I found my way out of the modern building and was about to cross the street when my stomach growled. Damn, with my morning mess, I had forgotten to have breakfast, and all I had was a large cup of coffee.

After checking my bag for coins, I headed to a little snack bar. Even though my sweet tooth almost drove me to get a Portuguese sweet called 'pastel de Belém', I chose something else. I had to make healthier choices now that I was about to carry a baby. A stranger's baby. A sigh left my lips at that thought. All I could buy with my four euros was a juice carton and a small cereal bar, and that would have to do.

Eating the cereal bar in a voracious way that would shock my judgemental cat, I started drinking the orange juice as I headed to the building. I knew better than to let Miss Rose wait, especially if she was anything like her colleague who didn't even tell me her name.

As I walked and sipped my juice, the sight of an absurdly handsome man knocked the air from my lungs for a while. My eyes flared open, and I stumbled on a stone on the sidewalk, spilling the juice all over my white t-shirt. For a moment, I didn't care about being dirty and wet. My eyes followed him, completely mesmerised as if I had fallen under a hypnosis spell.

My gaze roamed from his dark brown hair to his tanned skin, and my mouth watered. His muscles and even the way he carried himself did things to my body. Funny, hot things and I had to clench my thighs to soothe the feeling, the sparkle of fire.

Something about him was familiar. Could he be the man from my dreams? Nope! I was going crazy. Maybe I was so needy… that just seeing a man *like that* was making me hallucinate. My dear BOB, battery-operated boyfriend, wasn't doing the job anymore. It seemed like Portuguese men would ruin it for me, or at least a man, him. My hands moved through the air as I fanned myself. Wasn't it hot?

My gawking eyes searched for his, but he seemed too distracted to notice Miss Orange Juice here. His gaze was fixed on his phone and a smile stretched his lips. Swallowing deeply, I looked away. I knew I would end up alone with my cat and eye-stripping hot guys at some point, but it was still way too early for that. I was a lonely witch, and well… quite lonely, but still young. Maybe one day I would do much more than look at a guy. Only after the baby matter was settled though.

Crossing the street, I entered the archaic looking building. My eyes roamed the space, impressed by the imposing furnishings and the murals on the ceiling. This place looked completely different from the accommodation building.

Here everything exuded a classical vibe. This building was probably centuries old while the other one had a very modern edge. Before I could go to the reception desk and look for the bathroom, a lady stopped me.

"You must be Nicole Clerigh. I am Rose Vasconcelos," she offered me a smile. "Oh, what happened to your clothes? Nevermind, come with me, I think I can get you something else to wear. You don't have to stop at reception," she added, motioning for me to follow her.

A sigh of relief parted my lips at the realisation she was way better than the other warlock lady. How did she know I was the right Nicole? Maybe her powers leaned toward clairvoyance, or reading auras. My chest shrank at the idea. I only hoped she didn't read too much. I couldn't lose this opportunity. It was my only chance to pay the debts.

She didn't say anything, so my poor heart started beating normally again. As we walked into the building, a green light flared up, driving my senses to alertness. I felt like a thief about to be caught. Having so many warlocks around wasn't that safe for someone like me.

"It means that we have the authorization to come in," she explained, turning to look at me for a moment. "Don't be nervous. The interview will only comprise a few questions," she comforted me, a smile of sympathy on her face and her brown eyes filled with warmth.

"You can go to the bathroom, and I will look for a clean top for you," Miss Rose said as we entered a spacious office. Going to the bathroom, I cleaned my mess as a stream of frustrated sighs escaped my lips. I was a natural disaster!

"Miss Clerigh, we only have a shirt with one of our slogans," Rose said, and I opened the door and took a crop top from her hands. It had a sentence written in huge letters, *'Putting babies in since 1230.'* Cringy! I didn't even want to imagine how they put the babies *in* before the *in vitro* technology. Well, I knew, I just didn't want to think about it.

Gulping hard, I put the shirt on, as I didn't have a better option. Inspecting myself in the mirror, I inhaled deeply. The short top barely covered my ribs. It was only an interview and, soon, I would get back to my cat and my own clothes.

I left the bathroom and took a seat in front of Miss Rose's desk and she asked me some questions about my general health and habits. I answered everything honestly; I was healthy-ish, except for not sleeping or eating well. Afterwards, she started explaining a little more about the procedure.

"I am sure my colleague has talked you through the general contract terms when you went for your tests back in Dublin. This case is a little special. The client is paying a very generous amount, something we don't see very often, and that corresponds to five times our standard fee. In addition to the money, he will pay you with jewellery, runes, and potions," she informed me, handing me a piece of paper with an exorbitant value written on it.

My eyes widened. I'd never seen that many zeros after a five. A chuckle left me at the thought that Lucky would be able to have the royal life she thought she deserved.

"Miss Clerigh, are you sure about it? I have to ask. It is part of the protocol and we only contacted you three days ago," she asked me with a sigh.

Their agency had contacted me three days prior, telling me about a client looking for a Golden Dragon Summoner witch, the procedure, and their rules. After only a few minutes of hesitation, I said yes. I needed it. It was like winning the magical lottery without even having to buy a ticket.

"Yes!" Miss Rose moved her head back. She seemed shocked at my tone. "Yes, Miss Rose, I am absolutely sure. You have nothing to worry about." I gave her a little smile.

"There are also some special conditions since the insemination won't follow our normal protocol. Dragons can't be conceived in vitro. The semen can't survive even a minute out of the body of a dragon or a Dragon Summoner witch…"

"I know, Miss Rose. I did my research." I knew well what it all entailed. So far, all I knew about *the client* was that he was a Golden Dragon shifter, which meant that he was probably as old as dirt. My stomach churned, and I dreaded even imagining the type of male I would have to sleep with. Fortunately, it would only be once.

"The birth of a dragon child from a non-dragon female is also dangerous. You should summon your Spirit Dragon before labour and have her or him by your side the whole time. It will help you in case the fire of the placenta spreads through your body." I gulped hard at her words. Burning with dragon fire from the inside out seemed terrible. Yet, I had to swallow down the knot that formed in my throat along with my fear. Again, I didn't really have a choice.

My pulse stopped racing and my body calmed down considerably as I felt the Spirit Dragon roar within my soul. It washed over me in comfort, like an embrace.

I smiled inwardly at him. Azula was an ancient Golden Dragon, and I was very lucky to be able to summon his spirit. He was a beautiful and unique creature, even among the other Golden Dragons.

Every Golden Dragon had a gift, a special superpower while alive, and some of them also carried this power to their spiritual forms after they passed away. Azula's water powers were still strong and pulsating within his spirit.

He felt alive within me; I was his summoner, his channel to the world of living, and he was my miracle, the only thing that made me feel special and strong. Without him, I would probably be very lost right now. I sighed inwardly. He and Lucky helped to keep me sane and whole, even with the chaos my life had become and all the difficulties I had been through.

"I am aware of that, Miss Rose," I told her with a nod, and she smiled.

"That's all I had to ask and to explain to you today. There is actually something else, something that doesn't follow the protocol, but the client insisted. He wants to meet you, to talk to you now."

28

My brows arched in surprise. Now? Wait, what?

CHAPTER 5
Nicole

"Now? As in right now?" I asked like an idiot, a little shocked. Things were getting real. Well, it was good to have all my issues solved as fast as possible. It wasn't like I could wait very long, anyway. Yet the idea of meeting him sooner than I expected made my stomach churn nervously. The gulps of orange juice I had managed to drink suddenly roiled in my stomach.

"Yes, Miss Clerigh. He should arrive any time now. It doesn't mean that you can't change your mind anymore. Until the contract is signed, you can reconsider your decision and so can the client. However, he seems adamant about having you as his surrogate."

My lips opened slightly. That was unexpected, but good news.

Someone knocked on the door and Miss Rose asked them to come in. To my astonishment, the absurdly handsome man I'd seen walking in the streets and the cause of the orange juice incident, entered the room.

My eyes were fixed on him, as my arms automatically tried to cover my exposed stomach.

"Please, come in. Mr Alev Aureus, this is Miss Nicole Clerigh," Rose introduced us, a polite smile on her face.

Alev took a few steps towards us and beamed a drool-worthy smile, greeting Miss Rose. His hazel-green eyes kept my full attention, and I even stopped breathing. My body couldn't do anything besides look at him as if hypnotised. The colour in his irises was deep and lively, and they held tiny flames. For a moment of insanity, all I wanted to do was to burn inside of them.

My delirious gaze roamed down to his straight nose and his slightly fleshy lips. His chin was chiselled to perfection: square, and virile, and his dark stubble only gave the final touch to his Alpha Male vibe.

The man was worth me spilling my orange juice and, well, pretty much anything on me. He would surely cause many disasters.

"Nice to meet you. I am Alev."

He offered me his hand, and I looked between it and his chiselled face as if my brain had fled and left my body for good. His effect on me was worse than a paralysis spell! The two of them kept looking at me, and I stayed there frozen and immobile like an ice statue.

Clearing my throat, I snapped out of my daze and shook his hand.

"How rude of me... Nice to meet you. I am Nicole." My voice came out like a whisper. I wasn't the life of any party, but I was also not that shy. What was wrong with me? Why did he make my breath flutter and my cheeks heat up in some sort of puberty-kid insecurity?

"Nice to meet you, Nicole. I am Alev," he repeated, and I offered him a silly smile. *Get a grip, Nicole!* I bit my bottom lip to contain my silly smile. I had to look like someone serious and responsible and not some swooning teen girl. Was he the... Golden Dragon? He had to be! Who else could he be? Besides that, everything about him was so big and majestic, and his aura exuded something gold. No, he wasn't old and wrinkled as I'd thought, but a man in his prime. He did look mighty fiiiiiine for a centuries-old dragon, and making a baby with him wouldn't be an issue at all!

Alev sat on the empty chair to my left and Rose looked intently at us, her face growing serious.

"There is something I want to address that is of common interest to you both. Miss Clerigh, some of your magic blood tests had very inconclusive results. Our Alchemists can't pinpoint the cause of it. It might be an issue for your candidacy as a surrogate."

My face fell at her words. No! No! I needed this to work!

A sigh left my lips. Of course, it was bound to happen again. Things would go wrong because of what I was.

Ironically enough, I didn't know what I was or what was wrong with me. I always thought, no, I actually knew something was wrong. Ever since I could remember, the kids in my coven used to pick on me.

Unfortunately, it wasn't only the kids. The way the people in our coven treated my sister and me, they never let us forget that something was wrong with us, even though we didn't know what or why. The anger and disgust in their eyes were a heavy burden to carry, and it was also what made my sister lose her way, what made me lose her. For a while, I thought that it might have been because we were orphans, or because of my sister's exceptional powers and the fact that I was a so-called rare Dragon Summoner. Our conservative little coven couldn't deal with something *that* different from them.

My chest clenched for a moment simply because those memories hurt. Now those tests brought the hard reality back to me; our powers weren't the cause. There was actually something wrong with me, my magic, my blood.

"It won't be a problem for me." Alev's voice resonated with determination, bringing me back from my reverie. A sigh of relief parted my lips, liberating my bottom lip from the nervous scratching of my teeth. For a moment, Miss Rose seemed a little taken aback by his definitive answer, but soon her expression of surprise morphed into a nod of agreement.

"So let's address the other conditions," she said, giving me a brochure that I had already read, explaining about the bi-weekly prenatal check-up in one of the surrogacy centres for magical assessment once the conception was successful.

"So, according to this brochure, I will move to your place or the place you determine for a few days until the conception is successful and then I have to do the prenatal check-ups?" I asked, looking between Alev and the warlock lady.

"Not exactly. That is something I wanted to talk to Miss Rose about. Both this contract and my situation are special. Therefore, I will offer you adequate compensation for all the eventual inconveniences.

Golden Dragons are very protective and also possessive of their children, even when they are still in the womb. Besides that, my species faces many dangers and has many enemies. You would have to move in with me until the child is born. I can give you much more money, runes, and spells than what Miss Rose discussed with you. Nicole, this is very important to me and I will do everything in my power to make sure that this all goes well and smoothly. But even though I will protect you and keep you safe, you have to know that this agreement has an element of danger." Alev's voice was smooth and his eyes filled with hope, worry, and sympathy.

A little gasp left me. Wait, so I had to move in with him for months? Dangers? It all seemed too much.

"What do you say, Nicole? Can you agree to these terms?" he asked me, his gaze intense. My breath became a little ragged.

33

Alev

Even before I opened the door to Miss Rose's office, Nicole's sweet smell assaulted my senses. Soft, gentle, yet distinguishable. It couldn't be confused with Miss Rose's flowery perfume. Nicole smelled like wild lilies with a touch of seawater.

As I entered the office, my eyes roamed to Nicole. She looked at me, her mouth wide open and her eyes startled. What had surprised her so much? Hadn't she ever seen a dragon shifter before? I was taller and stronger, but not that different to other men.

My eyes travelled up subtly as I captured her features without gawking at her. She looked somewhat uncomfortable. Her long, dark hair was tied in a ponytail, and she was wearing a tiny top with a funny motto. I had to control my chuckles when I looked at it. The last thing I wanted was to make her even shyer.

I couldn't miss how the curves of her round breasts were accentuated by the top. My hands almost itched to touch them. No! That was not why I was here! Nicole wasn't a one-night stand. She and I had a much higher purpose: to bring my child into the world. My gaze quickly moved down to find the skin of her stomach exposed, which didn't do much to soothe the lust growing within my pants.

Her stomach, the place where my baby would grow, was a beautiful sanctuary. She was the one, Horus growled his agreement. There was no doubt.

As Miss Rose asked me if the inconclusive results of Nicole's tests would affect my decision, Horus replied in my mind with a deep roar. He had chosen her as our surrogate, and so had I.

34

I trusted my dragon and my instincts in almost everything. Horus had never failed me, but my instincts had only failed me once, with my ex, Niki. Love was something not even my primal instincts could understand, but it didn't matter. I was here for a reason beyond sex, love, and mating. I was here to create life and my family. Now, I just had to wait for Nicole to say yes.

"There is something else. I won't hide it from you, Nicole, not even if the truth makes you decline this contract. Scarlet Dragons followed me on my way here, so if you become my surrogate, for the security of both my clan and yours, you should come with me to my clan's house now. As I said, you would stay there under my protection until the baby is born. I know that is a lot to process. So, take a few minutes to an hour to think about it, if you can accept it all," I told her. I couldn't keep her in the dark, hide facts from her, it wasn't fair.

Another soft gasp left her as the reality of the situation set in.

Miss Rose cleared her throat, and we both looked at her.

"This is a complete departure from our normal protocol, but I understand your situation is special, Mr Alev. So, it can be done as you have asked *if* Miss Nicole agrees," she said, and all eyes were on Nicole once again.

Looking intently at her blue eyes, deep with sweet melancholy, I waited for her answer. Nicole seemed like a lovely girl, but also someone who had felt and experienced the rough side of life. Her eyes carried much more depth than a twenty-three-year-old should have.

There was something sad inside her, sad and beautiful. Horus roared within me, yearning to comfort her. He was already getting attached to the woman who was to carry our child. I had to keep him under control. Nicole wasn't ours, and we could only do part of what my dragon wanted. We

35

could only protect her and keep her under our wing temporarily.

She swallowed deeply, overwhelmed by my question. I knew it was too much to ask, but I had hope.

CHAPTER 6
Nicole

My mind raced with all the news and the unexpected ways the interview was going. Once again, I froze, lost in my confusion.

Alev's gaze bore deep into mine, waiting for an answer. Yet, instead of replying, all I could do was look at him.

"Miss Clerigh, do you need time to think about it?" Rose asked, bringing me back to reality. Darn! I had never felt so attracted to a guy before, and *that* wasn't exactly good. Things could get very confusing and messy.

His presence alone made me dizzy and clumsy; imagine living with the guy for months! How many things would I spill on myself? I would surely fall too, on my darn knees, much to the embarrassment of my cat. No! I had to pull myself together and keep in mind that all of this was just a business agreement. I had a higher goal: saving my butt and Lucky's entitled tail.

"I am sorry… It's just a lot to process, but no, I don't need time to think. I accept these conditions. I just have to fetch my clothes and my familiar," I said, looking at the warlock lady. Maybe that was why Lucky wanted to come.

Maybe she somehow knew things would take a hundred-and-eighty-degree turn.

"Very well. If you are absolutely sure, we can proceed with the contract signing. However, I recommend that you both take some time to think things through before signing." Rose's eyes were solemn, serious.

Alev's answer came immediately. "I've already made my decision. Now, it's up to Nicole." He turned to look at me, and I swallowed hard.

I wasn't proud of what I was doing, all this mess, but I had no choice. I had to embrace the chaos and the challenge in order to overcome a much bigger issue. My only choice was to stay strong and keep all my emotions in check, lock down any doubts and hesitation in a box within my heart, and throw away the key.

"I am sure, Miss Rose. You don't have to worry about me changing my mind. I talked to some psychologists from the surrogacy agency in Dublin yesterday, and I have no doubts," I told her, even though I knew she was aware of the procedure. Their psychologists tested my resolve, but nothing in the world would make me step back. I knew what I needed, and this was my last chance, my only hope.

"Very well," she nodded, giving Alev a slightly glimmering-green magic pen. I knew how magical signatures worked. The pen bound his magic, and his very essence to the contract, just like it would do to me when I signed it.

The pen felt heavy as I took it from his big warm hand, and after a deep breath, I signed it. It was done.

Keeping my facial expression neutral, I had to keep my heart from breaking a little after selling the only thing I had left, not that I was in a position to have any regrets. It would be over soon, and I would move on with my life, safely.

"Now, I will hand over the ovulation kits and pregnancy tests to you, along with more brochures with specifications and recommendations to achieve conception quickly," she told us.

These warlocks really liked brochures; they had one for everything, even about the best positions to conceive. Good Goddess Nyx! That seemed a lot! After she explained about the check-ups and gave us some tips, she walked us to the door of the building.

"As soon as you have your cat, I will transport you both to the Golden Dragon's mansion," she said, looking at me, and Alev nodded.

"That is the safest option, thank you, Miss Rose," he gave her a heart-melting smile. The hope in his eyes did things to me, unexpected things. He almost made me have hope as well, except I didn't know for what, but the strange feeling warmed my heart.

"Someone will fetch your clothes and belongings, Miss Clerigh; you have nothing to worry about."

She was right; I had nothing to worry about. Fortunately, Lucky and my most precious belongings were here with me, safe in my purse. As I walked to the other side of the street, Alev followed me. To my surprise, I didn't even have to turn around to know he was right behind me; the warmth radiating from his body was there, close, comforting.

My eyes clenched shut, and I shook my head. It wasn't right! I couldn't use his warmth, his comfort. I was out of my mind. Ignoring him and the feeling, the need burning within my cold soul, I entered the accommodation building and headed to my Lucky. She would know what to do. She always did.

As soon as I got to the living room where I left her, I took her from her carrier and held her in my arms. She didn't like to be held as she considered it a pet thing, too low for her, but this time she let me do it for more than a minute.

It wasn't supposed to happen. Darn! I would rather have to surrogate for an old creepy dragon than for a man that looked like that, who was already making me feel so many things I'd never experienced before, things I shouldn't feel. I bit my lip nervously, it could ruin everything. Breathe, Nicole. Don't feel, think!

Lucky meowed, climbing up on my shoulder and making me look over it. There he was, in his more than six foot-five inches of hot glory.

"So, that's your cat? We have a cat in the clan mansion too, Burbus, Alma's pet. Alma is our Duchess, which is like the queen of our clan," He smiled at Lucky.

Unlike me, she didn't melt at his smile but took it as an offence, frowning and growling at him softly. It was the growl of a lady.

"Her name is Lucky, and she doesn't like to be called a cat. She also doesn't like regular cats in general. She thinks she's furry magical royalty," I whispered the last part with a hand cupping the corner of my mouth, preventing Lucky from hearing my words. Nope, I didn't need a cranky cat now.

Alev offered me a hand to help me up, and I took it; his warmth stole over my skin and made my body tingle in funny places. Oh, dear Goddess, dear Nyx! I was lost!

"Nice to meet you, my lady Lucky. I will let you see for yourself that Burbus is not a regular cat," he smiled at Lucky's unfriendly face. I knew that face well. She liked him and was trying to pretend otherwise. The sassy pussycat was full of tricks and charms. I, on the other hand, couldn't contain my giggles at the way he addressed her.

Alev took Lucky's carrier, and I carried an annoyed-looking Lucky in my arms as we walked out of the building without exchanging a word.

I clung to Lucky's furry body. The whole situation was awkward. What should someone say to the man that was paying them to conceive and carry his baby? Well, the way

40

I felt made everything much more awkward; royally and magically awkward.

"We can't teleport directly inside the clan mansion due to the protection spells," Alev let Miss Rose know, and she nodded. The Golden Dragons seemed very careful about their safety, and they had to be. From what I'd read about them in the last few days, they had many enemies and the Scarlet Dragons had almost annihilated them. My chest clenched for their people. They had suffered a lot and lost everything, and I could relate to that. Yet they were trying to rebuild their clan and their lives again. They had hope, whereas I only had desperation.

As soon as we met Miss Rose in the old building, she opened a portal of teal-coloured light, and we walked through it, arriving at a warm and beautiful place.

Miss Rose bid us goodbye quickly and went back through her portal. I knew she had put us under a cloaking spell so humans wouldn't faint in shock at the light of her magic.

The crashing of the waves on the sand and the salty smell of freedom weren't things I could miss, and I immediately turned around. A smile formed on my lips as I looked at the sea.

It was even more beautiful than the coast close to my former coven. It looked warm, inviting even, not like the forbidden blue under the cliffs that I wanted to jump into when I was a little witch. Nope, I wasn't a depressed kid, and my sister took good care of me. She made sure I smiled more than I cried. However, I always loved swimming and wanted to go to the water, which was frowned upon in my coven. They were strange witches, maybe more in the sense of what humans called witches — or better said, bitches — than women filled with nature's magic.

Ever since I could remember, I loved everything related to water, its soothing, malleable nature. It was somehow related to my water-summoning powers, and even to the

41

Spirit Dragon, Azula. Funny enough, Lucky was the opposite to such an extreme that it seemed like she was allergic to water, and even doing water magic ruined her mood.

Walking or running on the beach also seemed like a great idea, much better than running in Dublin like I had every day, normally before sunset and just after my shift at the store. I didn't even work in the store, but on the streets as a mascot. I had to dress like a Leprechaun with boobs and try to attract tourists to the souvenir shop. The costume was so huge and loose that people couldn't see even an inch of my skin and they could only see that I was a woman because of the generous curves of my breasts. Lucky always judged me as I dressed in the huge costume. I was one of the rare witches to have a human job, and pretty much a human life, even though I never stopped practising my magic.

Inhaling the sea breeze alone was enough to fill my lungs with a sense of peace and contentment. Being in this house, in front of the blue infinity of the sea, wouldn't be half as bad as I thought.

"Do you like it?" he asked, gesturing to the sandy beach and successfully attracting my attention back to him.

"I love the sea, to swim, float, move within the water as if I could fly." I sighed, daydreaming.

"You can do that as long as I go with you. This house isn't meant to be your prison, but it's not safe otherwise, Nicole. We have to be cautious." His face contorted with frustration. He didn't seem like a man who liked to be constricted or held in a box either, but he was right. Safety came first.

I nodded at his words, and he led me into the mansion. His hand holding mine made it possible for me to enter through the many powerful spell barriers. I could feel them in my bones. The house was a fortress, surely impenetrable to unwanted visitors.

"Almost the entire clan lives here, except for Kemy, a female mated to a werewolf. You will probably meet them all today," Alev told me and I gulped hard at his words, pulling my cat closer to my chest, having to endure her silent protest in the form of her narrowed eyes. "Don't worry, they are all nice people and will welcome you," he added, and squeezed my hand in reassurance, noticing my anxiety. I wasn't very good with people since people generally didn't like me, not in my Coven and not in my former *human job or better said Leprechaun job.*

Taking a bit of air, I calmed down a little and fought myself for hope. It would work out well. I wouldn't be the orphan they called a bastard or the annoying Leprechaun handing out flyers. So, it would be different this time.

As we entered the house, we came across two beautiful women, one was very pregnant and the other carrying an adorable baby girl. My gaze soon roamed to their faces, their frowns. No, it wouldn't be better this time.

CHAPTER 7
Nicole

"Nicole, this is Marion and our Duchess Alma," Alev introduced us, as we walked further into their ample and luxuriously decorated mansion. The Golden Dragon's lair was filled with shining and expensive decor as golden as them. I'd heard that dragons liked to hoard and collect valuable things, jewellery, and stones. Yet they managed to keep it elegant and not over the top. The house was beautiful, cosy even. At least for them, not for an outsider.

"We didn't expect you here that soon, Nicole. It's a surprise, welcome," Marion said with a polite and somewhat artificial smile.

"Her name is Nicole?" Alma, the tiny redhead beauty with the baby in her arms asked, looking intently at Alev. Her face contorted with shock.

"Yes, it is," he replied. What was wrong with my name?

"Alev, I…" Alma gasped, shaking her head. She was clearly a witch. I could feel her astonishingly powerful magic. The tall, pregnant lady to her left was a dragon. Even with her huge baby bump, she looked like some sort of top model, too perfect to be real.

"Alma, please!" Alev gave her a pointed look, and she sighed.

"Welcome, Nicole," she said, looking at me, even though her face said otherwise.

A sliver of coldness went through my chest, and I hugged the life out of my cat. Lucky didn't take it well; it was too much for her. She mewed and jumped off my lap. Things got unexpectedly intense when I saw a ginger ball of fur come closer, swirling his tail and holding his head up. Did this one also think he was a member of the imaginary cat royalty? What was wrong with them?

Lucky meowed to him, which she never did to other cats. Flaring his round green eyes, the ginger bobcat leapt forward and ran after Lucky, chasing her. They ran in circles around the living room, mewling, shrieking, and making strange noises, maybe some sort of feline battle cry. Was it a fight? A game? A fight for the cat crown like the Game of Thrones Feline edition? I only followed them with my startled gaze for a moment, before trying to reach Lucky and help her.

"Burbus, stop! What are you doing?" Alma asked, moving around the room and giving the baby girl to Alev before she too went to try to stop her cat.

As I looked over my shoulder, I saw the little baby melting into Alev's arms and yawning in an adorable way. I'd never lived with a baby before and only seeing her cute face made my ovaries jump and my chest clench. But I didn't have time for that now; I had a cat conflict to stop. The ginger cat was surprisingly fast for one that was chubby and Lucky had to give her all to flee from him.

Moving as fast as I could, I crouched down and tried to grab Lucky, but all I could feel was her flashing tail slipping out of my grasp. Once again, I tried diving onto the floor like a crazy person. I surely was the queen of good first impressions. Panting a little, I succeeded in my capture mission and quickly stood up with Lucky safely tucked in my arms. She released low growls of threat, her narrowed eyes fixed on Burbus, who was now in Alma's arms.

"I am sorry, Burbus never does that," she said, panting even more than me and shaking her head at her pet.

Alev stepped closer to me and his gaze examined Lucky as if to check if she was fine. I was quite surprised that, in the desperation of her flight, she didn't use magic on him, since she could share a bit of my magic and do pretty much anything she wanted with it.

"No harm done. She is fast," I told him, and he nodded, the baby still snuggled into his strong arms. I had to pull my gaze away from them, or else I would melt like butter at the sight of the most absurdly handsome, big, and muscular man I'd ever seen with a tiny little munchkin in his arms.

The imposing presence of a tall, dark-blond man coming down the stairs with a baby in his arms attracted my full attention. The baby was the same size as the little girl cuddling with Alev. Were they twins? He looked regal and exuded power, even more than Alev. But while Alev's energy made me weak in my knees and tingling, this man commanded my respect and reverence.

"Egan, this is Nicole, my surrogate," Alev told him, then turned to look at me, "Egan is our Lord, a king if you will, and Alma's husband."

Egan stood close to his wife, and she let go of her complaining cat. The orange feline jumped to the floor, passing by Lucky and me whilst giving her a funny look. These cats were crazy! I hoped they wouldn't hurt each other or something even worse… Oh, Holy Nyx, Goddess of all witches and cats! Nope, I couldn't have anything happening to my Lucky.

Egan handed Alma the baby and cradled them both in his arms, almost covering Alma's small frame completely. I wasn't that tall at five foot seven inches, but next to Alma, I felt like a giant.

"It's good that you are here. I have an urgent matter to tell you both about. On the way to Lisbon, I met a few Scarlet Dragons. We fought, and I killed them, so that won't be a problem, but it means that they are close, maybe looking for us in the area," Alev informed them.

Egan exhaled sharply and pulled Alma further into his arms as Marion sat on the sofa and sighed, her hand over her swollen stomach.

"We can't stay in Marbella for much longer. The enemies are close and we aren't safe; it doesn't matter how many spells we have shielding this house. Spells can be broken," Alev added, patting the baby girl's back and holding her closer to his chest.

"Moving again! So much for giving the children a stable home." Alma sighed.

"Alev is right, Little Ruby. That dark witch Meghan and her partner also know where we are, and we don't know what happened to her. Maybe she is still alive," Egan told his wife, and she nodded.

Dark witch? What now?

CHAPTER 8
Alev

A frown formed on my face as I thought of Meghan. Only a few days after Niki had left, Meghan invaded our mansion, and not for the first time, looking for something in Egan's office. The last time was especially nasty for me. The evil creature and her sidekick brought a Succubus with them to distract us males as they roamed freely in our house.

My fist clenched into a tight ball, and I had to take a deep breath not to scare baby Amaris.

The Succubus made me fall to her devious feet and spell. I believed in her love and gave her my numb devotion. When Alma and the dragon ladies broke her spell, the other men had their mates, their bond and love to fill their chests and bring them back from the Succubus' darkness. I, on the other hand, didn't have anyone, only an empty hole in my heart. It took me days to recover from the she-demon's spell. It hurt even more than Niki's departure; it showed me how empty and meaningless my life was.

I remember what they told me about that time as I recovered with the help of a healer. This time we successfully managed to have Meghan and the other witch captured, but when they were being transported to the warlock prison to wait for judgement, someone broke into the transport unit and portalled both dark witches elsewhere. Everything had smelled like blood and felt like death.

That's why we believed they were either severely hurt or killed by their captors. I hoped they were killed. Their dark and taunted souls were beyond redemption.

Closing my eyes for an instant, it came back to me. I could feel the Succubus' dark spell filling my soul as she touched my arm. I tried to fight it, to find an anchor, something to hold on to, but I didn't have anything. So, I fell deeply under her spell, much more deeply than the others. Her demonic magic had filled me with an achingly intense and fake obsessive passion, with lust occupying the place in my chest that Niki left. The dark spell was devastatingly powerful, showing me somehow all I wanted to feel, being all I could feel: a passion that bordered on madness, unstoppable lust, and sweet devotion. Those feelings were all fake, and all I actually felt for the demon was repulsion. As the spell was broken, so was I. Horus let out a roar within me, his anger and pain were raw; we were still not healed.

"Things will be better soon," I reassured him inwardly.

I'd already lost too much, much more than Niki. I lost my family and most of my people in the war. I wouldn't lose anything again, but start anew, have a family, my child — a dragonling to curl up in my arms, just like little Amaris did. My love, protection, possessiveness, and devotion couldn't be put to a better use.

I wouldn't ever allow that emptiness to possess me again. My jaw locked with the determination I felt burning through my body. I knew I could experience the passion that intense, much more intense than I'd ever felt for Niki. I refused to love and lose.

Looking at Nicole, I couldn't not notice her reaction.

She looked slightly pale, and her pupils seemed dilated. Did she know the dark witch? Or was she afraid?

"You have nothing to worry about, Nicole. You will be protected wherever we go," I promised.

She nodded, the colour coming back to her pretty face, and she seemed relieved at my words.

"I know that safety comes first, but I wish we could stay." Alma sighed. Our hermit life wasn't that easy to follow and Alma had been with our clan for less than a year. She would get used to it. The first couple of times moving around were the hardest, but then we learned not to get attached to places and people that weren't part of our clan.

"I also wish we could stay here, since I like Marbella. I wish this could be our home." Marion sighed, her voice filled with longing.

Female dragons liked to stay in the same place while carrying and after having their drangolings; they needed their nests and so did the babies. How would my baby feel without a mother to nest him or her? Horus roared his complaint in my mind.

"We are a modern male, Horus! We can nest our baby by ourselves or… Nicole could stay for the nesting period, which never takes more than two weeks, as far as I remembered. It's up to her," I told him, and the second option pleased him more, making him rumble.

"Marion, we don't need a place to be at home. Alma is my home and I'm sure Adrian would say the same about you." Egan gave her a smile of sympathy as he snuggled Alma and baby Ethan further into his arms.

His words made Horus roar, his pain and longing were raw, almost palpable. Dragons' emotions are strong, always coming in a heated torrent, like their fire. Egan, Adrian, and the other male, Daniel, had a home for their hearts, Horus and I didn't.

"I don't want to be nosey, but why don't you mislead the Scarlet Dragons to think you moved, and stay here? You could cover the house with a *Masc Iomlán**, a cloaking spell," Nicole suggested, to my surprise.

"We already have many shields and protection spells around this house," Egan explained to her.

"Yes, but not the *Masc Iomlán.* It's the most powerful cloaking spell in existence. If the mansion is under it, no one can even see it, not even the humans. The place will disappear and be immediately erased from their memories as if it never existed. It's a powerful spell," Nicole explained. A smile formed on my lips as I saw the determination and calm in her words. She knew what she was talking about.

"I've never heard of such a spell," Alma's face contorted with wariness, her brows lifting slightly.

"Can you perform it, Nicole?" Egan asked her and she nodded.

"Yes, I've done it once before. I will need runes and crystals to draw energy from," she told him.

"I will ask a warlock to come in and help, so as not to wear you down," Egan added, and Nicole gave him a tight smile. She felt it, she knew it almost as I did, that Egan wanted to do it because he didn't trust her. Alma, on the other hand, seemed thoughtful, taken aback by Nicole's words. Maybe this spell was something unheard of in Alma's former coven. Nicole wasn't from the same place as Alma, and her people surely had other habits.

No one could blame Egan, or any of us, for wanting to be careful; that was what ensured our survival for over forty years after our Kingdom was destroyed.

Lucky moved in Nicole's arms, looking at her and narrowing her eyes. Nicole only nodded at her cat. They could communicate only with gazes. I knew little about the bond between a witch and her familiar, but it seemed quite strong.

"I think Lucky wants to see your room," I told Nicole, after pressing a kiss on baby Amaris's little head and giving her to a now smiling Marion. Soon, she too would have her little one in her arms, a little girl according to the doctor.

Nicole's eyes flared open. "How do you know?"

"After living with Burbus, I understand cats well, even those who don't like to be called cats." Chuckling at her, I took Lucky's carrier in one hand and placed the other one on the small of her back to lead her towards the stairs. After nodding at Egan, Alma and Marion, we climbed the stairs.

"You seem to know a lot about your magic," I told Nicole, the smile of amazement still clear on my face.

"Living alone among humans for the last five years, I've become quite good at being invisible." She gave me a smile that didn't reach her eyes as we went upstairs to the second floor. "Do you always have to move?"

"Yes. In our clan, we have only seven adult dragons and our enemies are countless… we have to move around and hide to survive."

I didn't have time to prepare for her arrival, so I led her to the guest room closer to my bedroom. That way, she could call me easily if she needed anything. Opening the door for her, I showed her the large bedroom.

"Here, you and Lucky can make yourselves at home, rest, or do whatever you want. There is a mini-fridge over there, and the bathroom is the second door on the left. The right door leads to the closet. You can, of course, go wherever you want within the house, but the bedrooms and offices. You can always use the gym, the swimming pool and the sauna, and, of course, the kitchen, which you'll find just behind the living room. If you need anything else, just ask me. My room is the second door on the left side," I told her and she nodded, still looking around the room.

"Thank you, Alev." She sounded lost in thought, sad even. Maybe she was tired. Closing the door, I let her rest and went downstairs. I knew my clan was waiting for me to have what would be an unpleasant conversation.

CHAPTER 9
Nicole

A deep sigh parted my lips as I let Lucky out of my arms. She jumped on the bed and settled on a fluffy pillow, stirring lazily. Now, she would have the royal cat life she thought she deserved.

Letting my body fall onto the bed, I sighed again. Why was I disappointed that I had my own room instead of staying in his? What was I imagining? My thoughts were muddled by the funny way my body reacted to him: tingling warmth and even some kind of ache. I wanted his hands on me; I wanted him to hold me like Egan held Alma. It was insanity! My body was pranking me with overwhelming desire. No! I should stop it, get a grip, take a cold shower and a sanity pill.

Like a little girl lost in a dream, I was imagining things. But fantasies didn't make it to the cold world of reality, they just didn't come true. Maybe if I had dated more, I would know better, and I wouldn't feed such silly hope.

Alev and I weren't a couple. I was just doing this out of necessity, and so was Alev. Barely a few minutes with the guy, and I was already going insane. How would I survive six months of pregnancy, plus the time we would take to conceive? The period app on my phone showed that my fertile day would be in a little less than one week. I had to get this baby inside my womb like the stupid slogan on my tiny top said and get the having-to-be-around-him over with. Move on with my life; a safer and better life, hopefully.

Suddenly, an intense grey light radiated from my purse. Opening it, I took the mirror in my hand and looked at *his* face. The silver mirror was just as small as my phone, but it always brought big bad news.

Lucky moved to my side quickly and quietly, sitting next to me. Her ears perked up as she got ready to pay attention to his words, his intentions, and his magic. Her eyes narrowed as her bushy grey tail held out stiffly, making it clear that she dreaded him as much as I did.

On the other side of the mirror, he was waiting for me, of course. The warlock lord gave me this little thing to facilitate *our* communication, except it was only ever used for him to make demands pretty much whenever he wanted to. Taking a deep breath, I looked at his cold silver eyes in acknowledgement.

"Lord Kadmus," I sighed, not making an effort to hide how much his call upset me. The man gave me all the bad creeps and the icy shivers. Unfortunately, I couldn't free myself of him anytime soon.

"I've been waiting to hear from you, young witch. Do you already have it? Can you already pay me what is owed? My patience is running low." His voice was dry and his gaze piercing. He knew well that I couldn't have gotten anything in only a few days. His true intentions were to hurry me up, make me nervous and make me fear him.

I did fear him, not because I knew he could hurt and kill me with a single spell. He was that powerful, dangerous and ruthless. I didn't fear for my life, but because he could take from me the only thing I had left. And although he could, he wouldn't, or at least, not yet. Besides, now that I had this surrogacy job kind of secured, I would find a way to pay this debt and soon I would keep my promise.

"Sir, I will pay for the debts. I still don't have any resources, I didn't have time... Please, give me a little more time?" I asked, trying to sound neutral even though I knew he could feel my desperation; he surely knew the way my hands were trembling as I fidgeted with my hair below the mirror.

A smile formed on his thin lips. He was an old man, much older than the mid-forties human he resembled. I knew well that for someone as powerful as Kadmus, time was not a hindrance. It simply didn't matter at all.

"Nicole, you know there is a much easier way to pay me. Yet you don't want to consider my generous offer. You are as headstrong as your sister, and we all know where it got her, don't we? She is lost because she didn't know when to stop, and how to obey. Do you want to follow the same destiny?" he asked patiently, almost teasingly. His proposal and his words made my stomach churn. I knew what he wanted, since he made it very clear the first time we talked about the debt and he gave me the silver mirror that I was holding now. He said that there were two ways for me to pay: either giving him what he wanted or giving him myself.

Clenching my fist tightly, my nails pierced my skin. I tried to keep my repulsion at bay. I didn't fully understand why someone as powerful as him wanted an outcast witch like me. I didn't miss the lust in his eyes. I knew that look from a few human men I had come across.

Also, I wasn't stupid. I knew I was different from the witches in my coven, more powerful than them, although still an outcast.

Being a Golden Dragon Summoner as well as a Water Elemental was very rare indeed. However, I was nothing compared to him and other noble warlocks.

Kadmus wanted much more than to use my body. He wanted to bind my soul and my magic to his for eternity and keep me as his puppet and some sort of slave. I would do anything to pay my debts and save my family. Anything but to agree to his absurd proposal. Even my desperation had limits.

"I will honour our original deal, Lord Kadmus. As soon as possible you will receive your payment," I told him and he nodded.

"Very well. If you change your mind, I will find you and bring you here, Nicole. Be quick about it; I am waiting and time is running out." His voice carried the undertone of dark warning.

"I will be as quick as possible," I reassured the warlock and his face disappeared from the mirror, with a dark and heavy fog replacing him for a minute until all I could see on the silver surface was the reflection of my pale face. Desperation was etched in my features like makeup, making me look dull.

If only I had done things differently, I wouldn't be in such a mess. Clenching my eyes shut, I returned the mirror to my purse and lay on the bed beside Lucky.

"I know, I despise him too. I will find a way to save my butt and your tail, Lady Lucky," I whispered to her, and she nodded her furry head.

If I stayed here, I would only get lost in my bad thoughts and give myself a headache. "Let's get some food, Lucky. I am sure they have the Hera milk you like. Hopefully Burbus can share it with you, even though you don't seem friendly towards him. What was that, girl? I've never seen you acting that way, like a... a cat before." I stood up and Lucky followed me downstairs, but the words I heard held me in place as if I was under a paralysis spell. No, everything was ruined now!

CHAPTER 10
Alev

Even before I reached the bottom of the stairs, all eyes were on me. The entire clan was there, all with the same looks of concern on their faces. Was this some kind of *intervention*? It was ridiculous!

My gaze roamed as I looked at each of them. Marion was on the sofa, curled up in the arms of her mate, Adrian. Alma and Egan had the little twins tucked in their arms on the sofa, opposite the other couple, while Mallory and Daniel stood. Daniel was the most suspicious among us, especially before he'd met his mate. Not betraying his character, his arms crossed in front of his chest and his brows lifted as he studied my face.

"This is too much!"

"I heard your surrogate is called Nicole. Really? Is that a joke?" Daniel snorted softly.

"It must be a joke," his mate, Mallory, added, looking between Daniel and me.

"It's not a joke. What's wrong with her name? Don't tell me you are acting like nosey children because you think her name is too similar to Niki's," I told them, walking forward and taking a seat. I would need some whiskey to get through this shitshow.

"Her name *is* similar to Niki's, Alev. That's a fact. My sister was just like that; after her mate passed in the war, she was so lost in her grief that she started to look for him in other males. She dated two other guys called Oswald." Marion sighed, and Adrian ran his fingers down her arm, soothing his pregnant mate.

"I am not like your sister. Niki wasn't my mate. Her name was Nikoleta, not Nicole; it isn't the same. Besides, the surrogate's name doesn't matter, and it isn't the reason I chose her. She is a powerful Dragon Summoner and Horus likes her; he chose her," I explained. Horus wasn't the only one, I, too, chose Nicole. It was because of her eyes, and not her name. Yet, I didn't expect my clan to understand my decision and my strange attraction towards her when I couldn't understand it myself. I just knew she was the one. "This is much bigger than my break-up with Niki. This is my family, our family. We need more children. I want and need a family. A surrogate is the perfect solution."

"Alev, I don't think you are wrong. I am just surprised at how fast everything is happening. You chose this girl within a few days and didn't tell anyone anything until yesterday. It all just seems too impulsive." Mallory breathed out softly, sympathy clear in her eyes.

"I've thought about it for a long time and contacted the surrogacy centre over two months ago, Mallory. It isn't something I decided overnight," I told her and she nodded.

"Months? But you and Niki only broke up three months ago. Alev, did you and Niki want to hire a surrogate together because she couldn't have your babies?" Alma asked, her mouth dropping open.

Niki wasn't a Dragon Summoner or a Golden Dragon. We wouldn't ever have been able to conceive a child, and she knew how much I wanted to be a father.

58

"We considered it, although it was only an idea. But that is not the point." I exhaled sharply, running my fingers through my hair in frustration

"It would be fine if the problem was only the name. The spell she mentioned isn't regular, Alev. I am sorry... I didn't want to intervene and disrespect your choice, but I am afraid there is something off with that girl. None of this makes sense. Don't let your desire to have a family blind you. Why would a witch need money? In our community, we use magic rather than money to do things, to survive." Alma's face contorted with worry.

"Exactly, Alma. In your community, in your coven. Nicole has no coven to protect her, to help her. That's why she needs money. She had to live among humans for five years and, probably, fend for herself. Miss Rose from the surrogacy agency told me that Nicole has no family left, no coven. So, she probably had to do very challenging spells, and there is nothing wrong with that. The agency investigated her, and you know how methodical and competent those warlocks are, almost anal. They wouldn't make a mistake; there is nothing wrong with her." My words came out with much more determination than I expected. They vibrated with such an intensity that I could feel a rumble forming in my chest.

"You are right, Alev. The warlocks are careful, and that's why we are letting this woman, this stranger, enter our house and our lives. However, we are still worried about you," Egan said firmly, his bicoloured eyes fixed on mine as if they wanted to test my resolve. There was no going back since I knew what I wanted and I wouldn't accept being treated like a lost and confused child, regardless of their good intentions.

"You are more than a dear friend. You are family, and we all care about you deeply," Marion added.

"I know and appreciate it, but you will have to trust me on this."

59

"Alev, you don't even know this woman," Alma shook her head. The pint-sized witch was the hardest to convince, which made little sense.

"Alma, we also didn't know you when you came to our clan. I welcomed you with open arms. You don't have to do the same to Nicole, given that she will only be here for a few months. All I ask of you is not to intervene or to make her feel bad or unwelcome. She is already visibly uncomfortable in this surrogate situation. Think about it: no woman would do something like that if she was not in dire need. We shouldn't trouble and humiliate her, adding to the burden she is already carrying," I told them. I had had enough of their words, so without saying another word, I left the living room.

As I headed upstairs, an annoyed breath left my nostrils, and a sweet feminine smell entered them. Suddenly, my body crashed into something soft. Nicole almost lost her balance, falling backwards from the impact, a gasp leaving her plump lips.

My arms went around her of their own accord, steadying her cold body. I could feel a shiver run down her delicate frame, and all I wanted to do was to warm her up. Damn, I wanted to make her hot. Horus roared in my mind, coming to the surface. He was about to possess my body and let instinct and raw need guide us.

CHAPTER 11
Nicole

"I am sorry! I wasn't looking," I mumbled without lifting my gaze. The words I had heard made me a little dizzy and a bit anxious.

I felt his chest vibrating with prowess, and it could almost start an earthquake. Yet, I felt safe in his iron grip. Stealing a glance, I saw his hazel-green eyes become gold and an inhuman slit replaced his pupil. Was he about to shift into a huge dragon and break everything around us, including my poor bones?

Alev took a deep breath as he pulled me closer to his chest, and his usually heated body felt a little cooler.

"Did you hear them?" he asked, tilting my chin up and looking at my eyes.

I had overheard, and it brought a bitter and familiar taste to my mouth: being judged by everyone, being the centre of all the unwanted attention intertwined with the fear that Alev would agree with them. That feeling was creeping through my heart until I heard his words. And more than that, I felt the resolution in them.

"Yes. I didn't mean to. I was going to the kitchen to get something for Lucky and me." My gaze darted down at the cat to my right. I knew I was a stranger in their house *and* they didn't know me *and* they weren't wrong; witches normally didn't need money. Still, nothing about my situation, or my life, was exactly normal. "I live as a human, Alev. I don't have a career or any financial stability. Leaving the coven school and going to a human institution did nothing to increase my chances. I can't be a real witch, nor a human… I don't have many options nor much hope. That's why I accepted this contract," I told him, my chin up and my emotions in check.

Maybe due to Alev's words and the way he stood up for me, I felt empowered. Determination coursed through my veins, warm like sparks of fire. I wouldn't take the humiliation they were shoving onto me or lower my head at their judgemental eyes. I was tired of that, and of letting people make me feel bad about myself. I was doing what I could, fighting the way I could, which they didn't know or understand. Sadly, I'd already learned, since I was a little child, that people didn't want to understand, to look beyond their assumptions. They wanted to judge you and put you in a box, except I wouldn't stay in anyone's box.

A sigh left my lips. I already knew about my sins and mistakes, and I didn't need their pointed fingers. More than that, I wouldn't let the coldness and suspicion in their eyes hurt me, or at least I would try my hardest not to.

To my surprise, Alev's response was to pull me closer to his chest. His warmth wrapped around me, and I felt a sweet sense of peace that I had never felt before. Alev broke the embrace immediately.

"I am sorry, Nicole. You are doing something very important for me and I won't let anyone make you feel uncomfortable or less for that. You don't have to face them now, I will bring you and Lucky some food," he said, and I nodded.

Darn, I didn't want to face the clan of gargoyles, at least not now. I was tired; talking to Kadmus and the intensity of the dark magic radiating from him always took some kind of toll on me.

Lucky and I went back to the room, and I took a good look around, only just noticing the details of the warm Mediterranean decor, the terracotta-coloured table lamps, the accent chair with warm and lively cream and orange pattern, and dark wood furniture. It also had a touch of elegant and classic English style, just like Alev's accent. A smile formed on my face as I recalled his sexy accent. Shaking my head as my face burnt with the heat it invoked, I opened the arc-shaped window and breathed in the cool sea breeze.

Lady Lucky surely loved having a fancy room that was twice the size of our little studio in Dublin, but I only cared about looking at the horizon and getting lost in the infinity of the blue sea. She was splayed out on the pillow she had claimed, enjoying the good cat life. The bed was big enough for three of me and at least five cats.

I couldn't stay there doing nothing, I wasn't the kind of person who could be still. I was used to doing everything at home with my sister and always kept busy. It always helped to relax my ever-busy mind and my whispering heart. Looking at the drawers of the mahogany dresser, I found a notebook and a pen, nice! That would keep me busy and productive.

I sat on the bed and started making simple and nothing-special sketches, but doing them and sewing my clothes always helped me to calm my racing mind. To top it off, while growing up in our coven, my sister and I only got food from the community, meaning that we had to get everything else on our own. So since I was twelve, I had made our clothes and cooked, and my sister took care of the rest and found a way for us to have books and whatever we needed for school. It didn't always work, but we did our best.

It was a good habit and skill for someone who didn't have much money like me. Besides not having to buy clothes, I sold some pieces online. After a few minutes, the maxi dress with flower patterns and an asymmetric cut was on paper and I smiled, looking at it. It was something that fit this place and if I could buy the fabric and have my small sewing machine here, I could make it.

A knock on the door attracted my attention.

"You can come in," I said, hiding my design under a small cushion.

Alev entered the room with a tray of food and a drool-worthy smile that made me feel the strange tingles creeping up my skin; remembering that I had assumed he would be a cranky old dragon made me chuckle inadvertently.

"I can't make anything in the kitchen other than this," he said, placing the tray on the top of the dresser.

It had a sandwich, a glass of orange juice, and a bowl of milk on it. Orange juice! I just hoped that this time I would be able to drink it without making a mess of myself. Alev placed the bowl of milk on the floor and Lucky jumped towards it graciously, sipping it and licking her paw in between. Even starving, she was a Lady.

"Thank you! This is more than enough." I smiled.

"The warlocks already brought your things; I will be right back with them," he said, leaving the room. He was so sweet and attentive, making me feel more like a guest than someone that was only here to provide some kind of service. A sigh left my lips. His smile fed my hopes in a way it shouldn't. Holy Nyx! I was eager to wear something other than this stupid crop top.

To be on the safe-and-dry side, I drank the juice before Alev came back. I was already eating my ham-and-cheese sandwich when he came in carrying a suitcase and a few boxes.

"Thank you so much," I told him, opening the boxes. A sigh of relief left me as I noticed that my old sewing

64

machine and my deceased mother's Spell Book were there. As I held the book against my chest, it brought back so many memories; not of my mum, though. I only knew about her from the stories my sister had told me, the bedtime stories. Mum was my favourite fairy-tale princess, but one that didn't have a happy ending.

She died when I wasn't even two and I could only remember, or maybe only imagine, her blue eyes in my dreams.

The book. It reminded me of my sister and me hiding it from the coven people and going to the extreme of burying it like a treasure. It was the only thing of mum we had left: our power, our heritage, our love. The coven leader took everything, but she wouldn't take that.

"After you finish eating and organising your stuff, meet me in the garden and put a swimsuit on. You've had a very challenging day and I am sure you could use some fun," Alev said, and my eyes shone with a smile, but it faded away as soon as I remembered all the impossibilities standing between us.

If this were a fairy tale, he would surely be the prince. But I, on the other hand, would only be the evil witch.

CHAPTER 12
Alev

Dammit! She shouldn't have heard them. I could see the sadness and pain in her deep blue eyes, and it affected me much more than I could have imagined.

I was in the garden, getting some distance from my overbearing clan while I waited for her.

After a few minutes, she appeared in a loose turquoise dress that both hugged the curve of her breasts and made her eyes less dull; she looked so beautiful in the sunlight, and in a reflex, my hands fisted. I needed to stop thinking about her *that* way.

"Are we going to the swimming pool?" she asked, looking around and trying to get her bearings.

"No. You can go there whenever you want. We are going to the beach," I said, handing her sunscreen to make sure she was healthy, safe, and cared for. For the next few months, this woman would carry my world in her body.

"You don't have to do that, not for me." She shook her head.

"I want to. Let's enjoy the sun, Nicole." My voice was filled with determination and I wouldn't have it any other way. I knew she wanted to go, and I wanted to give her something, a little fun to compensate for all the worry.

She beamed a small smile and nodded.

"This is a cloak rune; it will cover our scents and conceal our magic for two hours. You just have to rub it on your wrists and forehead. You will be safe as I will be right next to you all the time," I reassured her, placing a comforting hand on her shoulder.

"I know you will," her soft voice sounded firm with trust. Even though my clan doubted her so much, she trusted me. She, too, was putting herself in a risky position by moving in with strangers from an endangered species and having to conceive a child in a natural way. Yet she only showed genuine trust.

She did as I said, and we crossed the street, walking to the wide beach in front of us. As usual, at the end of the afternoon, there weren't many humans around; the place was almost exclusively ours.

Nicole looked with an intent gaze at the sea and took a lungful of air. Her lips curled into a smile I'd never seen before. It was sweet, vulnerable, almost innocent.

"This place is beautiful and so different from the sea in Ireland. I hope you guys don't have to move. This place is perfect!" she murmured, still completely enthralled by the beach.

"Spain is hot, that's why I like it so much," I replied, as we took a seat on the soft white sand.

Nicole pulled her dress up over her head, revealing a black bikini, beautiful curves, and her soft skin. I had to clench my hands to fight back the urge to touch her. What was happening to me? I'd never felt that way; I'd always loved and appreciated different curves and sizes of the feminine body, but I never felt the desire to touch it, not like that. I wasn't a perv!

As she spread the sunscreen over her skin, I tried to pull my gaze away. I didn't want to scare the poor girl and give her the wrong impression about me. Horus roared within me; he was all about giving her the wrong impressions. Which was odd, given that he had never before lusted over a woman this way. In the couple of centuries of our life, his only crush was a female in her dragon form, decades ago, way before the war destroyed the Golden Kingdom. As I took my shirt off to enjoy the sun, a chuckle left me as I remembered the weird way my dragon had looked at the female's tail.

"Do you need sunscreen too?" Nicole asked me, without looking up, too busy running her cream-covered hand down her beautiful long leg.

"No. We dragons can get a tan, but the sun never bothers or burns us. We are born to fly high, close to it," I told her.

"It must be amazing to fly. All I can do to defy gravity and move freely is to swim and float in the water." She smiled, her eyes once again fixed on the sea.

Horus sent me an image of Nicole riding him as he flew among the clouds and, soon after, he sent me an image of her riding me in a very different and naked situation.

Pushing both images away, I scolded him.

"What's wrong with you? I get that you are possessive over the baby that isn't even conceived yet, but this can't extend to Nicole. She isn't ours. She doesn't want to be ours. She is here to fulfil the contract and get what she needs. Respect her, lizard-head!"

He only roared in response, clearly not having it.

As I looked to my side, Nicole was heading to the water and, looking over her shoulder, she called me.

"Don't you want to come?"

"No. I will stay here. Don't worry, I will be watching over you." Staying close to her was dangerous. She was a heated and beautiful temptation. The things my dragon was literally putting in my mind didn't make it any easier. Horus was a damn tease, and not a clever one, since what he was doing was not only torturing me but himself as well. She nodded, apparently unfazed by my denial and, as my gaze followed her, she strode towards the sea quickly. I had nothing to worry about, right? She could surely swim as she was a Water Elemental, and could do whatever she wanted with the water around her.

She walked into the water with uncanny grace and only stopped when the water reached her waist, the swell of her breasts exposed to my hungry eyes. I wanted to kiss them, see the colour of her nipples and how they became pebbled under my tongue and lips.

Damn! I would soon do that, caress every inch of her body. That wasn't the problem, I had no issues mixing business with pleasure for a couple of nights. The huge and hard issue was the searing desire that exploded in my veins every time I looked at her, and just about every time I knew she was around.

Nicole let her body fall into the water, floating and giggling.

"So impossibly beautiful," the murmur escaped me. For minutes, I watched her, guarded her as I promised, my eyes hypnotised.

Nicole looked around and, when she didn't see any humans, she started magically playing with the water, making a small circle rise around her and due to my enhanced senses, I could hear her melodic laughter. Raising her hand slowly, she made the water move delicately as if it was made of crystals. The sun reflected on it, showing a prism of colours and making Nicole's smile fade. She looked pained. Was she hurt? Had any nasty sea animal stung her?

My lust was replaced by a strange intense worry, and I ran towards her, swimming closer, only stopping when I was in front of her.

"Nicole, are you okay?" I asked, putting my hands on her shoulders.

69

"Humm… yes!?" Her blue eyes were wide open with surprise.

"I thought you were hurt." I exhaled, and she shook her head.

"I am fine. You have nothing to worry about." She gave me a little reassuring smile that didn't reach her eyes, but soon she was making the water dance with the soft movements of her hands.

"It's been such a long time since I've done this anywhere besides the shower. I've missed it," she said, looking down at the crystalline water, following her fingers as it moved mid-air. Nicole made the water glide with a delicacy I didn't know was possible, it was almost ethereal.

"It's a pity you can't use your magic, practise your powers freely. You can do beautiful things," I told her and as she smiled, she moved her fingers slightly, splashing some water at me. My eyes were fixed on her. I wanted to kiss her smile, to bring her closer, taste her. I wanted it badly, but Horus' desire went beyond mine — he yearned for it so desperately. He was once again about to take control and take what he wanted.

CHAPTER 13
Nicole

My heart clenched as the light reflected on the droplets of water, forming a little rainbow. That was what my sister used to call me, Rainbow. She said mum was the one to come up with the nickname, and I loved it so much. Now they both were gone, and there were no rainbows, at least not until I could do something to bring her back.

Alev came into the water, surprising me with his warmth and closeness and making something flutter inside me with the way he worried. But as soon as I threw water on him, his expression changed completely, his face was tense, and the muscles of his neck flexed.

Alev's eyes became golden, and the reptilian slit crossed them once again. Something between a rumble and a roar vibrated through his chest. My legs walked back instinctively, my lips trembled slightly and my mind spiralled with unsettling thoughts. I had offended him and his dragon with the splash of water, and now he was furious. Of course, he wasn't as nice, easygoing and kind as he portrayed. He couldn't be; he was a force to be reckoned with. I knew people like him, Lords, Leaders, and Nobles. At first, they were nice, but soon they showed their claws, commanding submission and blind obedience. They only wanted to use people like me. That was how things worked. Yet, I'd always denied their desires — first the Coven Leader, then the warlock lord, Kadmus. I wouldn't be anyone's pawn.

Swallowing hard, I kept my head held high.

"I'm so sorry, my Lord." His eyes went back to their hazel-green colour and the heat rolling off his body decreased considerably. My words made him snap out of some sort of trance.

"For what? It's okay, and you don't have to call me that, Nicole. I'm not a stuck-up warlock noble," he told me, taking a step closer.

My muscles relaxed immediately, and a little sigh of relief left my nostrils. I didn't want problems, but I didn't want him to be a jerk. Just thinking about the possibility of it seemed to bring me lots of disappointment, and I didn't even know why. I must have been fantasising, dreaming again.

My sister always told me to stop doing that, otherwise, I would have my heart broken, yet she was the one who had broken my heart. Maybe dreaming wasn't so bad, at least if I kept in mind that it was only a dream. In this reality, it was impossible.

"I know… the words left my mouth on their own," I replied.

Throwing some water back at me, he laughed.

"Two can play that game, my Lady. Now it's your turn."

Giggling, I felt the droplets of water rising with my fingers and making them rain over him, as my other hand pushed a blast of water blast into his face. Distracted by the artificial rain, he didn't dodge my real 'attack'.

"In the water, I will always win." I raised a brow at him in a playful challenge.

"You will see, Lady," he said, lifting me by my waist and throwing me to the side with not much force. The splashing noise of water filled the air as I dove for a moment, already getting ready for an underwater move. Shaking my head, I tried to avoid the distraction of his perfectly sculpted abs and formed a blanket of moving water within my hands, intertwining it carefully. I could see Alev looking for me on the surface, I wasn't far away, but the water I wrapped around me like a burrito was the perfect cover.

Soon, I hit his chiselled chest with my water bomb, and surfaced, laughing.

"Nicole! I was worried. How could you remain underwater that long without breathing?"

My only response was to laugh at his surprise. I told him he couldn't win when we were in my element. I had no problem breathing or seeing under the water, as it was one of the perks of being both a Water Elemental and the Summoner of a Golden Dragon with water abilities. Uncommonly, Azula managed to lend me his abilities; we were one somehow, thus much more connected than the Summoners and their spirit animal normally were. Maybe because of the way I loved him. Yes, since the first time I summoned him by mistake when I was a wee child, we loved each other. Our souls are meant to be together.

"I will catch you and have my revenge!" he laughed, swimming after me as I moved away fast, my feet swishing through the water as fast as I could.

After a few minutes, I slowed down a little; part of me wanted to be caught. And everything in me wanted to feel this carefree, free as I hadn't been in as long as I could remember. He wrapped me in his arms, twirling me around, and making an almost forgotten sense of happiness bubble in my chest and come out in giggles.

73

"Maybe you used to win, Lady, but now you've met your match!" he laughed, bringing me closer to the shore, his arms around me strong, protective, and warm.

"I am not so sure about that." I scrunched my nose at him. "I am not an easy catch!" I laughed. After quite some time swimming, relaxing and playing, we walked back to the beach. The runes' effect was about to wear off.

As we walked towards the house, we saw a couple sitting on a blanket on the sand. They were Golden Dragons, two that I hadn't seen yet. The girl was on the guy's lap and he looked at her with extreme love and adoration. My lips curled up in a smile. These dragons knew how to treat their mates, it was beautiful to see. Alev took my hand in his warm, big one and led me towards the couple. Up until then, every introduction had been hard, so I braced myself; I couldn't let their words and judgement hurt me, and I wouldn't.

"Mallory, Daniel, this is Nicole," Alev introduced us.

"Nice to meet you. I am Mal and this is my Daniel." The beautiful blonde smiled at me. It wasn't the same confused and polite smile from Marion or Alma's suspicious gaze. Mallory's smile was small but real. Following her lead, her broody mate gave me a tiny smile, nodding at me.

"I've made a few tortilla sandwiches, do you want some? Spanish food is my new passion." Mallory offered us a sandwich and my growling stomach couldn't say no, so I picked one, immediately thanking her. She seemed nice, kinder than the others. I hoped she would stay this way.

"Thanks, Mal, now we have to go. The runes' cloaking spell is about to end," Alev told her.

"Sure. Go before your carriage becomes a pumpkin, Alev." She laughed and Alev nodded, chuckling at her and going to fetch my cover-up. I managed to put it on while Alev and I headed to the mansion, leaving the couple alone.

We went upstairs, and before I entered the bedroom, Alev spoke.

"You can always get whatever you want from the kitchen, because most of the time, we don't have meals in the house, but at work. So, I will leave a credit card for you. You can use it to order food or whatever you want and need, or whatever Lady Lucky demands." He chuckled, and my face fell a little.

"Thank you, but it won't be necessary. You don't need to worry about Lucky and me," I told him, closing the door behind me. I pressed my back against the door and sighed; I wasn't a gold digger. I didn't want his money this way. I wanted nothing more than what was in the contract, which I only accepted out of desperate need, even though I didn't like it.

Holy Nyx! I dreaded it, but there was nothing I could do. I didn't need anything. I could eat whatever was available in the house. Besides, I was willing to work and make some clothes to sell online; that should be enough for me to buy Lucky's milk, food and whatever else I needed.

After showering and eating the tortilla sandwich Mallory gave me, I drifted off to sleep. I was exhausted, much more tired than I had realised.

I looked up at him as his wandering hand cupped my sex. His thumb caressed me teasingly, opening my folds for his eager finger to enter me completely. A gasp left me, but soon it morphed into a moan as pleasure washed over every cell of my body.

"I told you this wasn't a bad idea." He laughed, caressing my bottom lip with his big thumb before thrusting a finger into my mouth in the same way he was doing with my core. I nibbled his thumb, throwing my head back as hot and thick desire coursed through my bloodstream. It only encouraged him to plough deep into me, inserting another finger into my greedy sex. Yet, my body felt empty, my walls wanted to clench around something bigger and thicker. I

75

*wanted him inside me with a desperation I'd never felt
before. I wanted to be completely his and lost to the world.*

*"You are mine, only mine, and no one else will have
you. It doesn't matter where you are. I will come for you.
But, now, you will cum for me," he whispered in my ear, his
arm firmly wrapped around my waist as he gave my butt a
light swat. The possessiveness in his voice was
unmistakable. This man would kill and die for me.*

Waking up with a start, I sat down, and a sigh of
frustration left my dry lips: why did I always wake up at the
best part? Even though it was only a dream, his words
resonated within my mind, and my heart. I was his only,
and he would come for me. The idea was scary and
enthralling, and my desire made my panties damp. Would
he come for me? Did I want this? Did I yearn for this man
from my dreams or someone else? No, Vasilis and Alev
were both dreams — one imaginary and the other
impossible.

CHAPTER 14
Nicole

It was hard to go back to sleep after such a vivid dream. My body was wide awake, burning with need.

My gaze wandered around the room and found Lucky's green eyes gleaming in the dark.

"Can you come here and be some kind of support anim-… familiar for a couple of hours?" I asked, and she jumped off the top shelf with the grace of a ballerina and walked, taking a few steps towards me. She offered me her extended lithe back to pet, curling her tail.

To my surprise, she didn't leave after a single petting. Instead, she made herself comfortable by stealing my pillow without shame and laying there as if she owned the place. After a deep yawn, she fell into a nap. A deep sigh parted my lips. I had to try to do the same, even though I both feared and desired to get back to my dream and lose myself completely in it. After a few hours, I fell into a dreamless slumber and woke up much more rested. I certainly didn't need those scorching dreams haunting me.

After feeding Lucky, and grabbing something to eat in the mini-fridge, I unpacked my sewing machine and the material I needed to get to work. Letting my imagination take control, I sketched a couple of dresses on paper. A few black cocktail dresses weren't hard to make with the help of some magic, and they always sold quickly on the internet.

I lost all sense of time while working, only stopping when I felt the judgemental weight of a pair of hazel-green eyes on me.

"Well, Lucky, we can't accept his money. You know very well what we need and we won't take more than that."

She shook her royal feline head at my words and narrowed her eyes at me.

"I know I am making another classic dress; there are no mistakes with those. Besides, they are easy to sell." The truth was, these little vintage dresses reminded me of my mum — I'd found a couple of them among her things when I was a teenager.

Lucky mewed, looking at the door.

"We can't, not like that," I replied with a deep sigh. I knew what she wanted. But I couldn't make my next move now. I had to wait and be cautious, especially because I knew that I could make no mistakes. An error would demand too high a price; something I wasn't willing to pay.

The door opened all of a sudden, almost making me jump. My eyes met Alev's, which did nothing to calm my racing heart. His hazel-green eyes locked with mine, bringing all the desire and the guilt I couldn't allow myself to feel.

"Nicole, did I scare you? Sorry, I should have knocked first. It's a force of habit. It's getting dark and you haven't left the room. I imagined you were hungry for something more substantial than the fruit and snacks from the mini-fridge." He handed me a small bag. "There is a wrap and some fries with aioli there. It's a typical Spanish dip, quite good."

"Thank you." I smiled, placing the food on an accent table.

"You should feel free to go downstairs whenever you want to and try to make yourself at home. If my clan people frown at you, you let me know. Their behaviour is really going too far, and that is making you uncomfortable," Alev said with a sharp exhale and a frown of his own.

How could he look so handsome even while making a grumpy face? I shook my head, trying to get a hold of myself.

"It's not that I am afraid of frowns. They don't scare or upset me, but I would rather be in a place where I feel comfortable," I replied. I was okay there, and I would be alright anywhere as long as I got what I needed. Besides, I was used to dirty looks and angry faces: growing up as the coven outcast taught me to live with it.

Alev took a few steps closer to me and the delicious warmth radiating from his skin made my silly heart beat faster. He was so handsome, big and powerful with his broad shoulders and strong frame, yet gentle and more considerate to me than almost anyone I'd ever met. *Alev, you are dangerous for my heart. You feed my hope and raise some kind of fire within me. I wish you could stop doing that. Please be kind and move this temptation of a body a few metres away.*

As he placed a gentle hand on my shoulder, I swallowed hard and looked at him like an idiot — half-paralysed and completely enthralled.

"You should feel comfortable anywhere, everywhere. I will talk to them again, Nicole. This is your home for the next few months, and it should feel as such," he reassured me. Looking around, he saw my makeshift atelier. The fitted bodice and flowing skirt of the first dress were almost ready and displayed on a mannequin.

"That's beautiful. Did you make it yourself?" he asked, amazement clear in his eyes. It wasn't a big deal at all, only a simple dress.

"Yes, but it's rather simple to make, especially when one sews with magic," I told him.

Alev shook his head.

"I think you are selling yourself short; it's really—," he stopped in his tracks, realising he didn't make the best choice of words, given my situation. My gaze shifted down, and I swallowed hard.

I could hardly wait for the moment it was all over, I would be free and his beautiful eyes would be only a memory. Hopefully, the days would pass quickly and I would resist all the temptations! My Goddess would help me!

"I'm sorry. What I mean is that you are very talented. Marion has a fashion brand, and she's always looking for new people to work with. New inspiration she says," he muttered.

My gaze remained down as I chewed the inner part of my lip nervously. If I remembered correctly, Marion was the pregnant blond lady that looked as perfect as a doll. She surely wouldn't want to work with the likes of me. In their eyes, I was some sort of gold digger or someone who sells herself for money.

"I'm not a stylist, I just sew sometimes. That's not something I want to do," I told him my half-lie, my eyes not quite reaching his. I was losing myself in my ironies. I hated to lie, even though it had become some sort of a habit lately. That would be a great job, but it wasn't for me. Maybe in another life.

"I just don't want you to be sad and lonely…" he murmured, looking around and furrowing his brows slightly, lost in thought. "There is something we could try."

Lucky seared him with her glare and mewed in protest. If I could read her mind, I am pretty sure I would hear the words, 'Submit to me, dragon!'

80

He chuckled at my annoyed cat and flashed her a breathtaking smile, but she seemed to be immune to his charms. Lucky cat, pun intended.

"I know she isn't alone, Lucky, but maybe she can make even more of your company. There is a rare talking rune originally used to communicate with spirits of nature, but I've heard it works on familiars too. We could try that on Lucky," he started looking at Lucky and finished looking at me.

"Do you really want to hear what Lucky has to say? She might offend you or order you around." I couldn't contain my chuckles. Opening that feline mouth would be the same as opening a Pandora's Box of mean remarks and entitled commands.

He furrowed his brows in confusion. "Wouldn't you like to hear her?"

"I would love to. She's my best friend, and we have been inseparable since I met her on my ascension day when I turned thirteen. Against all the odds and her queenly vibe, she chose me and I chose her as well," I explained to him. Every witch of our coven… was supposed to choose a familiar on the day they ascend to their full powers, their thirteenth birthday. Well, almost every witch; my sister and I were supposed to be the exceptions, but Lucky chose me.

"All the odds?"

"I—my big sister and I were the outcasts of the coven, orphans, and we didn't have the same upbringing as the others. I wasn't supposed to have a familiar, but trying to say no to Lucky is impossible. She chose me and not even our Coven Leader in all her power and outrage could deny the choice. It's said that the choice of a familiar is to be respected, and even though the Coven Leader tried to ignore such a tradition, Lucky wouldn't have it any other way. She refused to work with any other girl." I explained. She might seem a handful at times, but since day one, Lucky fought for me, to be with me, and I have always done the same for her.

"She is a great familiar and you are literally lucky. I am quite sure she won't have only mean-cat things to say." Alev smiled at me and my grey-furred friend.

"I hope so, but I wouldn't bet on it." I chuckled.

"We will see very soon, Nicole," he said before leaving to fetch the rune. Lucky gave me a funny look and shook her head. I didn't need words to know what she meant. He was a good guy, which made everything harder. The risk of me not only dropping orange juice but also my heart for him was real.

"I will keep my focus and I won't let myself fall. Don't worry," I reassured her.

Soon, Alev was back with the rune and a smile on his overly handsome face.

"Let's try it. She has to stand in the middle of a circle of crystals and have the rune brushed over her forehead. You surely understand more about spells than me," he said, giving me a little box with twelve translucent crystals and a beautiful, tiny rune. It was beautiful, tiny, and gold with a silver edge. My magic was connected to Lucky's, and while doing spells, we functioned as one.

"Come on, Lucky. I know you are itching to start voicing your orders and decrees," I chuckled, motioning for Lucky to stand in the middle of the circle of crystals Alev and I were making on the floor. With a look of half-indifference, she stood in the centre and started licking her paw as if she didn't have a single worry in her life. Great timing for cleaning! As soon as the circle was formed, I felt the energy of nature and the essence of the water in me stir up. Placing the rune on Lucky's forehead, I let my body channel and conduct the magic from the circle to my familiar. We vibrated as one and the curtains of water leaving my fingertips slowly surrounded us both. The small rune became liquid and was absorbed into Lucky's forehead, making her glow in an intense shade of silver for a moment.

My eyes blinked at the flare of light and when they opened again, the light was gone, and Lucky was once again licking her paw.

"Nicole, it isn't polite to stare. Especially not during my cleaning routine!" I heard a soft feminine voice carrying the undertone of a meowing, and even though I should have expected that, I fell on my startled butt.

Alev and I exchanged a look before we both started to chuckle. Those were really Lucky's first words? Alev offered me a hand, helping me to stand up as we continued chuckling like little children.

"Frankly, you both are so immature!" Lucky gave us a single gaze as she continued with her *cleaning routine*.

"It worked very well, and you were right," Alev said, brushing a stray lock of hair behind my ear. Didn't he know that his touch enticed all the feelings, sensations, and goosebumps?

His lips so close to mine made my brain turn off partially and the words left my mouth without even making much sense.

"My ovulation day is in four days."

Alev arched his brow in confusion at the weirdness and my sudden change of subject and I breathed deeply, taking a few steps away, creating some secure distance between us. That way, I could think straight, without getting lost in his warmth and the odd magnetic force that seemed to attract me to him.

"I've checked my period app. I will take the test the lady from the Surrogate Centre gave me as well, to make sure everything is right, and it works," I added, biting the inner side of my lip.

He gave me a small smile, unfazed by my awkwardness.

"That's great, Nicole. This baby is very important to me and I want to have him or her in my arms as soon as possible. I will let you and Lucky have a girls' talk. Don't forget to eat your wrap," he said, leaving the room. At least it worked and my sanity was once again safe, as his smell and his warmth no longer assaulted my senses and made my mouth water. Sighing deeply, I let my body fall and sink into the soft mattress.

"Some people are in need of a reverse talking rune!" Lucky remarked.

CHAPTER 15
Nicole

"Nicole, it's time for you to woman up. Go downstairs and get me some good milk."

I woke up to those words from an annoyed-looking Lucky.

The clock on the bedside table told me it wasn't even 7 am yet. Who thought the talking rune was a good idea?

"Lucky, seriously? Now you can talk, so cat up. Go and ask someone else," I teased her, getting up to change and do her bidding.

"You could've asked that handsome dragon to do it for you if you hadn't pushed him away by being awkward yesterday," she grumbled, giving me a dirty look. I had to push Alev away; otherwise, I would lose my resolve and end up jumping into his arms. I had to choose between awkward and crazy. Jumping his bones would make him give up on this agreement and look for another surrogate. I couldn't have that happening. I needed this to work.

"Since you are going downstairs, bring some dry food too," Lucky added, and I nodded with a sleepy frown.

"Do you want catnip as well, Your Highness?"

"No, Nicole. I am not a day drinker. Maybe later," she replied as she jumped on my bed and made herself comfortable on my pillow.

Throwing the first thing I found on, I headed downstairs. I heard a small gasp as I entered the kitchen, and there stood a wide-eyed Marion holding a bag of chocolate and a pot of ice cream. She almost jumped as if I had just caught her doing something naughty.

"I am sorry. I didn't mean to startle you," I said apologetically.

"It's okay, don't worry," she said, taking a bowl and mixing her sweets with orange juice. Sighing deeply, Marion sat in an armchair, adjusting herself a couple of times to find a comfortable position, which seemed hard with such a swollen stomach. Her due date was surely close.

"Please, don't tell anyone you saw me… eating this. I'm not supposed to, yet it's hard to resist," she murmured, looking between her sweet mix and me.

"Don't worry, your secret is safe with me." I gave her a small smile as I fetched Lucky's milk and dry food.

"Your cardigan is beautiful. Where did you buy it?" she asked, looking at my crochet off-white little coat. Just like most of my clothes, I'd made it myself.

"Oh, I made it," I told her, following her gaze to the simple piece of clothing.

Marion's grey eyes lit up with a gleam of excitement, and she smiled in approval.

"You are very talented. I design clothes as well, but I have zero skill in sewing them. Do you work in the fashion industry?"

I had to hold back a gasp of surprise. Was this elegant and graceful woman really praising my work?

"Oh, no. I just make some clothes sometimes. It's kind of a hobby." I gave her a shy smile.

"Well, you should pursue a career as a fashion designer. We can talk more about it later," she smiled. I was about to leave when her next words stopped me. "You should come downstairs more often. The clan was surprised and a little overwhelmed to see you. We are quite protective of our people since we've been through a lot in the last few decades: war, near extinction and betrayal, to name a few. However, our first reaction to your arrival… it shouldn't keep you away. This is your home now and the least you should be able to do is to walk around freely."

Nodding, I smiled at Marion. I didn't deserve her kind words, yet they made my heart a little warmer. My Spirit Dragon, Azula, roared within me, not happy about my thoughts. He was the only animal spirit I'd heard of that came without being summoned.

Marion wasn't wrong; I couldn't live in this house for months and keep to myself in my bedroom. It wouldn't help anything. Even though my now-talking cat would deny it, she, too, would like to walk through the house and meet up with Alma's orange cat.

Mallory

My mate Daniel and I were having lunch on the balcony, enjoying the view and the gentle sound of the waves crashing.

"Why are you lost in thought?" I asked, looking between his contemplative face and my empanada. Since we had left our hideout in London and came to Marbella, Spanish food became my favourite.

"I am thinking about Alev and his surrogate. I don't know this girl and what to think, but I can see something clearly. Yet it seems that everyone else refuses to see it. This situation might seem far from ideal, but Alev is happier with it. He is happy about getting his baby. Besides that, when he is with this girl, he seems much happier than he has been in months. He liked Niki and was in love with her. We can't deny that, but she made him tense, and different to his normally easy-going self. Somehow, Niki didn't bring out the best in him and didn't help him to be fully himself. I thought it was because they weren't a fated pair, but maybe it was their relationship. Yet, now, around this witch with whom he has no relationship, he seems much more relaxed, happy even; he seems more like himself," my mate told me.

It was clear from seeing a bit of their exchange at the beach the other day: Alev was happy and relaxed, maybe even more than that. Though I wasn't naïve to think he was in love with her. They weren't mates, yet there was a spark there, and little sparks could light intense fires of either passion or hell.

"You are right. I've never seen him that relaxed, enjoying himself that much. The fact that Niki left him suddenly, along with the Succubus' poisonous seduction, took a heavy toll on him and hurt him deeply. One way or another, either because of the hope of having his baby soon or because of Nicole's presence, Alev seems better now, lighter. His eyes are brighter and he smiles wholeheartedly again. This crazy situation is doing him good, Baby."

"Maybe the best outcomes arise from unexpected and somewhat unconventional situations." Marion's voice attracted our attention, making us look back. "And it isn't like Alev is the most conventional of the males we know. He seems happy and is behaving like himself once again. That's enough for me to give Nicole a chance," she added.

To my surprise, Marion stole one of my empanadas. As I looked at her with wide eyes, she glanced at her huge baby bump and smiled, making me giggle. At this point in her pregnancy, she had an almost divine right to steal all the food she wanted. This long-awaited pregnancy agreed with her and made her glow in many golden shades of happiness.

"I have the feeling that Nicole will be more than a surrogate to him, even though I think they both are still not aware of it. Maybe they need a little push *from destiny,*" she added, a naughty look on her face. Daniel shook his head but smiled.

Why did I get the feeling that by destiny, she meant us?

CHAPTER 16
Nicole

Today was the day. The test the Warlocks had given me only confirmed what my period app had already told me.

I slumped on the edge of my bed and sighed.

"Don't be like that. Sleeping with the hot Dragon isn't the biggest sacrifice we are making in our situation. It actually should be the easy and fun part," Lucky said as she jumped to my side. We? I was the one making all the sacrifices, while Her Highness was enjoying the good cat life.

"I only hope it works, so we can be done with it, and buy ourselves some time. I am sure Kadmus will contact me again through that bloody mirror very soon," I sighed.

"Right. We have to work on this Kadmus issue too. I will walk around the house and try to find something while you get ready for your Dragon. No one will suspect a beautiful and innocent-looking familiar lady like myself," Lucky told me, lifting her snout with pride.

"He isn't my Dragon." I shook my head and fidgeted with the blanket under my hands. Her idea wasn't bad and it could, hopefully, work. "Go, but be careful," I added.

She nodded with a matter-of-fact meow.

"I am always careful, Nicole. Felines observe, judge and then act. That's why we are at the top of the food chain," she told me, and I chuckled at how delusional she was. The only food chain she topped was her expensive milk from a supermarket chain.

My anxious eyes roamed to the clock; it was still before noon and Alev was working, so nothing would happen any time soon. These dragons definitely didn't have to work at all. Everything about them was golden, fancy, and privileged. Honestly, I think they worked as some kind of cover so as not to attract the suspicion of nosey humans. It was either that or they were bored with their long lifespans. A Golden Dragon could live for centuries, and I was sure that those here were all as old as dirt. Another sigh left my lips; here I was with no experience whatsoever, about to go to bed with an ancient Dragon.

It surely would be a fast ordeal, only enough to put his seed in and ensure conception. It should be done soon, and that was what mattered. So why did the thought of being close to him soak my panties? Could I conceal my desire as we got down to business? Maybe I could close my eyes and sing something stupid in my mind. Yes, that would be fast and, hopefully, work on the first attempt! I repeated it to myself as if it were a mantra.

It would be as romantic as any other business arrangement, but instead of shaking hands, we would shake something else. A humourless laugh left me at that thought because I never dared to be romantic or think about guys, let alone have any romantic dreams about my first time. Surviving and fending for myself always took all my time and attention, and now I had the debt to pay and no headspace for daydreaming or anything like that. Well, my slumber was something else. The dreams of this mysterious man, Vasilis, had haunted me my entire adult life.

My sister told me it must mean something, but I dismissed her. It couldn't mean something other than pain and frustration. That was what love did; it took my mother too and I wouldn't let her story repeat itself.

My eyes met her old spell book on the top of the shelf. I didn't know much about her or about her death. But I'd heard rumours around the coven, something about how a man ruined her life and took her from us. They also said that, just like a bad omen, I was born of my mother's misery. My sister insisted it was only gossip, but not even when I was a child did I believe her.

I jumped up and headed to the kitchen. Despite not being much of a booze girl, today I really needed a drink. I would drown all those thoughts and worries in the bottom of a glass of Guinness beer — or whatever I could find.

In the kitchen, I poured myself a glass of the first alcoholic drink I found — whiskey. They seemed to have lots of that in the house.

"Holy Nyx! That's pure alcohol!" I mumbled after taking a sip, frowning and biting my lip at how strong it was as it burned its way down my throat.

"Why are you drinking in the morning?" I whipped around as I heard Marion's astonished voice.

"It... today is the day of the first trial," I replied, looking between my drink and down my lap, anywhere but at her. Considering my situation, I shouldn't be ashamed of what I was doing; I should be beyond that. Yet shame consumed me, and it brought a bitter taste to my mouth, more than the burning drink. How I wished everything was different.

"Tea will do you better than morning whiskey. I will make you some camomile," Marion offered with a smile, and to my surprise, she squeezed my shoulder in reassurance.

"And homemade cookies always help too," Mallory added, and I only just noticed that she was there as well.

"I love this pencil skirt. Did you make this one yourself as well?" Marion asked as she boiled water just by holding the mug.

"Yes, it's a basic pattern," I replied, looking down at the dark blue skirt.

"It's classic and elegant. You really should think about working in the fashion industry, Nicole. I have a fashion brand, even though I don't plan to launch a new collection any time soon. My mate and I want to focus on our baby girl now. This baby is very precious to me; for years I tried to get pregnant without any success, so I want to give my little miracle all my time and love," Marion told me as her eyes shone with emotion, something between a smile and an unshed tear.

Marion placed the mug of tea in front of me and sat by my side with another mug in her hand. Mallory did the same, but instead of feeling overwhelmed by their presence, my heart felt warm. I swallowed hard the lump of unspoken emotions that formed in my throat. These two looked at me with kind eyes and even shared things about their lives with an undeserving stranger.

"Babies are really precious to our clan. We almost went into extinction and because we didn't have fertile females for many decades, our people had no hope. We were only waiting for our imminent death, our end. But one day a stranger came into our lives and small and big miracles started to happen. Alma was expecting her twins and soon we found Mallory and her sister and saved them from the Scarlet Dragons' captivity," Marion told me.

"We have hope, life and something to live for again," Mallory added with a teary smile on her face as she passed me the cookies.

"Now the house is full of babies, of new life," I told them, smiling as their pain and their joy tugged at my heart. This clan had lost almost everything, I could relate to that. Yet unlike me, they hoped, they thrived, and they found their miracles. In my case, only dark magic seemed to follow my path, and it had the name and the ugly face of Kadmus. A little sigh parted my lips; because of him, there was no hope for me.

"Yes, it is. We hope that it will continue, that our family grows with babies, friends and allies," Marion added, giving me a look that made me fidget nervously with a lock of my hair. Did she mean me as part of the family? No-no! She didn't know what she was asking for. Holy Nyx! These people deserved much better than me. I hoped and prayed to the Goddess that no one would harm this clan, as they had already lost so much.

I took a long sip of tea, trying to hide my flushed face from Marion's eyes.

"How about you, Mallory? Do you have children?" I asked, changing subjects.

"Oh, no… Daniel and I are newly mated and we… we have time," she replied with a small smile.

"I don't understand one thing, Nicole. Why do only certain witches have familiars?" Mallory asked.

"There are five different septs of witches: purple, red, green, blue and yellow. It is said each one comes from one of the original witches, and that the colours designate our aura and energy. Nowadays there are many covens around the world, still divided into colours and septs. The witches from different septs have different affinities. Purple Witches, like me, have familiars, while Red Witches, for example, are good with curses and blessings. Within the colours, witches have their individual talents, as you know. Your Duchess, Alma, and I are both Animal Spirit Summoners, Dragon Summoners. Normally each witch only has one talent, however, I have two. Besides being a Summoner, I am a Water Elemental," I explained.

"That's pretty impressive! Your coven must be very proud of you!" Mallory said, a smile on her lips, and I noticed as Marion touched her under the table; Alev should

94

have told her about my special circumstances. I was an atypical case of a witch without a coven. It was one more thing to add to how odd I was, how different to my peers, thus, never accepted. Ironic enough, these dragon ladies looked at me with more acceptance than the people of my own kind.

"I know that it's rather uncommon, but I don't have a coven. I have lived among humans since I was a teenager," I explained to her as I stirred my tea.

"Sometimes covens are overrated and we have to make our own path. That's what a witch friend of mine did, and now she is happily mated to a werewolf," Marion said, offering me a reassuring smile. She wasn't wrong, better alone than among those who don't like you.

We kept talking about Marion's impending due date, fashion, and how beautiful the city was. Unexpected smiles and even laughter crossed my lips, and I managed to relax, without needing the help of the tea or the booze.

"Nicole, I think I know something that will make you feel more secure about tonight. Every woman needs powerful lingerie to feel better about her body and intimacy in general," Marion told me, a brow arched and a funny smile on her face.

"Oh, no… that's not like intimacy. I am sure it will be quick, only to fit the purpose of natural insemination…" I mumbled awkwardly, once again playing with my hair nervously. My body wasn't what made me insecure, and I didn't even think about the way I would look. It didn't matter, he wouldn't care. His only interest is to get me pregnant, right?

My teeth grazed the inside of my lips as thoughts swirled in my mind. What I feared was the way my body would react, the explosion of desire that would erupt from every cell of my being. It was inescapable, unavoidable; my body craved him like it craved air and water. It was a basic, instinctive need. More than that, I feared getting lost in the hot sea of desire and never coming back. Burnt, drowned and intoxicated by him as he consumed all my dreams, thoughts, body and soul.

CHAPTER 17
Alev

As soon as I got home, I went looking for her. Fuck, I could hardly work or concentrate on anything else all day; I was too busy thinking about her.

I should have been thinking about the baby instead — it was so close, it could even be today — yet, Nicole occupied my whole mind.

She had firmly taken control of each one of my thoughts and even if I managed to think about something else, Horus would send me a mental image of her. I shook my head. Horus was a naughty beast, so he only sent images of her in her bikini or the swell of her breasts.

"You know our baby is the priority. Nicole isn't our mate, not even our girlfriend. She too will leave," I told Horus, and he roared in response, fury and sorrow spreading through him like wildfire.

To my astonishment, the prospect of having Nicole leave hurt more than when my ex-girlfriend actually left me. Why did I desire this woman so much? More than ever, more than anyone? That was it, lust. It didn't make sense for it to be anything else. Except I knew it wasn't only that; I wanted her beyond this scorching desire.

"What the hell!? I am going insane!" I muttered to myself as I knocked at her door and only heard Lucky's high-pitched voice accompanied by a meow.

"Alev? Is that you? Nicole isn't here. But please be so kind as to bring me some milk," Lucky said, making me chuckle.

"Sure," I replied, laughing to myself at Her Highness' meows and demands as I went to the kitchen.

Hopefully, having sex with Nicole would soothe my yearning and help me get used to the idea that she would leave my life soon after giving me something precious.

She wasn't here for me, but for the contract. All that mattered was my child and the fact that soon I would have him or her in my arms. Hopefully, the baby would have her beautiful eyes.

Nicole

After showering and putting on the ridiculously tiny black lacy lingerie Marion gave me, I put on the cutest summer dress I owned and went to the balcony. Leaning my tense arms on the white bannister, I watched the first lights of the sunset wash over the sky with vibrant shades of orange and golden. A smile formed on my face and I felt an almost unknown sense of peace.

All I wanted to do was to breathe in the sea breeze and let the sound of the waves crashing against the sand soothe my heart and relax my overextended nerves. The balcony was the closest I could get to the sea. Yet, I knew it was dangerous to go to the beach by myself; from what the ladies said, the Scarlet Dragons were insane and a real threat.

"Nicole?" His deep and sexy voice made my stomach churn with anxiety as moisture started gathering between my legs. There went all my peace and serenity.

Turning around, my eyes drank in his tall and broad frame. His hazel-green eyes looked even more beautiful in that light.

"I was looking for you," he said, taking a few steps closer. I shook my head. I needed to follow Lucky's advice and stop staring.

"Oh, I'm sorry. I came to look at the sea and lost track of time." I gave him an apologetic smile.

"No problem at all. I am glad you are venturing out of your bedroom. I wanted to ask if you took the test the Surrogacy Centre gave you," he said, and I nodded.

"Yes. The app was right; today is the day." I flashed him a nervous smile. My heart was beating so fast that it felt like it could leave my chest at any moment, and as a shifter, he could surely hear that.

"I think you need a sip of wine," he said, wrapping a strong and warm arm around my shoulder and leading me back into the house. His touch seemed to calm me down and arouse me in equal measure. I nodded, breathing deeply and trying to conceal both my nerves and desire.

"Have you already had dinner?" he asked as we passed by the kitchen.

"I ate something, enough." I tried to sound normal and calm, and Alev nodded. To be completely honest, given how nervous I was, if I ate anything, the food wouldn't even stay in my stomach for five minutes. I had to finish this natural insemination thing to regain my sanity.

"Can we start now?" My voice was no louder than a whisper. Alev stopped in his tracks and looked at me, his eyes wide open and his brows arched.

His reply only came after a few seconds of startled silence. "Yes, as you wish." We headed upstairs as a tense and expectant silence spread between us. The only thing we both could hear was the desperate beat of my heart.

Alev opened the door, leading us into his bedroom. It was bigger than mine and tidier than I imagined. I couldn't say it surprised me to see a hot tub, a hammock, and a mini-palm tree through the open door of his balcony. By the left wall, there was some sort of pub table and a wine rack. On the other side, the Greek-style sculpture of a semi-naked woman not only surprised me but washed me over with a sense of familiarity. Had I ever seen that statue before? Was it a replica of a famous masterpiece?

My eyes soon went from the old chest by the bed to a video game console. Most of the games lying around it were about fighting and assassins who were searching for something. I might have heard about these games and movies. To complete the very eclectic decor, there were beautiful paintings of the sea on the right wall. The oddest piece of the curious mix was a small, pink velvet chair. It was so small that it wouldn't ever fit a big man such as Alev. It was unexpected, and surely, it had a story.

"Make yourself comfortable," he said, motioning for me to sit on a chair by his private bar while pouring us both glasses of red wine. Letting my body sink on the chair, I took the glass in my hands and swallowed it in a single gulp. I really needed that drink, and no tea would cut it.

Alev took a seat in front of me and chuckled at my table manners as he sipped his wine slowly.

"I know it's an atypical situation, but don't be nervous," he murmured, brushing a lock of my hair behind my ear and making me gulp hard, even more nervous.

"What can we do to make you relax?" he asked, standing up and massaging my shoulders. His warm hands working on my tense muscles actually brought me some relief. A breathy moan almost left my throat, but I held it back, sealing my lips.

A pool of desire gathered in the tiny piece of fabric covering my sex, and goosebumps rose all over my skin. How could a simple touch feel so good?

"We can start," I told him, biting the inside of my lips and clenching my trembling hands.

"Very well," Alev muttered. Leaning down in front of me, he cupped my flushed cheeks and brought his face closer to mine. So dangerously close that the breath hitched in my throat. I noticed a shade of green radiating through his hazel irises like an expanding star and contemplated how his eyes looked even more beautiful from that close. To my utter shock, his warm lips brushed against mine as his tongue licked the seam of my lips slowly, reverently, asking for entrance and making my whole body submit in an uncontrollable moan. My lips parted for his tongue of their own accord as he wrapped his arms around my shoulders and brought me closer to him, our chests touching.

His tongue caressed mine, at first, gently. Soon his kiss grew bolder, and his tongue gilded mine, exploring, tasting and claiming every corner of my mouth. My numb tongue was coaxed by desire, and now it couldn't stop moving alongside his, trying to feel and taste his warmth. His wine flavour exploded in my mouth as our lips moulded against each other and our tongues danced together.

When he parted the kiss, there was no air left in my lungs or sanity in my mind. I was startled, dizzy, and lost.

"I-I didn't expect that," I mumbled like an idiot.

"If we have to do it, we should do it properly," Alev said, looking deeply into my eyes.

My breathing came out in trembling gasps, and my skin was burning with the unfamiliar flush of pleasure. All I could do was nod at him, giving in to my body and the desires of my soul. Tonight, I would be lost. I only hoped not to lose myself forever.

CHAPTER 18
Nicole

He brushed a lock of my hair behind my ear before standing in front of me and pulling his shirt off. My tongue ran over my dry lips as my eyes drank in the view, magnetically attracted by every rippled, every corded muscle of his I-don't-know-how-many packs and his well-built chest. Dragons were big, and Alev's body was chiselled to perfection by a very careful and inspired God — probably a Goddess!

As he took a step closer, his warmth assaulted me, hitching my breath. My trembling hands moved up of their own accord.

Alev chuckled lightly, taking my hand in his, and placing it on his sculpted warm chest.

"You can touch. Everything. No reservations, Nicole. We are doing this properly."

Holy Nyx! Doing. This. Properly — those words again, simple words that would be the death of me!

His hand slid to the back of my neck as he pulled me in for another scorching kiss. While my eyes were closed and my breathing was erratic, completely gone in the kiss, Alev scooped me up in his arms.

"Are you ready to start?" he asked, and I nodded nervously. I wasn't ready. I was still in the middle of having a meltdown while liquid desire warmed my panties. My body wanted him and everything he had to offer. My mind was a mess, yet I couldn't care less; I just needed him now.

Gently, he placed me on the bed, but instead of covering my body with his, he moved down. A gasp of surprise parted my lips as his lips glided from my ankle to my calf. His possessive kisses grew even more intense as he sucked and nibbled the skin along my calf and my inner thigh. My body undulated, and a soft sound left me as my eyes closed, and all sanity was gone. I was completely possessed by an unknown flame. Desire claimed my body, and I gave in completely.

Tonight, I am yours.

His lips stilled at my inner thigh, close to my panties line, and his gaze roamed up, meeting my semi-open eyes. He only flashed me a mischievous smile before giving the same treatment to my other leg. Except this time he didn't stop but pulled my dress up to my belly button. His wide eyes met mine, and a very satisfied grin rose on his lips. What happened? Did he notice I was enjoying this way too much? Much more than I should, considering our weird situation.

"You are full of surprises," he murmured, running soft fingers down the tiny panties. Oh, that was the reason for his reaction. I was in such a haze that I could hardly remember where I was, let alone what I was wearing. My butt almost leapt off the bed as he replaced his fingers with his lips and kissed me there, very close to my most intimate part.

"Alev," I gasped, and his response was to flash me another deliciously mischievous smile. I was glad I didn't have the cup of wine in my hands now; otherwise, it would be all over me. This man's touch was even more intense and unavoidable than gravity, and he made me drop things on myself. He made my jaw drop, and if he wanted it tonight, I would drop to my knees for him.

His hands worked up my dress while another smile tilted his lips up as he looked at the see-through lacy bra; though his gaze didn't linger there. He placed a soft kiss on my lips instead, just before his wandering tongue moved down to my neck. His teeth grazed on my skin slightly, making something between a gasp and a moan leave my slightly trembling body. Little did I know that he was only starting. Soon, his lips found the swell of my breasts, and he ripped the bra with such skill that I could hardly feel it.

His firm yet gentle hands moved from my waist to my hips as he smiled at my breasts as if they were his favourite meal. A groan left him before his tongue traced the curve of each boob carefully, reverently. Weirdly enough, his touch made me feel beautiful, feminine and desired as never before.

My breath came out in frantic gasps, and my hand clutched the blanket as Alev sucked one of my nipples into his mouth, caressing it with his tongue and grazing slightly with his teeth.

My reaction only encouraged his tongue to work faster, sending a jolt of electricity right to my clit and making another wave of wetness drench the thin lace of my thong.

My pebbled bud pushed towards his lips of its own accord, my breasts feeling heavier and more sensitive than ever. Every inch of my body felt more sensitive, as if a soft yet intense spark of fire lit my cells.

"Goddess!" I moaned, trying to get a hold of myself. My body squirmed against the mattress. Alev's firm hands on my hips kept me in place as he looked at me, licking his lips.

"No Goddess, tonight, Nicole. Only you and me." His voice was even deeper than normal, and holy Nyx, it made things down there even wetter. If I hadn't shaved, it would be a rainforest down there now.

My head nodded frantically; tonight, I would only pray his name. His hands moved down my belly and under the thong, causing my overwhelmed body to leap again. A little nibble at my nipple was enough to slow my trembling body down as my mind tried to take in all the new sensations, pleasures, and heat.

His fingers slid down my folds, parting me for him and making me curse under my breath like a witch-sailor.

"So wet for me, Dyek—" he stopped in his tracks, busying his mouth with my other nipple. With ease, his fingers slid down my slit and entered my opening, making me jerk at the low-burning sensation. How many fingers did he have there?

"You are so impossibly tight. Wait. Nicole, are you a virgin?" he asked, withdrawing his fingers abruptly and kneeling down in front of me, shock clear in his too-handsome face.

"I—" I couldn't lie to him, and it wasn't something I could actually hide, right?

I gulped hard and propped my body up by putting my weight on my elbows. "Yes," I nodded, looking away for an instant.

Alev exhaled hard, and his expression completely changed. He seemed conflicted, angry even.

"Why didn't you tell me you are a virgin?" he asked, cupping my face gently.

My eyes met his, and I sighed.

"Because it doesn't matter, not for me, nor for the contract."

It didn't matter. I needed this agreement to work, and I didn't really have any romantic ideas or anything. I was doing what I had to with all the dignity I had left.

"It does matter. Your first time has to be slow, gentle, and somewhat special," he told me before standing up. Even though it wasn't time for that, my eyes couldn't leave the giant bulge in his pants. Did I do that to him? All of that?

I was such a dork when it came to sex; Lucky would be so ashamed!

To my surprise, Alev simply turned around and left the room. Why did he leave? This was his room, not mine. My hands covered my mortified face and all that came to my mind was that I was about to lose everything — my only chance. Tomorrow, Lucky and I would have to leave this house with empty hands, and Alev would find another surrogate. It would be best for him to find someone without secrets and burdens. So, why did my heart clench when I thought of him with another woman?

Goddess! I was losing my mind completely.

She felt better than anything, anyone. Her skin, her smell, the taste of her mouth and the scent of her arousal were simply intoxicating. Horus roared within me, impatient to go back to her and have my lips on her perfect breasts once again.

Running downstairs with a painful erection, I looked for whatever I could find to make tonight a little more special for her. I found some old candles, and I knew well where Marion hid her chocolate; she didn't want her mate to know that she was sneaking out at night and filling herself with boxes of it.

Last, I ran to the garden and collected the first flowers I found. It wouldn't be enough, but it had to help a little.

As I ran back to the bedroom, Nicole was searching for her ripped bra. Horus roared louder than ever before in my mind. He didn't want her to go anywhere. This time, I agreed with my Dragon. Tonight, I couldn't let go of Nicole.

Her startled blue eyes met mine, and she looked from my erection to the chocolates, candles, and flowers in my hands.

"I don't know what else I can do," I told her frankly, exhaling and placing the candles on the table before I lit them with a touch of my fingertips. I had been with virgins before, but it was some decades ago and none of them was *her*.

I poured some wine for both of us and brought it all on a tray to the bedside table.

"Thank you." She gave me a shy smile, and when she was about to gulp her wine as fast as last time, I stopped her.

"I need you sober tonight, Nicole. No forgetfulness, no regrets," I wasn't only trying to be a half-decent man, but I couldn't have her forgetting my touch and how my dick stretched her for the first time. A possessive and carnal side of me wouldn't accept that.

She nodded and sipped her drink slowly.

"Thank you for the flowers and the chocolate," she smiled, and that was my undoing. I forgot everything else and let my wine fall as I captured her in my arms, making her straddle me.

Cupping the back of her neck, I traced her fleshy lips with my errant fingers, asking for permission. She nodded, covering my hand with her small and much colder one. That delicate gesture was all the consent I needed.

My lips captured hers, and my tongue swept into her mouth with an almost unknown urgency. All I wanted was to be gentle and do it slowly, but I couldn't. The all-consuming fire swallowed me, and I yearned for this woman, her taste and her skin. My kiss was possessive, seizing, as I explored and claimed every corner of her mouth, both tasting and devouring her. Horus let out a triumphant groan of pleasure within me. Placing her glass on the bedside table, I lay her on the bed slowly, hovering over her.

I needed more of her taste. I squeezed her boobs slightly, pinching and twisting her nipples as I watched her reaction. My dick twitched as she moaned at my rougher touch, her red nipples pebbled and the freckled skin of her chest flushed slightly. She was beautiful! She was pure beauty. My lips drifted down her belly, finding her underwear, and I pushed it off her slowly, admiring the view.

Fucking pretty pussy! She was completely wet for me, her lips glistening with arousal. I ran my fingers through her slit from the clit to her entrance, without entering her, only circling it with my fingers. Her hips bucked in response and her small hands found my hair as she entangled her fingers in it.

"Sorry," she mumbled, pulling her hands away.

"No, Darlin'. We are doing things properly. Do what you want, set your body free," I said, looking at her hooded eyes and she nodded while her pink tongue ran across her delicious dry lips. All her wetness was elsewhere, pouring for my dick.

Not able to resist any longer, I pressed a kiss onto her pussy. My tongue opened her for me and caressed her slowly, enjoying her tangy yet sweet taste.

My fingers replaced my tongue, massaging her clit and her labia as my tongue swirled into her delicious pussy.

Her moans filled the room and her whole body started to squirm until I held her down with a firm hand on her stomach.

"If you want me to stop, say the word," I told her and she nodded, opening her eyes slowly.

"No. Please. Don't. Please, don't stop," she cried out. She didn't have to say anything else; in no time, my tongue was gliding in and out of her as my fingers flickered her clit, alternating gentle and energetic movements.

Soon, my sweet Nicole was cumming in my mouth.

At first, her whole body tensed as if she were trying to control herself and silence the fire burning in her pussy. But within a few seconds, her body jerked down and her hips moved towards me as she rode my face.

"Alev, please. Alev!" My name flowed from her lips in moans and soft screams. It was the most erotic sound I'd ever heard in my couple of centuries.

Damn! I could, and would love to, spend the entire night eating her, but my aching erection reminded me of a more urgent need. I had to be inside her now.

CHAPTER 19
Nicole

As I opened my eyes, Alev was by my side, giving me a glass of water.

"Are you alright?" he asked, his eyes filled with both lust and worry.

Oh, I was much better than alright. I'd never felt anything that strong, overpowering, overwhelming.

My head nodded, and I sipped the water slowly before giving him back the glass. He wiped a drop of water that flowed from my clumsy lips, and to my surprise, he kissed me deeply. His tongue caressed mine and I could taste myself in his mouth. Funny.

Standing up, he pulled his pants down. Wait, was he going commando? Naughty Dragon. Yet that wasn't the main reason for my shock. It seemed like Dragons were extra big everywhere. I was in trouble with capital **D**: his monster wouldn't fit inside me.

"Nicole?" he called me, making me snap back from my monster-of-a-dick-induced haze. How could something that scary make my mouth water?

"Hmmm… I am fine," I muttered, shaking my head and looking away as I felt my face flush a little. With that thing, he could surely put many baby dragons waaaay deep inside me.

Alev chuckled, sitting on the edge of the bed next to me and pulling me into his arms. My naked butt was on his thighs, very close to his huge willy! He parted my lips with his thumb before kissing me again, his other hand on my breast, playing with my nipple.

"We can do it tomorrow instead," he suggested with a frown he was trying to hide.

"No!" The word came out much louder and more intense than I meant, almost like a protest. No, not tomorrow. I needed it immediately.

Those lips assaulted mine as he lay me down on the pillow, his body covering mine. He parted my legs with his knee before his wandering fingers caressed a straight line down my body until they met my wet folds. Alev's finger entered me, and he let out a groan of satisfaction into our kiss. Caressing me slowly, his fingers swirled and circled my insides - Oh, Goddess! A breathless gasp escaped me as he touched a magical place inside there. My whole body seemed to grow more alive, and jolts of electricity radiated through to my womb.

To my frustration, he pulled his finger back and licked it, his eyes fixed on mine — golden sparkles gleamed in his hazel-green irises, making his eyes look like something out of this world, gates to a magical dimension of dark promises and infinite pleasure. His intense, dark and completely overpowering gaze seemed to look into my soul, baring it completely.

"You are ready, dripping wet," his voice was deep, raw, almost a grunt. My dizzy head only nodded at his words.

My breath caught in my throat as he brushed the tip of his member against my entrance.

"Look at me, Darlin'. It's alright," he cooed at me, attracting my half-startled gaze towards his. He didn't move; he was waiting for my confirmation.

"Yes," I murmured, and before I could clench my eyes and brace myself, his lips touched mine in a gentle kiss. His fingers ran down my hair slowly as he entered me carefully. A gasp crossed my lips at the burning, stretching sensation, but Alev's skilled tongue caressing mine soothed me a little.

He slowly pushed himself deeper as a raw growl left him and his golden eyes met mine. Without losing time, he covered my face with gentle, soothing kisses. He stilled there deep within, his hands running down my arms and his lips kissing the tears that slid down my cheeks. No, those weren't tears of pain, but something deeper, something I couldn't name, or even understand. I felt something warm in my heart, a feeling of recognition as if having him in my body was something that was supposed to happen, over and over again.

After some time, he cupped my face, and his gaze was once again kissing mine, his thumb caressing my lips. I only nodded, coaxing him to continue, but it didn't seem enough for him now.

"Use your words, Nicole. You were crying, are you…" He sounded and seemed almost pained, like someone fighting against his own desires and instincts, and from the look of it, he was about to lose it.

"No, it's not that. You can move. I'm alright," I whispered. My hips moved towards his, and I further impaled myself on his penis. He groaned deeply, his firm hands moving down my hips. Pulling his penis out of me slowly, he spread my legs open and wrapped them around his body.

Alev looked intently into my eyes, trying to find any sign of pain as he upped his pace. It hurt since I was stretched open by a monster willy, yet I wouldn't have him stop. If he did, then I would really cry in frustration. Yes, I was that gone! His caresses moved up my body, and he found the pearl of pleasure within my folds and started massaging it.

As soon as I started moaning at the building pleasure, his thrusts became deeper and harder.

A deep groan left him as his eyes flashed golden for a moment. "You feel so good, Dyekhadee!" He thrust his rock-hard member all the way in, brushing his tip against my cervix and making my hips undulate towards him. My body wanted more, but his words snapped me back from the heated-cloudy state my mind was in.

"What?" I asked, confused. Dye-what? This word pierced through my chest, sharp, painful. Who was this person?

"It's a word in ancient Dragon language," his reply made my chest relax, and the air left my lungs slowly.

"What does it mean?" I asked, pushing my hips towards him. His huge willy, as we call it back in Ireland, was starting to hurt so good, caressing some magical spots inside me.

"It doesn't matter now," he replied, sealing my mouth with a deep kiss and making me forget all questions, words, and the thin thread of sanity I still managed to hang on to.

The deep strokes combined with the skilled work of his fingers pushed me to the edge, sparks vibrated within all my nerve endings and I felt something like birds of fire flying down my back as my body combusted in a scream of absolute pleasure.

Within seconds, I heard Alev's guttural groans and felt his warm seed flood me. He didn't move away or even out of me, only pulled me into his embrace, flipping me to my side, our bodies still united.

With a mind of their own, my fingers ran across his muscular chest, where beads of sweat gathered, making the tan on his golden skin look even better.

When my absent-minded fingers moved a little down, his hand stopped me. "If you keep doing that, I will have to take you again. You are way too raw for a second round, and I don't want to hurt you." I expected chuckles or even a grin from him, but no, he was very serious.

He did have a point since I was sore down there. But his penis was still deep inside, and it didn't feel limp or anything like that.

He pulled it out of me slowly, cuddling me in his arms, his lips seeking mine. After a few sweet kisses, I think I ended up dozing off. My whole body was sated, exhausted, and nicely sore. My soul was satisfied, feeling whole and floating in dreams of hot water, his eyes, his touch and yes, his willy!

Suddenly, I woke up with a start. I shouldn't be here; the deed was done, and I should leave. Yet when I was about to roll my way out of bed, strong arms pulled me back to his warm chest.

"Alev, I've got to go to my room."

"No," he denied, without even opening his eyes. He only pressed me even closer and covered my lips with his. A sigh left me, but I let his warmth and the incredible feeling of his strong arms wash over me, lulling me back to sleep.

Alev

A smile formed on my face as I looked at her serene and sated expression. She fell asleep in my arms, and all I wanted to do was to keep her there. Warm. Safe. Mine. fuck!

That shouldn't be happening! Horus roared in ecstasy; he had her exactly where he wanted. After watching her sleep for a little while longer and kissing her sweet face, I decided to try to get some sleep myself — not an easy task with my throbbing hard-on. Still, I couldn't leave her here to solve my issue by myself. Setting my cock between her buttcheeks, I closed my eyes and tried to think about everything but her.

It was impossible: her smell, her taste and the sweet feeling of her were consuming me like Dragon Fire and I only fell asleep after many hours.

As I closed my eyes, I was brought back to the hot and bare lands of my dreams. This time it felt odd, and I knew I was dreaming. I saw myself walking in her direction, the woman that had been haunting my dreams for weeks now. This time it was different indeed; the first time, I could only see her flowing dress, her dark hair and the sensual curve of her breasts. Tonight, my gaze could finally reach up to her face and I saw *her*. Nicole.

It was always her, and it had always been her.

I tried to say something, but this dream was different. I could only watch myself walking towards her as if it were some sort of movie and I was only floating over my body as a mere bystander.

"Come here, Dyekhadee. You know no one can see you there. It's safer in my chambers, in my bed." I saw myself striding towards her and a sweet, divine smile on her lips.

She giggled, "I disagree! I think you are dangerous, and your bed is hotter than a pyre of fire. What does Dyekhadee mean? You always call me that, but you've never told me what it means."

I pulled her closer, taking her in my arms to sneak her into my chambers, as I murmured in her ear, "It's the word a few Dragons call their mates, and it means fire of my soul in Dragon language."

"It's beautiful! Why do only a few Dragons use it?"

"Because it means a lot. It means everything. Their spirit, their hearts, their fire."

115

CHAPTER 20
Nicole

The surrounding warmth was gone, and my body felt colder, waking me. My eyes opened slowly, and I saw Alev placing a small tray with orange juice, cookies, and fruit on the bedside table.

"Good morning, Nicole. I am going to work now. Beside your breakfast is the little concoction the Warlock Society gave to increase our chances of conceiving," he said with a smile, motioning to the small blue bottle on the tray, "See you tonight?" he asked and I nodded, still half-dreaming about him, his kisses, and his willy.

Tonight would be the second day in my fertile window and to increase the chances of success, we should do the deed again. A pleasurable tingle exploded through my inner walls at the thought of it. My body already missed his.

My eyes blinked twice as I tried to situate myself a little. True, I couldn't forget about the Warlock's little potion.

"I will go back to my room. I shouldn't have stayed..." I mumbled, regaining my bearings fast.

"No, please stay. Sleep more, and take your time. Of course you should have stayed. Remember, we are doing things properly." His mischievous smile was doing things to my fanny*. He surprised me with a lingering kiss on my cheek, inhaling my smell before leaving the room. Sitting down, I took the funny-tasting blue potion in a single gulp and had breakfast. Last night's activities made me hungry and especially thirsty. Now all I wanted was to get back to Lucky; staying in his room being surrounded by his delicious and sensual manly musk wouldn't be good for me — not my heart nor my throbbing fanny, not to mention that the latter decided to have a mind of her own.

Putting on my clothes, I headed to my bedroom, and before Lucky could say anything, I went for a long shower. His smell was embedded in me and it only made me more confused.

Wake up, Nicole! Nothing more will ever happen. Alev is a Golden Dragon, pretty much Dragon royalty. Handsome, tall, gentle, honest, and perfect. Besides, if a rogue witch had any chance with him, it would be ruined as soon as he learned the truth about me.

My clenched eyes started leaking into a vortex of emotions, with tears and shower water washing over me. To my surprise, my powers seemed to act on their own accord, forming a cocoon of water to envelop me.

All girls, well, all people that didn't have a pineapple in the place of their brains, would want their first experience to be somewhat special, involving love, lust and dreams. For me, it was all broken since my life turned even more upside down a couple of years ago when my sister and I met Kadmus, and I gave up on those expectations. I knew that my life didn't belong to me anymore.

Still, here I was drowning in myself, even though I could breathe underwater, because contrary to any logic, and lost expectation, my first time was exactly that: passion, desire, love and everything that romantics dream of. Come on, no one could do better than Alev.

Yet, those dreams were only meant to be shattered.

117

This love was only meant to become disappointment and pain.

My water cocoon held me tighter, keeping me upright even though my wobbly knees were about to fail. I was doing what I had done since my sister had gone; catching myself from falling. But I couldn't help myself when the fall was down an abyss of passion, when I was falling in love with Alev.

He should be angry that I didn't tell him about my virginity. That would be a prelude to what was about to happen, and eventually, he would end up hating me.

After a few more minutes of cocooning myself, I stepped out of the shower and dried my body. Crying over something I couldn't change was exhausting. I wouldn't shed any more tears.

A sigh left my lips, making a small hole of clarity in the steam-covered mirror of the bathroom. I looked into my eyes, and despite the cascade of tears, they seemed lighter and clearer. There was hope in them. But I shouldn't nurture any hope.

Love was impossible, especially with someone like him.

No secret could remain a secret forever: I've learned that the hard way.

I went back to the room, ready to face the scrutiny of one of the most judgemental creatures in existence: a cat.

"How was it? Are dragons as big as people say?" Lucky asked casually, after stretching and jumping from my pillow.

My eyes narrowed, and I shook my head at the nosy feline. So, now she knew about dragons' willy size. Why didn't she tell me before the act?

"What? We aren't having this conversation, Lucky!" I shook my head again, noticing that her bowls were both filled with dry food and milk.

"Alev is a gentleman; he already fed me this morning. At least someone treats me right and doesn't leave me to fend for myself," she meowed in annoyance.

Her words made a silly smile find its way to my face. Alev even came here to give my mean girl cat her breakfast.

"Rest for round two, Nicole. I will do some work, go around and investigate. Someone has to save our tails," she told me, motioning for me to open the door of the bedroom for her, and so I did. I let my body fall to my bed slowly, and when I was about to close my eyes and take a little nap, a loud and high-pitched meowing made me jump off the bed.

My legs took me to the door as fast as possible. All I could see in the hall was a blur of orange fur running away as Lucky stood pretty much on her claws, ruffling her tail up and raising her back in an arch as if a strong electric shock had coursed through her furry body.

"What happened?" I asked, leaning down close to her.

"I came across the fat bob, didn't you see? Do you think that cat knows about us?" she asked, walking back into the bedroom. A deep exhale crossed my lips. Burbus wasn't a familiar, only a regular cat with a certain magic sensibility, according to Marion and Mallory. He surely couldn't know anything.

"He doesn't know anything. Don't worry. I think the real problem is something else." I smiled, arching a brow at her.

"Pray tell me, what's my problem, oh wise witch?"

"You like Burbus, don't you? You can't lie to me! If you want to talk about guys, you have to spill the beans too." I chuckled, sitting on my bed.

"That would be an impossible lust story. I'm a familiar, whereas he is a simple cat. I am way out of his league, Nicole. We are worlds apart. Besides, he isn't my type. I'm not into chubby cats, and orange definitely isn't the new

119

black!" she said, licking her paw before running it across her lush fur.

"Keep lying to yourself, Lady Lucky."

"My dear peasant witch, I could tell you the same."

A deep breath left me as I let myself fall into my bed.

"I'm trying to deal with it and stop these feelings." Last night was of no help, and I feared nothing would help me. Staying close to Alev was dangerous. He was hotter than a pyre of fire, irresistible, inescapable.

"You better find a spell for that because, on your own, you will fail miserably, Cols. Something about him calls to you, and it's not his six-pack."

Mean girl cat was right! However, I didn't know any spell to make someone less... well, less like I was feeling. So, I had to do what I had done my whole life, fight tooth and claw to survive, survive this all-consuming passion.

My eyes found the clock once again. I could hardly focus on my work. As hard as I tried not to, my thoughts always swirled back to her. Perfect breasts, tight pussy clenching around my cock, sweet moans and those eyes!

At least I could have a relaxing and dreamless night. For the first time in days, I hadn't dreamt about the mysterious faceless woman.

Horus roared within me. Normally I could understand his grunts, but this time it was as unclear as if he was trying to tell me in an archaic, unknown language. He was going crazy.

I left the meeting room, knowing Egan could take care of everything since it was only an everyday meeting.

Staying was pointless, I wasn't productive at all and I was struggling to pay attention.

Heading to my office, I fell into my armchair and poured myself a drink. Fuck! I should have stopped and not taken the poor girl's virginity. She must have been even more desperate than I could've ever imagined, or else she wouldn't have put herself through this situation without ever being with a man before. I should give her the money and let her go, find someone else, yet I couldn't stop. Something in me wanted to be her first, her last, her one and only.

Hell, I didn't know why, but I wanted to have my child with her, with her eyes, with her smile. She was the one to bring my child into this world, and I knew it by instinct. The same insane instinct that demanded me to claim her, keep her in my bed, and in my arms all night, every night.

This instinct and desire made me act like a dork. My hands covered my face as I exhaled, gulping more whiskey.

What the hell was I thinking? I collected random flowers for her and got her the first romantic things I saw. I was acting like a clueless teenage Dragon, lost and out of control. Horus roared some kind of draconian laughter within me.

"I know, Horus. She is different."

She wasn't only the most delicious and fascinating woman I'd ever met, but also the only one I couldn't have. Nicole was the one to conceive and carry my child, and only that.

Horus roared in protest, sending me a very vivid image of him flying away with a semi-naked Nicole on his golden-scaled back. He wanted to steal her away, make her ours. This was his beastly way, but things didn't work like that. I refused to be in another relationship that was fated to fail. She wanted the money, I wanted my child, and that was it. Everything else was only the flames of desire fucking consuming my mind, body and spirit.

121

Egan opened my office door after a knock. "Are you alright?"

"As well as someone can be after they take the virginity of their surrogate and get completely pussy-whipped." I took another sip of whiskey, and Egan sat with me after cursing under his breath and motioning for me to pour him a drink as well.

"Alma doesn't trust Nicole. Our clan has been through a lot lately, Alev, and so have you. My Alma only wants to protect both our family and you. You are a grown man, old friend. You know what you are doing, just make sure you are acting for the right reasons, be it having this child or even starting a relationship with your surrogate. When business and pleasure meet, chaos can arise quickly and consume everything with its lethal fire. You have a lot to lose, especially with a child involved, and none of us wants to see you either lost or depressed again." Egan squeezed my shoulder and emptied his whiskey glass.

Egan was right. Still, all I wanted was to, once again, play with fire tonight.

CHAPTER 21
Alev

When I finally got home, I found Nicole in the same spot as the day before, gazing at the sea from the downstairs balcony with Lucky by her side. Her dark hair flowed in the wind, and her distant and lost look was enough to make my dick hard.

What kind of power did she have over me? Not even when I was a teenager did my body react that way to any woman. Horus roared in my mind; she also affected him a lot.

"Nicole," I called, attracting her eyes to me.

"Oh, Alev. You are back. Let's go to your room?" I almost chuckled at her words and how direct she was. Eager much, pretty witch?

"Let's go. This time I brought something for you. I will wine and dine you before we start," I told her, wrapping one arm around her back while the other carried the bags of food.

"You two don't mind me. I can find my way back to the room. Wait, I can't. I have short paws and I can't open the door!" Lucky's annoyed meow made me chuckle.

"I can open the door for you on the way, Lady Lucky," Nicole said with a sweet giggle that drew a smile from me. Tonight, I planned to enjoy having her — tasting, touching and fucking her to exhaustion. I would worry about Egan's words another day.

After taking Lucky to Nicole's bedroom, we headed to my room.

"I have something for you." I guided her to the balcony, where I set out the food I had bought.

"This smell? Is that what I think it is?" she asked, taking a lungful of air and glancing at the restaurant packet.

"Yes, Irish food. I imagine you miss it," I told her, going to pick a bottle of red wine, glasses and cutlery for us. She had left her home in such an abrupt way and surely missed the small things.

"I do! Thank you so much! Oh, you even got soda bread! And Colcannon and Champ, my favourite!" she exclaimed with excitement.

"Among other things that include potatoes in the many varied ways that the Irish could imagine possible." I chuckled. Irish people really seemed to love their potatoes.

After pouring us some wine, I pulled out the chair for her to sit on and took a seat in front of her. I couldn't stop smiling at the excited and quick way she devoured the food; she even moaned. *Your moans of pleasure have only begun, Beautiful.*

As soon as she finished, I scooped her up in my arms, earning a sweet chuckle from her. Now it was my turn to have my favourite meal.

"I need my dessert," I murmured in her ear, nibbling at her earlobe lightly and making goosebumps rise across her smooth skin.

I laid her down on my bed and took her lips in a kiss. My tongue thrust into her mouth, caressing and tasting hers as my hands worked on lifting her dress to reach and pull her panties off. I was starving and so was the fire beast

124

within my soul. Running my fingers down her slit, I drew a sweet whimper from her. She was already soaking wet for me and I wouldn't waste any time. As my lips devoured hers, I pulled her dress up only stopping to let her pull it all the way off. Now I could feast on her skin. My kisses drifted down her body, from her lips to her chin, reaching the soft skin of her neck, only stopping when my mouth was drawn to one of her perfect nipples. I sucked it into my mouth while I teased her sweet pussy, circling her opening without entering her.

Nicole dug her fingers into my locks as she pushed her breasts against my face. She felt and tasted perfect, but that wasn't how I wanted her. I flipped us over, lifted her by her waist, and placed her on my face. This way, I could devour her completely and drink every droplet of her arousal. My tongue pumped into her, and her whimpers of pleasure grew more desperate, becoming loud and breathless moans. She was close. I worked her faster until she came into my mouth, flooding me with her delicious essence.

Moving her down, I wrapped my arms around her trembling little frame, my hands playing with her nipples, tugging and pinching them lightly whilst making the sweet woman in my arms moan my name.

"I need—" her words came up in a gasp.

"What do you need? Are you alright?" I asked, cupping her face gently and trying to find any sign of discomfort in her expression.

"I need you now," she added, and a huge smile tilted my lips up.

"Yes, Darlin'." Sitting up, I placed her on my lap, facing me.

"Wait! Shouldn't I do the same for you?" her voice wasn't louder than a shy whisper as she touched her lips with quivering fingers.

"Don't worry about that. I'm more than ready to thrust deep into you," I replied, eager to be inside her and have her come around my dick over and over again.

My teeth grazed her bottom lip, opening her lips for my avid tongue to fill her and taste her delicious flavour.

I aligned my cock with her slick pussy and entered her slowly. So fucking tight! Nicole felt better than anything I had ever experienced; she was some sort of dream of a lost paradise, and I was completely high on her taste and the feeling of her.

Once I entered her completely, my mind couldn't form coherent thoughts anymore. So I only thrust deep and slow while my kisses devoured and claimed her and my hand massaged her perfect boob.

She started moaning senselessly, her nails sliding down my back as she moved her hips towards me. My hand roamed down to her clit, and I massaged it, pushing her over the edge.

"Alev, I—" she cried out. Her body tensed and shuddered as she lost control, taking me with her. Those clenching walls around my dick made it impossible for me to hold it any longer.

"Darlin'." My voice and body called for her as I filled her to the brim with my seed. Caressing her pretty face, I pulled her closer and kissed her over and over. To my luck, she wasn't tired or too sore after this time, and I could have her once again before we fell asleep in each other's arms.

It was the first time in my long life that I almost passed out from too much pleasure. Nicole was pure magic, ecstasy. Sex with all the other women wasn't bad, but nothing compared to what we had; they were nothing compared to *her*. I'd always felt like I could go more and blamed it on my shifter stamina. For the first time, I felt like I didn't have anything else to chase. I was completely spent, fully satisfied.

126

Nicole

"You shouldn't make any noise, they don't know you are here," Vasilis told me and I nodded, biting the fingers he placed over my mouth and giggling at his growl of lust.

"You are very bad, Agapiti. Maybe I should spank this naughty ass before I take you."

His words only made me giggle more, as I would welcome his spanking or anything this man had to give me. I was his.

"Vasilis," I moaned as he took my aching nipple into his mouth. He also couldn't wait any longer for this. As soon as he entered my body, I woke up with a start.

This again! It was like sweet torture, and I always woke up as soon as we started.

"Lucky, sorry if I moaned in my sleep. These last nights had been hard, between missing his wi-... Alev and all of those scorching dreams." My subconscious was adding the last straw to drive me crazy. I covered my eyes with both hands, trying to avoid the bright light. It was already morning.

"You are a loud one, Cols! Try to bite something during your wet dreams; that way, you won't disturb my sleep." Lucky replied with something between a yawn and a meow.

"Sorry," I murmured. I was traumatising my familiar!

"Tell me more about this Vasilis. I've heard so much about him, mostly in the language of moans and whimpers!" she laughed a meow, and she seemed fine with it. I guess I was the one being traumatised.

127

"I know nothing about him, only what I see in my dreams, and it's been happening even more often since Alev and I…" I sighed.

"Yes, that I can tell. At first, it was once a week, but now you are moaning like a cat in heat twice every night and really disturbing my beauty sleep."

It had already been thirteen days since my first time with Alev. Since our third night together, I've been trying to avoid him along with my fast-growing feelings. While he was at work, I spent some time with Marion and Mallory, but at night I came back to hide in this bedroom.

Avoiding him was ripping a hole in my heart and even making me feel a little cranky. I almost had the same mood as Lucky on a good day.

Following the demands of my bladder, I went to do my morning business. Another day waking up completely damp and in need of a cold shower. Looking down at my panties, I realised that it wasn't only arousal making them damp, but blood as well.

My period had come.

"No! It didn't work." I rested my head in my hands, my elbows on my knees, and sighed. Alev would be heartbroken. I knew how much he wanted this baby soon.

Well, I should be happy because the added cycle would buy Lucky and me some more time for our searches, except I felt like I had lost something. My chest was clenching for him, and at that moment, it seemed that his happiness was more important to me than my own safety.

CHAPTER 22
Nicole

The cool water soothed my hands and my face as I washed them; I breathed deeply and looked at myself in the mirror. I had to tell Alev the news, and I shouldn't delay it, as he deserved to know the truth. At least all the truth I could tell him. It was Saturday, so he would be home.

Lucky's soft snores permeated the room as I changed. Of course, she was snoring like a lady, comfortably lying on my pillow.

I grabbed the first dress I found and went downstairs. Alev was there drinking a large mug of coffee, with his headphones on, and fully dressed. Did he just get home? It wasn't my business... but still.

"Nicole." He took off his headphones and stood up as soon as he saw me. "What's the matter? Why do you look so sad?" he asked, wrapping his arm around my shoulder and leading me to a comfortable armchair.

"I got my period." I sighed. Why was I so sad about it? I couldn't understand myself and the cataclysm of emotions surrounding me.

Alev's face fell, and he took a seat next to me, placing his elbows on his knees and his crossed hands at the level of his lips. A sad sigh left me, and I looked away until the feeling of his warm hand on mine attracted my eyes back to him.

"How are you feeling?" He gazed at me.

Goddess, I didn't know why, but his gaze melted me a little, and a few tears left my eyes. I wasn't one to cry that easily; what was wrong with me?

"I am... feeling a little weird. I have cramps, that's it." I tried to give him a smile, but I probably looked like a struggling animal.

"I know what can help; come with me." He took my hand in his and stood up, leading me to the kitchen. To my surprise, he filled a huge bowl with ice cream, lots of chocolate sauce and chocolate chips, and gave it to me.

"That's what my sisters used to eat when they had their period. They had Godzilla moods; my father and I were afraid to approach them, so we just stayed away and fed them sugar," he explained as I started devouring the ice cream. He was right; it did help a little.

His words made a soft chuckle leave me.

"They are... were girls, not zoo animals." I shook my head.

"I am not that sure. You have never seen my sisters. For a few days of every month, they were the most terrifying Dragons of our land. I miss them, even their craziness and bad moods," he said, looking away and pouring himself some Irish coffee. "A long time ago, before the Scarlet Dragons sneakily attacked and almost annihilated our people, I had three younger sisters. They died when our hideout was ambushed, along with my mother. My father died a few years earlier. After losing her mate, my mother went through a profound depression, as no Dragon should be able to survive the loss of their mate, their beloved. Yet, contrary to nature, she did. She was a shadow of herself, an ash of her fire. That was when she surrendered her position in my favour."

"Position?" I asked.

"Yes, my father was a Count, part of Egan's Noble Council. My mother was his successor, at least for a few months. She couldn't take it any longer, so I had to step up and succeed her. Only after I joined the council when I was quite young, a child in Dragon years, Egan and I grew close and became friends. It was a hard time for the Council. We had to make hard decisions about the war. At those times, we didn't know the actual source of the attacks. The Scarlet Dragons made it seem that packs of werewolves had ambushed and killed our people in cowardly attacks on hospitals, schools and public squares.

A sob hitched in my throat and, without realising it, my fingers were drawing soothing circles on the back of his palm. Tears slid down my cheeks at the understanding of how much he had lost; he'd lost everything. His family, his people, and the life he used to have. Now all he wanted was to have a family again, a child of his own, and it wasn't happening. Holy Nyx! I was a crying mess now!

I also lost my whole family, and even though Alev was honourable and kind and I was... me, we both were driven by the same idea: family.

Except I was very different from him, and I didn't do things right. I was as bad and rotten as my coven had deemed me. My heart clenched painfully in regret because of the crime I still had to commit. Something I couldn't escape from. I had no choice, yet it still hurt.

His clan had been through a lot. Mallory told me they found out that one of the main goals of the Scarlet Dragon King wasn't to bring the Goldens to extinction but to perform scientific experiments to extract their power and transfer it to them. They were like sci-fi movie psychos.

"Don't cry, Nicole. I don't know why I told you that. I am sorry. I rarely talk about it. In fact, I never talk about them. Although now the words seemed to find their way out, I am sorry they upset you," he shushed me, wrapping one strong arm around my waist as his other thumb gently wiped my tears. I had to pull myself together and stop the waterworks. *You are a fighter, Nicole. You don't have time to break down and cry.* Maybe if I repeated that mantra to myself over and over, I would get back to normal.

"No, I am glad you could get it off your chest. Talking about the past can be good," I murmured, knowing that I, myself, had to keep my past a secret.

"True, thank you for listening. Now let's do something that will actually cheer you up. A comedy movie?" he asked, taking me and my ice cream bowl downstairs to the home theatre.

"Alev, I am truly sorry it didn't work this time." I knew it wasn't my fault, but I couldn't stop feeling bad for him and his broken hopes.

"It's alright. The Warlock Society said that the chances of it working at the first attempt were low. We will try again, try harder," he tried to smile, but it didn't reach his eyes and now it was my turn to squeeze his hand in reassurance.

After we watched a romantic comedy, Knight and Day, and ate all the ice cream in the house, I went back to my room to take a proper shower and talk to Lucky. She wanted to walk around the house again on her spying mission. Her only problems were her fear and secret desire to meet Alma's cat, Burbus. Nothing I said convinced her that he didn't know about our secret agenda.

As I entered the room, her eyes focused on me. "Where were you? And why didn't you bring breakfast?"

"I can bring you something after I shower. Lucky, my period came. I am not pregnant," I told her with a deep exhale.

She narrowed her eyes at me and stared for quite some time, but before I could say anything, she beat me to it.

"Are you sure you aren't pregnant? Lately, I've noticed some changes in your scent, and you are as moody as me."

132

"Why didn't you tell me that before?" I arched my brows at the staring cat.

"I don't say things unless I am absolutely sure; that's what the wise ones do. You should follow my ways, young witch," Lucky patronised me. "But now, taking another sniff of you, I am almost completely certain that you smell different. There is something draconic about you. Besides, as your familiar, I am especially sensitive to any change in your energy and magic, and I can feel some fire vibe coming from you," she meowed, her tail swishing in the air. "Just call your Dragon, pee on a stick or two and tell me I am right," she added with a small smile.

"He is not my Dragon!" I argued, going to look for both Alev and pregnancy tests.

After I told him what Lucky said, we both rushed to my bedroom, carrying a handful of pregnancy tests. I was about to enter the bathroom, and Alev was standing there, dumbfounded, about to follow me.

"Daddy, let the lady pee alone. There are some things that a man should not witness, trust me," Lucky told him. He shook his head, scrubbing his face with his hand.

"I didn't mean to go with her. I am just lost and a bit overwhelmed." He exhaled sharply and Lucky meowed in agreement.

"Now, now. Pour yourself some hard alcohol and get me some catnip while we wait." I heard her say before I closed the door of the bathroom behind me.

After using all the pee-sticks, the result was the same: pregnant. Lucky was right, but something was wrong. I wasn't supposed to be bleeding.

A heartfelt smile surged to my face as I looked in the mirror, and my hand roamed down to my lower stomach. I was happy only imagining how this news would overjoy Alev.

I was happy, confused, and shocked. A vortex of emotions consumed me. I was chaos.

Alev

I'd tried to distract myself in the previous few days to avoid thinking about her, but no loud music playing non-stop in my headphones or high-end parties were enough. All I could think about was her naked body, her smile and her eyes — and this time, it wasn't even Horus' fault. It was all me. I couldn't sleep with anyone; it didn't even occur to me, and even if I wanted to do it, Horus wouldn't allow it. Our Dragons were completely faithful to our mates, and even though Nicole wasn't our mate, the big golden beast refused to accept it.

An exhale left my nostrils as I looked at a very happy Lucky eating her catnip.

"Don't judge, Daddy. That's like cat wine. I am not much of a day drinker, but this is a big moment," she told me with a look of pure judgement.

Nicole left the bathroom, and both Lucky and I stilled, our gazes glued to her.

"I am pregnant; all five tests were positive."

Horus roared, overjoyed, and my tense expression morphed into a giant smile. I couldn't stop grinning. Running towards her, I wrapped her in my arms and lifted her by her waist, covering her lips with mine. My tongue parted her lips open, caressing her tongue. Nicole took a while to kiss me back, making me aware of my mistake. In the fire of my excitement, I let my feelings reign freely, controlling me.

I put her down gently.

"I am sorry, Nicole," I said. I couldn't take advantage of her, especially after taking her virginity. That wasn't fair to her, since she was only on board for what was contracted.

"I…" she mumbled, confused.

"Can I kiss your belly?" I asked this time, unwilling to cross any more lines and disrespect the woman that was about to give me everything I'd dreamed of, a family. She nodded, and I went down on my knees, my arms circling her waist as I kissed her stomach over and over. This close, I could hear a soft heartbeat. My child was indeed growing there, inside this sweet woman.

Happiness dominated all my thoughts until the realisation hit me and made dread wash over my mind as my blood ran colder in my veins.

"You shouldn't be bleeding." Scooping her in my arms carefully, I laid her on her bed and covered her with the comforter. "I will ask Marion to teleport a healer here now. Stay there, Darlin'. Don't make any effort. Lucky, please take care of her."

"She is fine. My girl is tough!" A completely drunk Lucky meowed, licking her paw as if it were a lollipop.

"Alev, Marion is heavenly pregnant. Please don't trouble her! Maybe there is a witch healer in the region…" Nicole started. Even in her state, she was extremely considerate. Sweet witch! Yet, I couldn't agree with her. She and my baby should have the best healer, someone we knew and trusted: Jen.

I wouldn't risk my baby's health and life. I also wouldn't accept anything happening to Nicole. I had to protect and look after them both.

CHAPTER 23
Nicole

"He kissed me, Lucky!" I whispered, still startled.

For almost two weeks, Alev had hardly been home, and we hadn't seen each other in the hall or living room more than twice. I thought he was done with touching me since the baby was actually already inside of me. Rationally, it was better that way for all of us, and that made it easier for me to avoid him, but then he kissed me!

"You both should get a room!" she meowed, rolling the catnip around, completely lost. Only I felt much more lost than her.

Before I could recover from my shock and process all the emotions swirling inside me like wildfire, Alev came back to the room followed by Marion and a witch, the healer he had mentioned. His handsome face was still contorted with worry, and the muscles in his neck looked tense.

"Alev, you don't have to worry that much. Some bleeding can happen," Marion tried to reassure him, placing a hand on his shoulder. Luckily, someone still could act rationally in the middle of this mess.

"We should have been able to notice the changes in her scent by now, but it didn't happen. Something could be wrong, Marion," he dismissed her, pushing a chair next to me and sitting there. He took my hand in his and squeezed it gently.

"You both will be alright, Nicole. This is Jen. She is a very talented healer and she will take a look at you."

My eyes met the brunette witch's warm smile. She must have been in her early forties, and despite my inability to read auras or anything, I could feel that she was a healer, someone filled with kindness and light.

Before the healer could take a step closer or even say anything, Alev flared out, tension clear in his voice.

"Is she in danger? How about childbirth?" Now he really didn't seem like the laid-back guy I'd met.

"New daddies are cute, all worked up! I will take a look at her. As you know, this kind of birth is risky. She has to summon her Dragon spirit to be with her the whole time," Jen told him and he nodded, looking lost in thought.

"We will have time to prepare for it, Alev," Marion reassured him.

"I am so glad that one more Golden Dragonling is about to come to this world! You guys work very fast! So, that's your mate, Alev? Beautiful!" she commented, looking between Alev and me and our joined hands.

"We aren't mates, Jen," Alev replied, looking away from me, though his hand remained attached to mine.

"Let me take a look at you, Nicole, and at your little dragon-grape," Jen added with a smile, hovering her hand over my head and closing her eyes for a while.

Opening her eyes, she started talking.

"Alev and Marion told me about how far along you are and the bleeding. You and your dragonling are fine and healthy. Your change of smell was harder to detect than in normal dragon pregnancy. It wasn't like that when Alma was carrying her twins, but that's not necessarily a problem.

137

Still, we should be careful and pay attention to any blood discharge and cramps. For a couple of days, you should avoid stress and try to rest. Expecting a Dragon child can be very demanding on your body; it's not like a regular pregnancy, dear. If the blood discharge and cramps stop in the next few days, you can resume your normal activities. And don't worry, Alev, sex is allowed." She chuckled, winking at Alev and making me shake my head. I guess Alev had some sort of fame for his great performance with the ladies. Holy Nyx, why did thinking about him with someone else make my heart shrink? I had to stop these feelings, especially now that I couldn't avoid him any longer.

Lucky let out a laughter-meow from where she was rolling on the carpet.

"As you know, the pregnancy should last around six months. Oh, something important: in a few weeks, you should watch your body temperature too. The dragonling needs heat to develop, so the naughty little babies steal the warmth from their mamma's bodies. Hence, you will feel very cold, especially during the night. It is imperative that you and the little grape are kept warm," Jen explained.

The confusion on my face was so clear that Marion stepped in and answered my unspoken question.

"It's a problem for all mums of dragons… for everyone expecting a dragon baby, I mean. Even though I am a dragon myself, my little girl absorbs so much warmth from me that I would shiver at night if it weren't for my mate's hot embrace."

Marion was right; I was not the mum of this child, only a surrogate, and I had made my peace with that. My needs spoke louder than any risk of attachment I could develop, yet her words unsettled me a little. Maybe it was the hormones and soon, I would feel normal again, or at least more normal.

"I will keep you both warm, Nicole. You have nothing to worry about." Alev ran his fingers up my arm and gave me a small smile of reassurance, even though he still looked a little tense himself. He would make me warm using his body warmth? Sure, now I had a reason to freak out. If he did that, how could I ignore my thoughts and feelings for him? I would rather shiver a little under a fat pile of blankets if it kept my heart safer.

"You should move to my room now. I don't want you or the baby going through any kind of discomfort," he said.

"You still have a couple of weeks before it starts, Nicole. But well, who doesn't want a hot, naked man to keep you warm at night?" Jen chuckled, and I noticed a small frown forming on Marion's face. What was on her mind?

Jen definitely didn't know about my arrangement with Alev, nor did she have a filter!

"It's your choice, Nicole. Do what's most comfortable for you, moving to my room now or in a few weeks," Alev told me, and I nodded. To save my sanity, I would stay in this room with the mean-girl cat for as long as possible.

Marion took a few steps closer to the edge of my bed and smiled at me.

"How are you feeling? Try not to worry too much and rest. I know it's hard, but it's the best thing you can do," she said, her voice laced with sympathy. I was aware of her complicated pregnancies and miscarriages before her current pregnancy, which meant she understood this situation.

"I am okay, I think." I was completely overwhelmed and not used to the attention and having so many people caring for me.

"All is good, my dear. Nicole, hon, if in three days you don't feel better, call me again. Rest, no stress, lots of vitamin D, and those are all the recommendations!" Jen smiled, saying goodbye to us before Marion accompanied her out.

"I will be back soon and bring you something to eat. For now, rest." Alev placed a kiss on my cheek before leaving me.

Closing my eyes, I took a deep breath, knowing that it would be impossible for me to fall asleep any time soon. Lucky and I should act fast and find what we were looking for. This pregnancy promised to be much harder than I could've ever imagined, and resisting this irresistible man would be impossible.

Alev

Taking a deep breath, I headed to the nursery, where I knew I would find Alma. She was always with her babies because they were still too young and her nesting phase was not completely over. Dragon mums nested their babies for a while.

I knocked on the half-open door softly, not to wake the dragonlings up. After motioning for me to stay quiet, Alma walked to the door.

"Alev, are you okay? You look worried," she asked, closing the door behind her.

"Nicole is pregnant and is bleeding. The healer, Jen, said that it might not be anything serious, but I want to ask you, Alma! Please, help her and my baby. Heal them with your Great Spirit Fire if needed. I know you don't like her, but we'll need you there during labour. I am not sure things will go well without your help." A worried exhale left me.

"Alev, it is not that I don't like her. I have trouble trusting her because I can feel within the Fire Spirit

140

pulsating in my soul that Nicole is keeping secrets." Alma sighed, placing her hand around my arm and taking a few steps away from the nursery.

"Secrets? What do you mean?" I asked, shaking my head.

"She isn't telling us something. I don't know exactly what, but the Great Golden Fire Spirit tells me that Nicole's past is cloudy and her intentions could be the same."

"Alma! I know you have the babies to protect and that our clan has been through many betrayals. But you should give Nicole a chance. She hasn't told us about her past because she doesn't feel comfortable enough to do so. If our clan showed more trust and acceptance towards her, she would open up."

"Maybe, Alev. I don't want to be unfair, but I am following my intuition and listening to my magic, and as life has proved many times, they are rarely wrong. I am happy for you. You will have your baby and get the family you yearn for. I just hope..." She stopped in her tracks, looking into space for a moment.

"What?"

"Nothing. Don't worry, I will be by her bedside during her labour and ensure that she's completely fine. She and your baby will be fine; we will protect them. The Great Golden Spirit Fire will protect them through me. I can go see her now as well, to give you some peace of mind. Dragon daddies are always so edgy when it comes to their babies," Alma told me softly, placing her hand on my shoulder.

Horus almost jumped in relief within me, and I could feel a burden leaving my chest as we walked towards Nicole's bedroom. I knew that with the help of the Great Golden Fire Spirit, Nicole and the baby would be okay.

That was what helped Alma deliver her dragonlings safely and healed Marion, allowing her to get pregnant and have a healthy pregnancy. It was the very presence of our

141

Gods among us, in the blessing of the spiritual fire Alma harboured within her small frame.

Entering the room, I noticed that Nicole was still awake and Lucky was even higher on catnip. The grey-tabby cat was rolling around the carpet and meowing, which, of course, she did in a gracious way only a lady could. Nicole turned to look at us and sat up with a jolt as her blue eyes widened with surprise and her pretty lips opened in a gasp.

"Nicole, I am here to take a look at you. I am not a healer, but a Spirit Dragon Summoner, like you. The difference is that the spirit I can summon is the Great Golden Spirit Fire, which reunites the spirits of all Golden Dragons that ever existed. It enables me to summon some sort of spiritual fire that can heal and examine Golden Dragons. So, I hope the Great Golden Spirit Fire will help me see how the little one in your womb is." Alma gave Nicole a small smile and Nicole only nodded. Probably more surprised about Alma's words than her presence here.

"Can I hover my hand over your belly?" Alma asked, taking a few steps closer to the bed.

"Yes," she replied, laying down once again and pushing the blanket down her stomach.

Alma placed her hands over Nicole's stomach whilst closing her eyes. Within seconds, the Spirit Fire left her palms, touching Nicole's belly. Suddenly, Alma's lips opened with a huge gasp, and she had to steady herself so as not to lose her balance.

CHAPTER 24
Nicole

My eyes were glued to Alma; it seemed like her shock was contagious. The plasmatic thing resembling golden fire touched my belly and warmed me as if something deep inside me was embraced. Azula, the Spirit Dragon that lived within my soul, almost purred like a cat.

His presence in my soul and the cosy feeling of the spiritual fire were the only things that prevented me from panicking at Alma's expression.

"That's so strange! Something isn't quite right... it's like something is lacking, but not with the baby. I think it's actually within your soul, Nicole, as if a part of you is missing. For now, you have nothing to worry about. The Great Golden Spirit Fire and I will ensure that you and the baby will be okay. I can run some spiritual fire through you from time to time to compensate for the missing part, whatever it is. Trust the Spirit Fire, Nicole. And you too, Alev. Baby and mu–they both will be okay," Alma's voice was soft but filled with certainty.

Something missing? A part of me? What was she even talking about?

"Are you sure, Alma?" Alev asked, sitting by my side and taking my hand in his. Worry radiated from him in heated waves. Did all his emotions feel that hot?

Before Alma could say anything, we all heard a meow.

"I know what's missing!" the drunk cat started speaking, and I was afraid she would reveal something about our searches, except that had nothing to do with what could be possibly missing within me. "She misses a willy! A spec–" Lucky meowed to my deep embarrassment.

"She doesn't know what she is talking about! She is as high as a kite!" I cut her off before she made things even worse. I wouldn't have her near catnip ever again, not now that she could talk and liked to talk much more than she should.

"She speaks!! Burbus would love to meet her. Kitten, why don't you leave the room more often and make friends with him?" Alma asked Lucky, a fascinated smile on her lips.

"I might be single, but I don't mingle, so I'm not available. I am a cat-familiar dedicated to a mission and now we are expecting a baby. I have no time to date the orange-striped Bob!" she told Alma, while still rolling around on the carpet. She would lose one of her nine lives from embarrassment when I tell her about her misdeeds after she sobers up.

"I understand. You are a modern and independent cat who isn't looking for a guy." Alma chuckled at her own words. After reassuring Alev and me once more and saying goodbye, she left the room.

Alev brought me some Irish food and stayed with me until I fell asleep. It wasn't easy, both his presence, his smell and Lucky's annoying drunk snoring kept me awake for hours.

144

The next days passed in the same way, with Alev coming back from his work early to keep me company and bring me food. He was sweet and amazing like the damn dream I had to force myself to wake up from. At least the bleeding stopped, and I was feeling better. I knew it was because of Alma's spirit fire. I could feel it flowing through my veins, making Azula warmer and filling a hole within my soul I hadn't even known existed.

Alev, Lucky and I were on the balcony. Lucky made Alev bring the television there because she wanted to watch her favourite: spy movies. I wondered if she was looking for some inspiration for her *mission* — as she liked to call it.

Suddenly, Alev's arms went around my shoulders and my surprised eyes met his hazel-green ones. What was he doing?

"Aren't you cold? This sea breeze should feel cold for those without fire in their veins," he told me, pulling me close to his chest. It was warm and felt so good. No, I couldn't leave his arms; I refused to. May my sanity be damned, little by little. I needed his embrace for a few minutes more.

"It's warmer now," I told him, snuggling further into him and his other arm came around me as well, his hand now resting on my belly. That was why he was doing it, not because he wanted me closer, but to keep *his* baby warm. My silly heart couldn't and shouldn't convince me otherwise.

Someone cleared their throat and Alev and I turned our heads around to see Alma, Egan, and Mallory.

"Alev, we are going to a club tonight. Marion and Adrian will watch the twins as practice for when their baby comes," Alma said with a little giggle. Marion was surely about to give birth at any time. The fact that she was about to pop was popping to the eyes. "Egan and I want to dance again, just like the day we met," Alma added, looking over her shoulder and giving her husband a loving smile, who then wrapped his arms around her.

"We are all going. You two should join too!" Mallory exclaimed.

"No, I am not interested. As you know, cats are homebodies. I won't leave my comfort to go to a place full of humans!" Lucky told them. Alev and I exchanged a funny look and started chuckling.

"Lady Lucky, Mallory wasn't inviting you but rather Nicole and me."

"That's rude, doesn't she see that there are three of us on this balcony!" Lucky grumbled, giving Mallory her best judgemental-cat look.

"Sure, Mal." Alev replied, looking at me and waiting for an answer. I only shook my head. It wasn't that I didn't like to dance, but I wasn't there for that. I was there as his surrogate and if I didn't keep that in mind, I was only bound to hurt myself deeply.

"Come on, Nicole, let's go. Burbus will keep Lucky company," Mallory insisted, a sweet smile on her face.

"You always stay at home; you can use some distraction and fun," Alma said. Even she was on board. We were on better terms now, even making some small talk here and there. She didn't seem as suspicious as she was before, even though she had reasons to be wary.

"Go Nicole, I could use some "me" time," Lucky said, and I knew exactly what she had in mind. It was a good way to buy Lucky the time she needed since she was almost never alone in the house. So, I had to go, and when we were about to come back, I had to warn her through our magical connection, so that she would stop her treasure hunt.

"Fine," I agreed, and Mallory's smile grew brighter. She was so kind, and it only made me feel more guilty.

146

After putting on a dark blue strapless dress and not-so-high heels, I was ready to leave, but a demanding meow stopped me.

"Stay there as long as possible, Cols. I need a lot of time and I'm counting on the fact that the Bob-cat will be sleeping like he always does. Plus, Marion and her mate will be very busy with Alma's babies," she told me, always bossing me around. But I couldn't complain, since she was doing it for me, to help me get out of my mess. It was my responsibility to give Kadmus what he wanted, not Lucky's.

"Bye Lucky, good luck," I told her and headed downstairs, where Alev was waiting. Wearing a fitted white buttoned shirt that hugged all those muscles and dark denim pants, he outshone the others who were there. I only had eyes for him and how good his butt looked in those pants. Holy Nyx, Goddess, protect me against temptation!

His eyes lingered on me for a moment before a smile surged on those sinful lips.

"You look beautiful."

Oh Goddess! His smile and words made something melt down there. I was getting wet. Shaking my head, I tried to think about Lucky's litter box — the least sexy thing that came to my mind.

"Let's go!" Alma sounded excited. She and her husband couldn't take their hands off each other. He even squeezed her butt before we got into the cars. The truth was, they looked adorable together, she in her cute red dress and Egan completely suited up like the duke he was.

The two couples were driving together, and lucky for me, I was alone with Mr Sinful Dragon.

I tried to keep my eyes focused on the window and the beautiful cityscape. It was a pity I hadn't seen much of Marbella yet. At least I had already seen the best part: the sea.

"Nicole, are you worried? You are oddly quiet. Don't be afraid, we are safe. There are many protection runes in the car. Here, take this little rune. You can put it in your purse. It will work for more than ten hours. With it close to your body, no supernatural creature will be able to smell the baby. They won't find or hurt you. I won't ever let it happen," he told me as we stopped at the red light, taking a small rune from his pocket to give it to me. I knew that some creatures with an enhanced sense of smell would be able to scent the child growing in my womb.

My head only nodded before my gaze roamed to the window again. "Thank you."

When we arrived at the club, I had to stay as far away from him as possible. I was sure that if the man as much as danced with me, my body would erupt like a volcano.

CHAPTER 25
Nicole

To my relief, we soon arrived at the fancy club. And as I suspected, we didn't have to stand in line as we headed directly to the VIP area. Servers came to us, bringing expensive drinks and even some snacks. I was definitely not used to the VIP treatment and to my surprise, Alma didn't seem comfortable in that luxury booth either.

"Egan, let's go to the dancefloor like the first time we kissed. I want a replay. Maybe we can make more babies!" She giggled after finishing her third shot.

"I see that the tequila shots are already having some effect. I can't say I don't like it." Egan chuckled. "Just no more babies, Little Ruby. However, I want every second of this replay you have in mind," he replied, taking her into his embrace. I wondered why Egan didn't want more children, given that their kind was almost extinct. Wasn't having as many babies as possible supposed to be a good thing?

I turned around, trying to avoid hearing their exchange, but on my other side was *Temptation* — him.

No, Nicole! You won't have those warm and big hands on or in you ever again; you won't feel him deep inside you or have his lips on every inch of your body! My heart hurt

149

and my pussy clenched at the thought. I was going insane, but I would rather blame the draconian hormones. Yes, that was a good idea.

"Let's all go downstairs to the main dancefloor," Mallory suggested, and we all followed her as I tried to keep my distance from Alev.

Downstairs was much more crowded, with many people drinking and moving their bodies to the sound of reggaeton. The loud sound and the intense neon lights of the club overwhelmed my senses, making me feel a little numb even though I hadn't drunk anything.

"I love this song!" Alma giggled, pulling Egan to the dancefloor with her. She moved freely, following the rhythm of the music perfectly as her husband moved his hips against her butt in what seemed like a very sensual dance. Now she was in her element!

"Alma and Egan met in a club less than a year ago and came together after their one-night stand went wrong," Mallory murmured in my ear, her words carrying a giggle.

Alev came closer, so I could hear him over the music. His proximity distracted me from the world and took my full attention.

"I am getting myself a drink. Do you want something to drink? Juice? Water? *A virgin cocktail?*" Alev whispered in my ear while the tip of his nose touched my neck. His touch rendered me speechless and all I could do was shake my head in response. I stayed in the corner next to Mallory and Daniel, dancing alone and enjoying the music. My body moved in circular motions, my hips rolling and my legs bending as the song overtook my body. I sang the unknown Spanish words under my breath, moving faster, feeling the sweet adrenaline move through me. I felt almost as good as when I was swimming or using my Water *Elemental* powers. The song and dance were as fluid and soft as the water.

150

Alma was right when she said it was good! There was something hot and sexy to it. It only made my hormones flare up, but I would breathe deep and keep myself under control as I always did. Everything was fine; I just had to stay and make sure the dragons and Alma remained in the club for as long as possible; that way, I could buy Lucky some time.

After some time, an off-balance smiling Alma came closer to our little group. First, she wrapped her arms around Mallory, and they both danced together between giggles. To my surprise, as soon as the song changed, Alma came closer to me.

"Nicole, I know you think I don't like you. It's not true. It's just that our clan, and especially Alev, has been through a lot. I am protective like a lioness, a dragoness mamma now. So, please don't break his heart. He likes you," she whispered close to my ear, placing her hands on my shoulders, more to steady herself than anything else.

"What?" I asked, dumbfounded.

He liked me? Had she lost her mind, or was it the truth? That was bad! I couldn't have him developing feelings for me. I didn't want to break his heart. Breaking his heart would shatter my own heart and soul. I clenched my fists into tight balls. I really needed a drink now, whiskey, neat. Except I couldn't have it. Well, I couldn't have anything I wanted tonight, be it Alev or hard alcohol. Both were equally intoxicating and dangerous.

"Little Ruby, come here. Let's wash this tequila down with a glass of water," Egan said, approaching us.

"I don't want water, Egan. You are not my daddy! I want kisses!" she grumbled as Egan wrapped his arms around Alma's waist and took her to the bar counter, leaving me alone with my confusion.

"Come on, Nicole. Let's dance," Mallory told me, wrapping a hand around my arm. Following her and Daniel, I walked to the dance floor. Daniel didn't let her out of his sight and, actually, didn't take his hands off her for even a moment after we entered the place.

Looking to my side, I saw Alev already dancing, surrounded by ladies. One of them was dancing with him while the other girls were pretty much dancing on him. My chest clenched and my nostrils flared. I could feel Azula come closer to my soul and roar in anger. Why was he that riled up? As a Spirit Dragon, Azula came forward only when I called for him and sometimes when I needed him. And, well, when Alma's Great Golden Spirit Fire touched me.

Oh, Nyx! Why did that make me want to scream, pull him to me and tell those humans that he was mine? He wasn't mine, nor did I believe he liked me. Alma was simply just too drunk to know what she was saying. The only thing that brought us together was a contract, an agreement. No love. No lust. No hope.

"Mallory?" I looked around and noticed that Mallory was dancing with her mate in a less crowded corner. As I headed her way, a human guy wrapped his arms around my waist and pulled me against his chest as he moved his hips.

He reeked of alcohol, and his breath, so close to my face, was making my poor stomach churn.

"No, I don't want to…" I started, but he only chuckled and said something in Spanish about *gringa.* I couldn't understand anything, but there was no way he could misunderstand what I meant as I tried to push him away. Yet, he insisted, pulling me closer.

I had to control myself not to use my powers when the jerk squeezed my butt. His hand roamed all over my backside, and I tried to pull him away again.

"What the hell!? Get your hands off me!" I protested, ready to use the best magic humans could come up with: a good old kick in the bollocks.

Suddenly, a roar louder than the reggaeton filled the room. My entire body froze, responding to it before everything felt hot again, hotter than ever.

Alev

As I went to get myself a drink, I took another look back, almost staring at *her*. Her hips were moving slowly, following the rhythm of the music in perfect circles. I wanted her dancing with me, in my bed, moving her delicious body as I thrust deep into her. My hands were itching to touch her, to hold those hips. I wanted to press my cock against the sweet curve of her ass as my hand roamed around her slightly swollen breasts. Horus roared his agreement within me. How could he do otherwise, when she was absolutely beautiful in that little dress? All I wanted was to leave the damn club, go home and peel the fabric from her body.

Suddenly, I was run over by a group of girls. One of them placed her hands on my chest, halting me. If it were a few weeks ago, before Nicole came into my life, I would have danced with the girl and probably ended the night in the room of my favourite hotel. But now, it wasn't even an option. The young and overly chuckling blonde was as appealing as rubbing my dick on a cheese grater.

"No, miss," I told her, and she chuckled again.

"Pretty please! Just one dance? It's my bachelorette party, and I want to dance with you. Please, one single song!" she asked, jumping up and down like an over-excited rabbit.

"Sorry," I shook my head.

"Come on, a single dance, Mr Hottie. I won't take advantage of you. You see, I am almost married." She giggled, showing me her engagement ring. The three girls with her giggled, clapping their hands. They were all tipsy.

"Fine, one dance!" I told her, and she clasped her hands too, almost like a child. Moving with the song, I shifted her hands away as mine went to her shoulders. The little bride-to-be moved them to her hips, and exhaling sharply, I set them on her waist, putting some distance between us. Her friends started dancing around us enthusiastically. Some even rubbed their sides or butts on me. What were these girls doing? It was almost unbelievable, but I was less than pleased by their advances. Even when I was with my ex, Niki, I would only laugh about this kind of situation and not mind those ladies. The difference was that now I was single and lost in love with my surrogate.

Where was Nicole? As my gaze roamed across the club looking for her, I found her almost in the same corner I'd left her. My blood boiled, and I saw red when I noticed what she was doing.

CHAPTER 26
Alev

Mine! The word echoed within my mind. Horus took control for a moment, pushing the annoying ladies away, and released a loud roar that made the walls and pillars of the building tremble. He was infuriated and his possessiveness raged into my bloodstream, mixing with mine. Dragons were very possessive of their treasures, and the baby in her belly was my most precious treasure. Horus roared again; this time he was angry at me for lying to myself.

It wasn't only her belly, but every inch of that woman's body and soul was my treasure. She was mine, and no one was allowed to touch her. My legs took me across the room so quickly that I was by her side in seconds.

Powered by raw instinct and an unfamiliar stir in my soul, I wrapped my arms around Nicole and spun her around fast. The guy dancing with her disappeared into the crowd before I could do anything, probably threatened by the feral look in my now golden eyes. Good, all that mattered was her, to have her close, to have her. Mine.

"If you have to get off, I can help you. You will be aroused because of the pregnancy hormones caused by carrying my baby inside you. So, I should be the one to help you." My voice was guttural, almost animalistic. I wasn't myself, not entirely.

"Why can you dance with someone else but I can't?" she asked, raising a brow at me. Horus didn't take her question well. We didn't want to dance with that girl to start with! We wanted Nicole.

"You signed a contract, Nicole. You can't have intercourse with anyone until my child is born, clause number seven." I didn't even know why I said those words.

Everything about me now was illogical, atypical. This woman had the power to turn me into a beast! One that wanted to prey on her tonight, eat her, take her and make her scream my name.

She gasped at my words, but I spun her around, slowly this time. Leaning over a little, I pressed my erection against her butt, earning another gasp from those sweet lips. My hands roamed from her waist to her hips, and I moved with the rhythm; it didn't take long for her to start moving with me. My bold hands wandered up, and I cupped her breasts. She moved faster, pressing her body against mine. She wanted it too. I brushed her dark locks aside and my lips found the crook of her neck, pressing open-mouth kisses on it, nibbling and tasting her skin. How I missed the feeling of her, her smell, her taste, the sound of her gasps. Mine.

Neither Horus nor I could wait any longer. Taking her in my arms, I headed upstairs, where I knew I could make all those desires come true deep inside her. Entering the bathroom, I locked the door and placed Nicole on the stone sink, my arms still around her waist.

"Alev, what are you doing?" she asked, confusion clear in her eyes; only the lust shining in them was even clearer.

"I am kissing you, pleasuring you, calming the rage of hormones in your body." I murmured in her ear, licking her earlobe and making her breath grow a little erratic.

"What you said about the cont–" she started.

156

"I am sorry! I shouldn't have brought up the contract. It doesn't matter, not at all. I didn't want to dance with that woman. I only wanted to dance with you, Darlin'. Dance with me only, in every way," I whispered again.

Now that the ability to think rationally had come back to me, I didn't care about the contract. I didn't care about anything but Nicole and the baby. Not that I had a choice or any control over it since my body, my beast, and my soul only wanted her.

Nicole gulped hard and put some distance between us.

"I didn't want to dance with anyone else either. I–I shouldn't, but I want you close. Will you dance with me?" she asked softly, licking her lips nervously.

I quickly captured her pink tongue between my lips and invaded her mouth in a scorching kiss. My hands worked on pulling her dress up and ripping her underwear in a way that wouldn't hurt her. She was precious, always to be worshipped, never to be hurt. Unless she liked a little pain with her pleasure, and if so, I would have fun spanking her sweet ass until she came.

Horus roared in approval. He was still on the surface of my mind, intervening with my thoughts and making me feral — more dragon than man.

After getting rid of her thong, my fingers tried her pussy. Fuck! She was already dripping with arousal, ready to take me deep.

Parting the kiss, I gazed into her blue eyes. "I want to dance with you now, Darlin'."

"Here?" she asked, her eyes wide and her pale cheeks blushing in the sweetest way possible.

"I can't wait, can you?" I asked, thrusting two fingers into her. Her sex clenched around them, coating them with another wave of wetness.

"I can't–"

I stopped at her words, pulling my fingers out. I would never do anything against her will or without her clear consent.

"I can't wait either. We should dance now," she added, to my relief. I took my fingers into my mouth, tasting her arousal.

"You taste so good, Nicole," I said before taking her lips with mine once again, unbuckling my pants as fast as possible to free my throbbing dick. My fingers roamed down, caressing her clit as I slid my cock deep into her, filling her completely with a single thrust.

She moaned into our kiss, undulating her body and moving her hips, effectively dancing for me.

"Come for me," I murmured against her lips as I unzipped her dress and pulled the top down, exposing her perfect breasts to my ravenous eyes.

"I–faster, please," she cried out. I wasn't going as fast as I wanted to, afraid of hurting her and the baby. But she didn't sound like she was in any pain. A grin spread on my face at her eagerness. My little water witch was all fire tonight, and I would add to her flames and make her explode in a raging inferno of pleasure and desire.

As my fingers tugged and pulled her pebbled nipple, I thrust deeper and faster. Nicole's hips did the best they could to follow the reckless rhythm of my pumping. Her breath came out in short gasps, and her sweet pussy started clenching around my dick. She was close and about to take me with her. I couldn't wait, I couldn't contain myself as my thumb flicked her clit vigorously, frantically. Without delay, my Darlin' cried out her pleasure in melodic moans. Her delicate body worked fast, dancing into our rhythm, consumed by our joined fire. As her pussy walls strangled my dick, I filled her with my come, releasing a feral groan.

Now Horus was calmer — reassured — and so was I. It seemed like deep inside her was the only place my dragon

158

and I could find peace and placate this all-consuming desire.

Before we could steady our breaths, my lips caressed hers and I leaned down to capture a nipple into my mouth, and I licked, nibbled and sucked at it. I wanted to eat her. Soon.

As she let her exhausted frame fall onto my chest, I closed my pants, zipped her dress up, and adjusted it, taking her in my arms.

"Let's go home, Darlin'. I am nowhere near done with you," I muttered in her ear and she nodded, wrapping her arms around my neck. Leaving the club, I headed to my car without putting her down. She was safely wrapped in my arms. *Mine.*

"Egan, I am leaving with Nicole," I let him know via mind-link.

"Alev! You losing control has created a mess. The humans would believe that the roar was part of the song, but your speed when you moved is problematic. The Warlock Society will have to come here to clean up this mess." Egan exhaled sharply. *"Going home is the best thing you can do. That and stop lying to yourself. We will talk later."*

My eyes roamed to the sweet witch in my arms; I didn't care about any mess. Having her was worth anything. I wouldn't ever allow any man to touch her, not while she was carrying my child. That had to be the main reason for my feral possessiveness.

She was mine now, mine for the next few months. Somewhere inside me, I hoped to make her mine forever. Yet, recalling Egan's words in the office, I wondered if that wasn't such a good idea.

Fuck! Having her was the best bad idea I'd ever had.

I placed her in the passenger seat and started driving.

"How are you feeling, Darlin'?" I asked.

Nicole sighed. "Dizzy, but more than anything, horny."

"We will be home in no time," I said, running my fingers down her thigh.

"Home?" it seemed like the realisation only hit her now.

A chuckle left me. "Where did you think I was taking you?"

"I have another idea." She gave me a little smile, looking fully awake now. "Let's do it on the beach."

"Nicole! I love the way you think!" I chuckled again, and Horus hummed in satisfaction.

Nicole

Freeing my mind from the frenzy of passion, at least partially, I understood the meaning behind his words. The first time he said something about leaving, I was too hypnotised by his deep voice and at the peak of insane pleasure to understand things fully.

We couldn't go home yet. Lucky needed time to walk around and go treasure hunting — as she liked to put it.

A long sigh left me. Now that I was thinking clearly, I wanted to facepalm myself! What I said in the club made no sense. Why was I so jealous when I saw him dancing with that girl? Why did I confront him about it? I had no right. I was out of my mind. I was only his surrogate.

He was right when he said this was only a contractual thing. Well, that and the all-consuming desire, insane attraction and pleasure rushing and undulating through my whole body and soul.

Alev caressed my thigh again and as soon as he parked in front of the mansion, his wandering hands found my aching breasts, making all rational thought leave my torn mind. Now there was only one certainty within me, the certainty of desire. Making love on the beach and listening to the waves crashing on the sand as he thrust deep into me seemed like a great idea. It was all I could wish for now — perfection.

Alev cupped my face gently, kissing my lips before he took a rune from his pocket.

"If we brush this rune on our foreheads, we will be invisible to human eyes and ears. I don't want anyone to see every gorgeous curve you have or hear the moans I will draw from those lips. Dragons are very possessive of everything beautiful they hold dear."

His words made the breath hitch in my throat for a moment before I nodded like an idiot, brushing the white rune on my forehead. Alma was right, and I couldn't deny it anymore. He liked me. He wanted me. And I... I was in love with him. I had already fallen; there was no edge to hold on to. I was already so far down this *bottomless pit* of passion; falling even further with every touch, every word, each moment with him.

We left the car and headed to the small walkway on the beach. Alev took his shirt off and spread it on the ground, exposing his perfectly sculpted chest. My greedy hands ran down his rippled abs, making him moan. In an abrupt movement, he took me in his arms, leaning me down and diving in for a kiss before he lay me over his shirt carefully. His knees straddled my hips as he helped me to get rid of my dress.

I wanted more! After I gave him something between a shy and a naughty smile, my fingers unbuckled his belt and opened his pants, pulling everything down and letting his cock spring free in his legendary glory.

My tongue roamed across my bottom lip. I wanted him in my mouth.

Holy Nyx! His next words took me into a fiery haze as my sex gushed with arousal.

161

"Darlin', I know you are hungry. Don't worry, I will take this mouth and then your delicious pussy. Afterwards, we can talk *ass*. I want to lay claim to everything, every inch of you, Nicole."

CHAPTER 27
Nicole

My hands wrapped around his thick willy and I used the moisture leaking from his tip to slide my fingers up and down his length easily. Alev groaned at my touch, leaning forward and clenching his eyes. He was so handsome under the penumbra light. Only a couple of lamp posts around the beach were on.

Sitting up, I brought him closer to my face and brushed my lips against his tip, tasting the salty and transparent fluid. Closing my eyes, I took a few inches of him in, only hoping I was doing that properly.

"Look at me, Darlin'. I want your eyes fixed on mine as you suck my cock." His words were both a plea and a command as he tugged at my hair gently.

My eyes opened immediately, and I looked at him, taking in more of him. His hazel-green irises were now surrounded by a bright and beautiful golden circle.

My tongue caressed the smooth and very warm skin of his willy as he stretched my mouth. A guttural groan escaped his throat as I took all I managed to and started to move my lips up and down.

Placing his hands on both sides of my head, he guided me gently as his now almost completely golden irises didn't leave mine. Looking at him felt almost as erotic as sucking his willy. I could see how much I was affecting him, pleasuring him. The way he grunted and groaned, how the veins of his forehead became evident and the muscles in his neck tensed.

There was an intense and feral gleam to him that made me hotter, wetter and lost. He was now both man and beast and I loved seeing him lose control and crumble to his most raw side at my touch. Every little reaction from this handsome and incredible man was because of me, my lips, my tongue, and my gaze. For a moment now, he was mine.

Finally, I managed to take more of him in and his tip touched the back of my throat. I breathed in and out slowly, focusing on keeping him deep. I wanted it all.

"Fuck!" he groaned, sliding his member in and out of my mouth.

His groans were growing louder, and he looked very tense, about to explode, when he suddenly pulled it out of my mouth. No! I wanted it back!

"No, Darlin'. I won't come in your mouth tonight," he said, to my frustration. I didn't know he was about to climax, but I didn't want to stop and break the sweet spell of pleasure I had him under — I wanted to pleasure him and make him feel the same intoxicating desire I had for him.

Alev leaned down, his penis now close to my burning sex, and replaced my frustration with yearning. I wanted him inside me there and then. Laying on my back, I parted my legs for him, earning a naughty grin of satisfaction.

The sky above was clear, filled with stars, a real wonder. Yet, all I could and wanted to see was the wonderful man in front of me, on top of me.

"No, the ground is too hard for you, Darlin'." He flipped us over and helped me to sit up and straddle his hips.

Darlin' — when he called me that, I could feel something breaking in my heart and pooling in my panties.

"This way, you will be more comfortable," he added, cupping both my breasts with his big and broad manly hands. My nipples became two pebbled points, aching for more of his touch. These two never seemed to get enough of Alev's attention. How I loved it when he tugged and swirled them, sending a jolt of electricity straight to my clit.

He pulled me down for a kiss and adjusted his langer*, entering me in a smooth thrust and making my whole body quiver. His hands moved from my boobs to my hips, and he pulled me up and down his member, impaling me over and over deliciously. I threw my head back, holding onto his shoulders, and tried to get a grip on myself. My whole body, my whole being wanted to melt, to explode.

"Ride me, beautiful. I want to see these beautiful breasts bouncing."

I'd never done it before, but using his shoulders as support, I rocked my hips as I moved up and down. Alev leaned my body back slightly, and he knew exactly what he was doing. Now his shaft was brushing a sensitive place inside me and pushing me closer to the edge.

His skilled fingers reached for my breasts, playing with my sensitive buds once again. A rougher tug seemed to be all I needed for the knot starting to form in the pit of my stomach to unravel. My whole body spasmed, and a senseless moan parted my dry lips as I climaxed hard.

Alev thrust into me fast, deep, and hard, making my ecstasy linger, whilst I rode wave after wave of overwhelming pleasure. Within a few minutes, I felt him splash my insides with warm spurts. It felt so good.

My body fell limp against his chest and I closed my eyes, completely exhausted and spent. Fully satisfied and lost in some kind of dreamy paradise. Undisputedly, Alev was better than any dream I could ever have.

Without opening my eyes, I felt my body being lifted. My head snuggled into his chest as he carried me home.

Alev

"Lucky," Nicole called in her sleep as I carried her upstairs, taking her to my room.

"I've been called many things, but Lucky? That's a first. Though I do feel even luckier than your cat." I chuckled quietly. I was very lucky to have my sweet witch in my arms, and I wouldn't let her go, at least not in the next few months, anyway.

Entering my room, I placed her on the bed and ran my fingers through her silky black hair. As if she had a magnetic power over me, I couldn't take my eyes off her relaxed sleeping face.

"So beautiful," I murmured, cupping her chin and placing a kiss on her red lips. They were raw after she sucked my cock and looked even better than usual. I intended to always have her lips like that: red and raw after taking me in or after I devoured them with kisses.

"Where are we?" she asked, opening her eyes for a moment and looking between the bed and me.

"In my room. You should stay here from now on." Her eyes sprang open at my words. My hand reached to her lower abdomen. "This way, I can keep you both warm and take care of this sweet and hungry pussy of yours. You will be safe, comfortable and sated, Darlin'." I said, moving my hand down and cupping her pussy.

She gasped, nodding in agreement before she snuggled into my chest and fell asleep again.

"Good night, Darlin'!" I whispered, closing my eyes as well.

When I opened my eyes, I was in Horus's skin. He was in his reduced form, probably twice as big as Lucky, lying in the bed with Nicole. His left wing was covering her still flat belly while his head nested in her collarbone. Every Golden Dragon had a gift, and mine and Horus's was to change sizes — he could be as big as an Alpha Dragon or as small as Lucky and many sizes in between.

Cunning dragon! How could he shift in my sleep? I tried to shift back to my form, but I found an impenetrable blockage. He wasn't letting me do it.

"Horus, shift back now. Nicole will be scared if she wakes up next to you!"

He only roared in protest within me, making the blockage even stronger. He was out of his golden mind!

"Horus! You don't want to scare or startle her!" I insisted, but he only roared in response, and this time it was out loud. Nicole opened her eyes slowly and glanced around, confused. To my surprise, instead of screaming or being frightened, she smiled at him.

"You are Alev's dragon? I didn't know you could be so small. No offence, wee one, but I imagined you way bigger. Come to think of it, I like that you are small and cuddly. You are so golden and beautiful," she said, and the stubborn reptile purred like a cat at her words, making her smile grow wider.

"Oh, do you want to listen to the baby's heart?" she asked, looking at the wing over her belly. Horus moved, placing his head over her stomach and whimpering at the sweet sound of the baby's heart. He was beyond himself, even smiling in a weird draconian way and swishing his tail like an over-excited dog. Lucky would give him one of her judgemental looks if she saw that.

Nicole giggled at his antics, and that earned her another whimper. It was ridiculous that one of the biggest and most

167

feared golden beasts was acting like a puppy dog. Nevertheless, I understood him; he was fascinated, lost in love and would do anything to see her smile and hear her giggle.

Hesitantly, she placed her hand on his scaly head, and Horus purred again, now moving closer to Nicole's face and licking her cheeks.

"You are the sweetest!" she giggled, running her fingers across his scales. Soon, she started yawning and couldn't keep her eyes open. We had probably only slept for a little less than two hours, and she was still exhausted and well-spent.

Horus settled between her collarbone and her neck once again, and she cuddled with him. Within a couple of minutes, her breath became shallow; she was asleep, and Horus was happier than ever.

Contrary to any logic, he still thought she was his mate. All he wanted was to stay close to her, and I couldn't say I wanted something different. At least in that, we both agreed. Nicole was a treasure, a pearl, and dragons were famous for two things besides our great performance in bed: breathing fire and guarding and worshipping their treasures.

CHAPTER 28
Nicole

I looked around to check if the other kids were still behind me. It seemed like my sister had forgotten to pick me up from school today. She had been so busy trying new spells and learning things lately, and I knew she was doing it for me, for us to have a better life. I also had to do my part since I was a big girl now, almost eight, and I could do it!

Gulping hard, I looked around again and took the next road. Good, in just a few minutes I would be at home. Sighing in relief, I wiped my eyes and tried not to cry. No one was around, so I wouldn't have to hear the kids saying how old and oversized my clothes were and asking me why no one in the coven liked my sister and me.

Murmurs and chattering attracted my gaze.

"It's said her mother was ruined by a man, and died in misery after being forced to have the child of a rape," I heard a man telling his wife as they walked away from me quickly.

I didn't know what that word meant, but I was sure it wasn't something nice. Did they think I hurt my mummy?

As I walked, lost in thought, I almost crashed into someone.

"Watch out, kid!" this big, and probably as old as my sister, girl yelled.

"Look, it's the Clerigh girl. Don't get close to her, Sweetie. She is the fruit of a crime and brought a curse upon her family. She won't ever bring anything good to anyone," a woman told her, pushing her into their house and closing the door behind them.

Just a few more minutes, and it would be over. I breathed deeply and let the tears flow freely. I just had to stop them before arriving home. If my sister saw that I was crying, she would be sad.

Breathing deeply, I stopped crying and wiped my face with the hem of my large shirt. It was even too big for my sister, so for me, it was even longer than a dress.

As soon as I knocked on the door, and my sister opened it, she wrapped me in her arms.

"I am so sorry, Cols. I was about to head to your school. Were the kids mean to you today?" she asked, cupping my face and looking at me carefully.

"No, it was a good day," I told her, biting the inner part of my lips. I didn't like to lie, but making her sad was even worse.

"I need enough power, Nicole, and when I have it, we can leave this bloody coven! Only then can I give you a great life where you will want for nothing! No kids will laugh about your old and oversized clothes ever again!", she reassured me, taking us further into our little house which comprised a single room with a bed, a small table and an oven.

"I don't need pretty dresses; I need you. But now you spend so much time hiding in the forest to try new spells and potions that you barely have time for me. I miss you, Sis," I muttered, unable to contain my tears.

170

"Don't be sad, Cols," she comforted me, while taking me to sit on the edge of the bed, *"It's temporary, Cols. Soon, I will have enough for us to have everything. I miss you too! I love you, my Rainbow!"* she smiled, placing a kiss on the tip of my nose and hugging me tightly.

"Love you, my Sunshine!" My sister said that mum used to call us these pet names too.

Suddenly, I could hear them again, the kids, the coven people and even the teachers; their words resonated in my mind.

"Low-blood!"

"Cursed girl!"

"She shouldn't ever have been born!"

I couldn't understand everything they said, but the anger and hatred were so clear in their looks and their voices that it always broke my heart and made me lower my gaze. Something was definitely wrong with me. I was bad.

Gasping for air, I woke up with a start, and before I could say anything, his strong arms were around me, pulling me onto his chest.

"Darlin', are you alright?"

It wasn't just a dream, but the replay of a few merged memories. It had been quite some time since the last time these memory-filled dreams haunted me, but they seemed to have found their way back to my mind.

In response, I only nodded, and he ran his fingers down my hair gently, fetching a glass of water from the bedside table for me. Water always soothed me, even if it were only by drinking it or letting it flow from my eyes in the form of tears.

"Did you have a nightmare?" he asked, cupping my chin and lifting my face.

"Yes. It was more like a memory from when I was little in my coven. The people there weren't kind," I sighed.

"Did those jerks hurt you?" he asked, anger clear in his voice.

"I… only with words," I mumbled. The kids pushed me around sometimes and bumped into me way too many times *by accident*, but what hurt most were their words.

"No one will ever hurt you again, Nicole; I will protect you," Alev told me, placing me on his lap and enveloping my body with his hot and large arms.

"Only until the baby is born, and it's all over…" I sniffed. Damn! My feelings were way too raw, just under my skin now. I shouldn't have said those words.

Alev gazed into my eyes and shook his head. "No, forever, regardless of the contract. Even when you are away, and go on with your life, I will always ensure that you are safe and sound."

I let my head sink into his chest as a turmoil of thoughts and feelings surged into my mind. Did that mean he had feelings for me? That he felt something beyond desire and the "*liking*" Alma mentioned. Something I noticed pretty quickly was that dragons were intense; their emotions were like fire, much stronger than those of humans or witches. Even in his liking, Alev was so intense.

"You are giving me the most precious gift ever, Nicole. The least I can do is do that for you."

A sigh left my lips, and I took all the comfort his warm chest and reassuring embrace could give me; it wasn't more than liking and desire, still I would enjoy every sparkle of this fire.

These last two weeks, sleeping in Alev's arms every night and spending the evenings together, had surely been the best time of my life. I was happy, warm and surrounded by the fantasy of my love. He didn't love me back, and it was okay; the feeling burning in my chest was enough to keep my life alight and warm.

These dreams made so many deeply buried feelings come to the surface — all the sense of inadequacy and the fact that no matter what I did, I would always be a curse, a bad Nicole.

A sad smile curved my lips. Ironically, those times in the coven were the good times before Kadmus entered our lives and took my sister away from me. No, it wasn't enough for him. He wanted me now, my services, body, soul, and magic.

I would give anything to have my sister back, everything but that. I knew that if I gave in to Kadmus, I would be the eternal prisoner of his dark magic, which was much worse than what he did to my sister. It was much worse than dying.

Strangely enough, I knew that my value lay only in the fact that I was a rare witch with two abilities, an Elemental and a Summoner. Still, I couldn't ever give my soul and my heart away to him.

"Do you think I am cursed?" I asked out loud, attracting Alev's shocked eyes to me.

"Of course not. You are blessed, Nicole, a powerful and beautiful witch, inside and out. You are bringing a beautiful miracle to my life and my clan, to help not only me but to save my kind," he said, and I remained silent. He didn't know the real reason I was in this house to start with, and if he knew it, he wouldn't think that highly of me.

"Believe me, Beautiful. But if you can't trust my opinion, believe the fact that if there was anything cursed about you, the Warlock Society would have found out; they are absolutely meticulous and thorough with all their exams. Maybe this feeling is related to the missing part of you that Alma mentioned. I am sure that there is something special about you and your powers; you just haven't found it yet," he added, caressing my face and making a sweet and sad smile curl on my lips.

Suddenly, Alev seemed distant, looking away for a moment. I swallowed hard, unsure of what he would say next. Maybe he realised something about my lies; I shouldn't have brought up the *curse* matter.

"Egan just mind-linked me, saying that Marion gave birth to a beautiful and healthy baby girl a few hours ago and he is asking if we want to see the dragonling," Alev told me with a drool-worthy smile.

"That's great!" My smile mirrored his. I was so happy for Marion, especially knowing how long she had tried to have this baby.

After putting on some clothes, we headed to Marion's room. She was on her bed beside her mate Adrian and with the little bundle in her arms. A heavenly smile shone on her face and her mate looked at both of them with so much love that my heart melted.

"Nicole, Alev, meet our little Lorelei," Marion beamed. She looked a little tired but completely radiant.

"She is beautiful." I smiled as I looked at her perfect tiny face from afar, fearing that if I took a step closer, my feelings would get to me.

No! I couldn't feel it; I couldn't want it. I had no right to, but still, a piercing pain made my heart quiver.

Without wasting time, Alev went closer to the sweet little family, beaming at little Lorelei. "Marion, Adrian! Congratulations! Your little fire angel is perfect!" His smile was so beautiful, yet so painful for me.

Fidgeting with my hair, I tried to remain impassive and keep my tears at bay. I had done it so many times, but now it felt even harder; all I wanted was to sob wholeheartedly.

The baby cooed, moving her little hand, and I had to swallow back my tears, while my heart broke slowly. I wouldn't ever have snuggles with the baby I was carrying. To start with, he or she wasn't my child.

My hand moved to my lower stomach, and I had to use my Water Elemental magic to keep the tears inside my eyes. I couldn't do it. I couldn't do it anymore.

CHAPTER 29
Nicole

"She has your eyes, Marion. I can't wait to see what my baby will look like and have him or her in my arms," Alev beamed, completely absorbed by the newborn.

Goddess, even imagining the baby's face was too hard for me. It hurt; it burnt a hole through my chest. No, I couldn't. I wouldn't be the baby's mum since I was only the carrier. Alev would be a great dad and surround this baby with all the love and care a child needed or could wish for. I, on the other hand, never considered being a mum. I hardly remembered my own mother to start with. So, why did it hurt so much? Why did I want to be this baby's mother?

My hands fisted into balls, and I swallowed hard, trying to get a hold of myself. I knew that leaving the baby after carrying him or her for months in my body would be hard, but I wasn't even a month along, and it already felt impossible. I was being selfish! I couldn't be fully happy for Marion because I was devastated for myself; I wanted the same thing that she had now. My heart was heavy, and my stomach churned a little as my hand caressed my lower abdomen. I was already in love with this baby, with this little dragon-grape in my belly.

"Nicole, are you okay?" Alev asked, closing the distance between us with a few quick steps. His face creased with worry. He lifted my chin up gently and looked into my eyes, making it even harder for me to contain the stream of tears threatening to flow from me.

"I am fine. It's just morning sickness," I murmured the half-truth as I freed myself from his warm touch and strode to the bathroom adjoining my former room — now turned into Lucky's royal territory.

"Nicole, why are you here disturbing my beauty sleep? Go back to your dragon." Lucky yawned, looking at me from between the pillows. I didn't even have the strength to answer, so I only entered the bathroom and closed the door behind me.

Breathing deeply, I pressed my back against the wall and let my body slide down until my butt met the floor. Covering my face with both hands, I let the tears flow freely. I couldn't hold them inside me anymore.

Since Kadmus told me about this plan and this mission, I knew what I had to do and all I had to sacrifice. Yet it was impossible. I couldn't do it. I couldn't lose this baby. I couldn't lose Alev.

But I knew deep down that Alev was already lost to me. I never truly had a chance with him. Even if he wanted me, he would change his mind after knowing the real reason I became his surrogate. I had entered his life and his house with bad intentions. I was a curse within myself, and no one could forgive someone like me. A sneaky thief, a liar, someone helping a dark warlock infamous for hurting people.

I wasn't naïve to think I could have a sweet little family such as Marion. I knew I didn't deserve that.

More sobs broke through my throat as I tried to breathe slowly and calm myself down. I had to stop it before Alev knocked on the door.

Standing up, I washed my face and looked at my reflection in the mirror.

"What if I could stay? Maybe in another life; in this one, I don't have that option!" I whispered to myself.

Suddenly, I felt another wave of nausea creeping up and crouched down next to the toilet, emptying my stomach contents.

"Nicole? Do you need anything? Are you alright?" Alev's voice brought me both comfort and heartache.

Breathing deeply, I replied, "I am fine. I will clean my face and go back to the room." After brushing my teeth and washing off the proof of my emotional breakdown, I exited the bathroom.

Without saying a word, Alev took me in his embrace and scooped me up in his arms, taking me to "Lucky's bed". Keeping me in the warmth of his arms, he covered my body with the blanket and placed a kiss on the top of my head.

"Sure, you both can lay here! Good, that you asked before," she grumbled, jumping to the armchair.

"Sorry, Lucky," Alev whispered, pressing me against his chest and rocking me back and forth gently, "Mallory is making you some tea. You will feel better soon, Darlin'," he told me and I nodded. I wouldn't feel better. My situation was impossible. I hated lying, but the truth was unforgivable. To my surprise, the warmth of his arms and the peace his touch brought me were enough to silence my swirling mind, aching heart, and to make me sleep.

A sad and sweet thought filled my almost-dreaming mind — *I love you.*

Alev

I was so excited that I woke up early and couldn't get back to sleep. A few weeks had passed, and today would be Nicole's first ultrasound. We would see the baby for the first time. A smile broke on my face as I looked at her peaceful, sleeping face — so beautiful and a true angel in my life.

Horus roared within me, telling me something I already knew: we couldn't let go of her. We had to ask her to stay. Yet this question was risky as she could say no. On top of that, my request would make my deep feelings for her known.

If she saw what we had only as a business arrangement and a lustful need, she wouldn't only break my heart with a single hit. If she realised that I had deeper intentions regarding her, she would leave my arms and not accept my kisses and caresses, causing a lingering pain in my heart. Damn! I couldn't risk losing those lips and all the kisses and smiles they entailed.

I didn't give a damn about this contract. She would have the money she seemed to need so desperately, and I could have her, her love, giggles and the gleam in her sweet blue eyes.

Horus whimpered in agreement. The mere idea was enough to reduce my huge dragon into some sort of pet lizard.

Snuggling Nicole further into my chest, I covered her head with soft kisses. Careful not to wake her up, my hand caressed the belly that was already showing a little. She was around two months along, which corresponded to almost four months in human or witch pregnancy. My poor Darlin' had been struggling with morning sickness in the last days and seemed quite tired and down.

An exhale of guilt left my nostrils. This pregnancy was taking a heavy toll on her body.

Enjoying every second of having her in my arms and drinking in her beauty with my avid eyes, I watched her sleep until it was time to wake her up and head to the clinic. Marion was very kind to take a few minutes away from her nesting dragonling only two and a half weeks after giving birth and teleport us to Doctor Emily's clinic in London. She was a trustworthy witch and the one who took care of both Alma and Marion during their pregnancies.

We arrived at the clinic early, and Nicole seemed a little nervous.

"Darlin', are you alright?" I asked, taking her delicate hand in mine. She felt cold and looked a little pale.

"Yes, I am fine. Don't worry," Nicole gave me a small smile.

"Mr Aureus, Doctor Emily will arrive in twenty minutes, but you can go inside and change," the receptionist let me know, and Nicole and I walked into the examination room.

After changing into a hospital gown, Nicole lay on the bed, and we waited. She seemed anxious, and so was I, but I knew a good way to relax the both of us. A mischievous smile lit my face as I lifted each one of Nicole's legs and placed her cute feet in the stirrups; even her feet were beautiful!

"Alev, I know that smile! What are you thinking?" she asked, her eyes widening slightly. I chuckled at her reaction.

"My sweet little witch, I'm going to eat you," I replied, my fingers running down her inner thighs and caressing her already naked pussy. My Darlin' was good at her water magic, and her pussy was already wet for me.

"Holy Nyx! Alev, are you insane? We can't do it! Doctor Emily will come and…"

"No, Darlin', *you* will come. We have plenty of time," I reassured her. My thumb massaged her engorged clit as my finger circled her leaking opening.

"It's a bad idea. She will notice… that I've just orgasmed." Nicole shook her head.

"I will clean you thoroughly. Let me take care of this pussy, will you?" I flashed her a smile whilst thrusting a finger into her clenching warmth.

"Okay. Do it," her words came with a moan.

CHAPTER 30
Alev

A smile of lust surged to my face. She was so beautiful, completely open for me.

Without wasting time, my lips dove into her pretty pussy, licking her from clit to opening before my finger slid deep, curling to touch her sensitive spot.

"Alev! Oh, Goddess!" she cried out, rocking her hips on my face. My grasp on her hips kept her still for my ravenous mouth, allowing me to lick, suck and tease her sweet clit and folds to my heart's content.

Adding another finger, I worked fast, finger-fucking her with reckless abandon. We didn't have much time.

Hearing a muffled noise, I looked at her. She was nibbling at her lips in an attempt to contain her cries of pleasure. I couldn't have that; I needed to hear her moans and feel her pleasure.

"Don't hold back, Beautiful. Give me everything, or I won't give that hungry pussy what she craves," I teased, knowing that nothing in the world would stop me from eating her.

Nicole nodded frantically, and her teeth released her now red and raw bottom lip.

Her greedy walls were clenching around my fingers, wanting more. How I wished I could give her something bigger now, stuff her with my cock. Soon.

My grazing teeth on her clit seemed to be the last push she needed to fall from the edge. Undulating her body and crying my name between moans, she came into my mouth. My tongue cleaned her dry of her juices, making the aftershocks of her climax linger while my sweet Darlin' trembled beneath my kisses.

"Alev, I think I will... again, please don't stop," her sweet begging voice made my cock even harder. I didn't care about the time, Doctor Emily, or anyone else in this world. I couldn't deny my Darlin'.

My tongue thrust into her walls, and I tasted her delicious arousal direct from the source, my frantic fingers massaging her clit.

She was quivering, gasping and mewling sweetly. Once again, she was very close.

Damn! She felt and tasted so good. I didn't want to stop, ever, but my woman needed her release now. Circling her butt hole with a finger coated in her own arousal, I teased her and watched for her reaction. Her moans became breathy screams, and that was all I needed. My moistened finger slid into her tight virgin hole, and within seconds, she climaxed for me. Beautifully.

Looking up at her face, I had to control myself not to wet my pants like a teenage dragon. She looked heavenly, lost in pleasure, eyes closed, cheeks flushed, lips parted and red from her nibbling, breathing still erratic.

Striding closer to her face, I crashed my lips onto hers, invading her mouth with my tongue.

Not even the sound of a door opening and the approaching steps stopped me. Only when a startled-looking Nicole pulled away, I let go of the kiss and rushed to her legs, taking some tissue paper and trying to erase the proof of our little moment as fast as possible.

Doctor Emily cleared her throat, attracting my gaze to her shocked face.

Soon, a frown replaced her startled expression.

"Alev! You shouldn't pleasure your mate in my practice!" The corner of her lips tilted up, and a chuckle escaped her.

I couldn't miss the way Nicole's face fell, and her cheeks became bright red.

"We are not mates," she whispered, her voice laced with embarrassment.

Not yet, Nicole. We aren't mates yet. Horus roared in victory, approving my thoughts.

The doctor shook her head. "Very well. I will clean your mess and examine the patient. Nicole, I am Doctor Emily."

"Nice to meet you," Nicole's voice was small. She was still mortified, and I had to hold back my chuckles since I knew Doctor Emily would be okay. Plus, what mattered the most was the lingering taste of her pussy in my mouth and the fact that my sweet witch was well-satisfied and relaxed now.

After cleaning Nicole and showing me where I could wash my hands, Doctor Emily started the physical examination, checking on her breasts and lower abdomen. Horus growled in my mind, wishing that I were the one to examine our Darlin'.

"Everything seems normal. You are almost ten weeks along, which means roughly sixteen weeks in a witch or human regular pregnancy. Your due date should be in between twelve to fourteen more weeks. Now, we will take a look at your dragonling using a transvaginal ultrasound due to the thick membrane of the dragon fire-placenta," the Doctor explained. I took Nicole's hand in mine, more to reassure myself than her. She seemed calm, still riding the effects of her two powerful orgasms.

The warlocks of the Surrogacy Society wanted to run an extensive range of tests on Nicole every week, but I opposed that because I didn't want her to be treated as an incubator and spend her days at the warlock clinic. She just needed the same treatment Alma had to make sure she and the baby were healthy and alright. Anything more than that was excessive.

After some time, the image of the baby appeared on the screen, and I couldn't stop smiling. It was the second most beautiful thing I've ever seen, only losing to his or her mother. My glance roamed to Nicole for a moment, and I realised she wasn't looking at the screen. She seemed rather distant, maybe still lost in pleasure.

"Nicole, look!" I beamed, over-excited, my eyes fixed on the screen.

"The size, weight and development seem normal, yet the heartbeat is not as strong as it is supposed to be. I will run some magic and blood tests," the doctor said.

"Is that enough? Will they be okay?" My voice carried worry as panic washed over me and my hold on Nicole's hand grew tighter.

"Yes. There is no reason to worry. We will wait for the results of the tests. If there are any problems, I will let you both know. But I don't think it will be a problem, nothing Alma and the Great Golden Spirit can't fix," Doctor Emily reassured us with a little smile. "Oh, someone is moving and opening their little legs. Do you want to know if it's a boy or a girl?"

"Yes!" I replied, looking at Nicole and waiting for her reply. She was surely confused now, but soon after we talked and I told her what I had in mind, things would be clear. With every passing second, it seemed more clear to me: I wanted her completely, not only as my surrogate.

"It's your choice, but yes, why not?" She gave me a small smile, and I planted a kiss on the top of her head.

"It's a little girl!" Doctor Emily told us. My chest expanded, filled with the bright fire of joy. It was happening, it was real, and my daughter would be in my arms very soon.

"I am done here. After the blood sampling, you both can go home. Send my regards to Marion and little Lorelei!" Doctor Emily smiled.

After the final tests, Marion fetched us and teleported us home. Nicole went directly to the bedroom; she was very tired and needed a nap.

As I went to the kitchen to get her some food before I joined her and made sure she and my daughter were both warm and comfortable, I came across Egan.

"Alev, I've wanted to talk to you for quite some time. It's about what happened in the club," Egan exhaled sharply, placing a hand on my shoulder. Between work, Egan spending all his time with Alma and the twins, and me staying with Nicole every possible time, we hadn't managed to talk.

"I won't do something like that again and risk exposing us to humans. It was irrational and completely unreasonable. I am sorry, Egan. I will be more cautious and carry an invisibility rune around from now on to use in case of another emergency," I told him, giving him an apologetic look.

"That's a good idea, undoubtedly. Yet, that wasn't what I wanted to talk about. It's too late, my friend. There is no safety, reason, or caution for you anymore; you are in love with Nicole. I've never seen you like that about anyone else, not even in the times before the war. Embrace it and claim your woman; otherwise, Horus won't calm down." Egan's words surprised me to such an extent that I took a step back inadvertently.

He was right and talking from experience; he was the same with Alma! His fire was unruly, and he was pure chaos and desperation, a true ticking bomb before he and his dragon had claimed Alma.

My head nodded. There was no time to lose, even though it could make me lose the little I had, her kisses, her giggles, the gleam of happiness in her eyes and the sweet way her legs opened for me. I had to talk to her immediately or as soon as she woke up.

"Thank you, Egan. You are right," I told him. Forgetting about the food, I headed up, my heart beating faster with each step.

Horus was roaring in my mind like an untamed beast. He couldn't lose Nicole, and neither could I. To my luck, she was sitting on the bed, looking wide awake.

"Alev," she called me, patting the place on the bed on her left.

Taking off my clothes and keeping only my boxer shorts, I sat next to her. This way I could warm her up with my body better.

I couldn't tell her that she was my first and last thought every day or that she was the very material of my dreams.

I shouldn't tell her that I craved her smiles, her giggles and her pleasures more than I yearned for my own happiness and satisfaction. It was too much, too sudden, and it would scare her away.

Damn, I wanted her to be my mate, my wife. Yet our situation was so unconventional that the smartest thing was to approach it carefully, only this way I wouldn't risk losing it all.

Exhaling deeply, I took both of her hands in mine and started.

"I have something to ask you. Nicole, we don't have a normal surrogate-client relationship. I like you a lot. I desire you. I am falling in love with you." It was much beyond that; I had already fallen completely and irreversibly for her, but judging by the way her eyes widened and the colour on her face drained, it was good that I was going with less.

"Alev, I…" she didn't finish her sentence and started fidgeting with her hair nervously instead, her teeth chewing the inner side of her lips.

"Nicole, I want you to be more than my surrogate. We can forget the contract and start over. I want you to be my girlfriend."

CHAPTER 31
Alev

Looking intently into her blue eyes, moistened with unshed tears, I searched for her answer.

"Goddess, Alev…" she ran her hand down my arm and pushed her body away a few inches, taking a deep breath.

"I think we should… let's just keep doing what we are doing now, enjoying each other's presence and warmth. I'm not ready to take the next step," Nicole mumbled, almost hesitantly.

Horus whimpered within my soul like a wounded beast.

Even though these words left her lips, I could see something gleaming in her eyes: passion and pain, so clear it was tangible.

"I am sorry," she whispered, and to my surprise, she threw herself in my arms. Wrapping her in my embrace, I tried to comfort both Nicole and myself. Why was she so conflicted? Didn't she know what she felt?

"Nicole, you have nothing to be sorry for." I ran my fingers down her dark and silky hair as my other hand caressed her little belly.

Maybe Nicole needed time, or perhaps once again, I was in love with the wrong woman.

Yet, what I felt for my ex was only a spark of fire that held no comparison to the blazing inferno that exploded in my chest at the mere thought of Nicole.

A sharp exhale left me; she wasn't the wrong woman. No one else I met in my couple of centuries of life even held a candle to the burning star that my Darlin' was. Everything about her felt right; Nicole was my own perfection. She was mine like no one else ever was. She was mine, body and soul, and even if I had to let her go, she would always be mine.

Even though it made no sense, I felt like Nicole had always been the mysterious woman in my dreams. And surprisingly, Horus roared in agreement.

I didn't know what was wrong, but unless she really didn't want to be with me, I would burn half a world to keep her where she belonged, by my side, in my arms, smiling at me and calling my name between moans.

"I have to go to my... to Lucky's room," Nicole murmured, looking away, hiding her eyes from me. But it was of no help, I could smell her tears.

"Darlin', we have time. We can keep our relationship as it is now, don't worry about it," I reassured her, caressing her cheek and turning her face towards me. After I wiped her tears gently, she nodded and left me alone with the cold emptiness that filled my chest.

"I won't give up on you, my Pearl," I added.

Nicole

Trying to breathe deeply between my sobs and tears, I headed to Lucky's room. I needed both to be away from Alev and to be close to my familiar.

Saying those words to him broke my heart completely. He offered me what I wanted most; the chance to be with him and the baby, of being his. I wouldn't only have a family, but stay with the man I loved with every cell of my being.

Yet, I couldn't say yes. I couldn't be his girlfriend and keep lying to him, or else the betrayal would cut even deeper. It would be cruel, and when he found out the truth, he would be devastated.

The truth he surely would find out at some point, but not through me. I knew well that if I failed in Kadmus' mission, my sister would be as good as dead.

A quivering sigh parted my lips. No one could help me, no one other than me would help my sister. I was all she had, her only hope. My Sunshine might have done many bad things and lost her way in her addiction, but she went that way because of me, to protect me and give me a good life.

Even though she never said so, I knew that she had sacrificed everything for me, starting when our mum died, when I was only two and she was eleven.

Entering Lucky's bedroom, I closed the door behind me and let my back fall against the soft surface of the bed.

"Cols, you know that's my bed now, right?" she asked, leaping from the floor to the bedside table. "Wait, are you alright? Didn't your dragon want to give you his willy? Is that why you look like a mushy Sphynx cat? You know, the weird fella without fur that looks like a hybrid cat-zombie," Lucky started blabbering as she moved closer.

"Lucky?" I called for her, needing my fluffy and too opinionated best friend.

"Do you want *me* to cuddle with *you*? That's not in my job description. I'm not a dog, Nicole! But okay, only this time," she grumbled before sitting close to my chest and placing a paw on my belly. Lucky tried to hold back, but I could hear her purring.

As soon as I managed to stop crying, I told Lucky what happened.

"It's hard. If you tell him the truth, Kadmus can turn your sister into dark ashes with a few curses and waves of his hand. If you don't tell him the truth, you will lose him. In technical familiar-feline words: you are deeply screwed. Worse than that, Kadmus' mirror device was shining on your purse again today; he wants to talk to you. I am sure his patience is running short and I haven't found anything yet. It's not like we can ask them like, *hey dragons, what's your most precious treasure? It's not like I want to steal it and hand it to a dark Warlock or anything like that. I am just asking out of curiosity. You know, I am a cat, and cats are curious, hence the curiosity killed the cat*," Lucky mumbled.

"Don't you even have a clue what it can be and where it is?" I asked with a long sigh.

"No. I am sure it's not in Egan's office, though. I've looked around all Daddy-o's things, and there is nothing there, just runes and spells. I am trying to look in Alma and Egan's bedroom, but the orange Bob-cat is always stirring his fat tail there. I think he is following me, Cols. First, I thought he knew something about our mission, but now, I am sure he is obsessed with me. I get that I am all *fiiine* and furry and hard to resist, but can't he see that I am way out of his league? Some males have too much self-esteem for their own good, even the ones with small wings!" Lucky sighed, shaking her head.

I had to contact Kadmus soon and try to appease him, yet Lucky and I weren't making any progress and I had nothing to tell him, no news to give. Wiping my tears, I sat up slowly and tried to think straight.

Kadmus was a dangerous man; I knew for a fact that he had done many bad things in his centuries-long life, including creating a dark magic dimension to hide criminals, the *Lux Dubia*. He was powerful, clever and evil, a lethal combination. I couldn't stop wondering why he wanted the Golden Dragons' most precious treasure and what he planned to do with it.

Such a treasure wasn't easy to find, and many had searched for it and failed. How could we find something when we didn't even have a clue as to what we were looking for? Even though I loathed Kadmus, and even more the idea of doing that to Alev's clan, I didn't have an option.

I was afraid for Alev and the clan, their safety, the safety of this poor baby I was carrying. I had to know why Kadmus wanted that treasure and what he would do with it.

"Lucky, we have to research, go to the library, the Witch-net, look everywhere. We need to know what Kadmus wants with the Golden Dragons' treasure," I told her.

"It's not like we can stop him, Cols. It's better not to know," she mewed sadly. I knew well that even though she tried to keep her impassive cat face, she too really liked the dragons and was worried about them.

"Depending on what his purpose is, I am not sure I can hand it to him," I murmured, a fresh batch of tears flowing down my cheeks.

"If you don't give it to him, he will kill her, Cols. She is your family, your sister, and was like a mother to you." Lucky's eyes went wide and her meow was high-pitched.

192

"I know," I replied, swallowing back my tears and standing up to get my computer.

Suddenly, I felt the baby fluttering inside me and my heart leapt. No, I couldn't lose this baby or allow anything to happen to her. She was not only growing in my belly but also in my heart. I tried not to look at the ultrasound; I tried not to get even more attached. Yet, it was impossible, just like how it happened with her father; I already loved her completely.

My hand roamed to my lower stomach and more tears flowed down my cheeks.

"The baby is fluttering, Lucky. For the first time," I sighed, caressing my stomach and trying to show that sweet baby how much I loved her.

"Cols, don't cry. Probably, it's only gas," Lucky meowed.

A piercing pain spread through my chest, making my stomach churn. I was torn and desperate. I couldn't lose my sister, yet I couldn't let Kadmus hurt this clan, hurt Alev and the baby.

CHAPTER 32
Nicole

I feared that Alev would grow distant and things would be weird between us after our talk, after I said no to the many things I only wanted to say yes to. Yet, he was as doting and as present as before.

A sigh left my lips coming straight from my heavy and guilty heart. Holy Nyx, I didn't deserve this man and this love at all.

Alev adjusted me on his lap; we were on the balcony watching the sunrise after a busy night of fire. He was insatiable, and I was completely addicted to everything about him — his smell, his warmth, his willy.

A yawn escaped me, making Alev chuckle.

"I think I should start letting you sleep at night. Only sleep"

"Don't you dare!" I chuckled back. I needed his touch, his warmth, every spark I could get from his fire and his love.

Crashing his lips on my pout, he scooped me up in his arms and carried me upstairs, to our room, to his room. It wasn't ours, it could never be ours.

Putting me down to my feet, carefully, he took my lips with his.

"I think we need a short vacation, Darlin'. You seem so tense and exhausted lately. I know this pregnancy hasn't been easy for your body. I want to indulge you, to have you relaxed and smiling again," he said, running his fingers down my hair, his other hand caressing my little bump. It was probably much bigger than if I was carrying a witch baby. Everything about Alev was big, including his baby.

"I don't need a vacation; I'm fine. Don't worry about me," I told him, holding back the sigh that wanted to escape my lips.

"Darlin', I can read your eyes; you can use some relaxation. Besides that, I was planning to take you to the sea. What do you say?" He turned my face towards him gently.

"The sea? Can we not go to the beach in front of the house?" I asked, arching my brows in confusion. We haven't been to the beach very often since it was too dangerous for me to go there alone and Alev was only back from work in the evening.

If we travelled, we would be alone and together all the time. It would be too much for my heart; I would end up jumping into his arms and saying that I wanted to be his, his now. His forever.

Not when Kadmus was very close, very dangerous and surely very impatient.

No, I couldn't do that to him.

Alev

I knew well how my water witch loved the sea, and even though it was in front of our house, it was inaccessible to her. I wouldn't have her going there alone with Scarlet Dragons roaming the peninsula. But since I wouldn't work in the next few days, Nicole and I could spend as many days by the sea as she wanted.

"Yes, we can. But we also can go somewhere much more beautiful," I replied with a chuckle.

"Even more beautiful?"

"Yes, not a touristy place, but wild, untouched and untamed nature," I added, wrapping my arms around her and letting my hands slide from her back to her pretty ass.

"Yes!" She smiled, making my chest leap. That was all I wanted.

"We will go tomorrow. For now, it looks like you need your rest." I smiled at her and she nodded, sitting on our bed.

The next day couldn't come quick enough and after breakfast, I took Nicole out and introduced her to my third girl.

"This is Bonnie," I introduced Nicole to her.

"Are we going on this thing?" she asked, looking between my face and the dope motorbike.

"Yes, Darlin'! It's very safe, don't worry. I wouldn't put you or the little princess in your belly in any danger. With my enhanced senses and reflexes, an accident is impossible." If something were about to happen, Horus would shift within seconds and take Nicole in his embrace. I had the Rune of invisibility on me in case I needed to shift.

"Okay, let's do it! I've never been on one of those things before!" To my astonishment, a smile formed on her beautiful face.

After putting on the helmets, we climbed on the motorcycle.

"I will show you Marbella, mi Bella!" I told her with my best Spanish pronunciation and she laughed in response.

I took her to the main touristy spots of the city, the Plaza de Naranjos and the old town. In each spot, Nicole took a vintage camera from her backpack, and to my surprise, instead of taking photos of herself or places alone, she took photos of me everywhere.

"Sorry for acting like paparazzi." She giggled.

"Don't worry, Darlin'. But don't you want to be in the photos as well?" I asked before she climbed on the motorbike again and we headed to the final destination of the morning.

"No. I just want to collect memories," her voice sounded almost distant.

"Anything you want, Darlin'." I squeezed her delicate hand in reassurance before I started the bike, both enjoying the high of feeling the wind on our skin.

Finally, we parked in front of a five-star hotel.

"The food here is amazing, Nicole," I told her, taking her hand in mine and leading her to the restaurant.

"That's great! The baby is starving." She giggled. "but isn't this place too fancy? I'm not sure if I'm dressed appropriately," she murmured, looking around.

"You look perfect, Darlin'."

Didn't she know that despite what she wore, she would always be the most beautiful woman in this place?

Horus roared in agreement; he spent the entire morning grinning like a gecko, overjoyed to be with her and making her smile.

She nodded, and we took a seat.

I was about to call the server to order my steak when I noticed that Nicole was having trouble choosing. She stared at the menu, looking distant and thoughtful.

"I want to be healthy for the baby and order grilled fish and salad, but this lasagne is calling my name. It's so hard to decide."

"You should find a compromise, Darlin'. Be both healthy and happy. Let's order both and we can share the dishes."

"But do you even want fish or lasagne?" she asked, placing the menu on the table and looking at me.

I wanted Nicole, her happiness.

"Sure," I replied, and we both ordered.

I had other desires, another taste that I wanted to have exploding in my mouth.

As soon as we finished eating, I exchanged some words with the concierge and stood up, offering a hand to Nicole to do the same.

"Now it's time for dessert," I told her, guiding her towards the elevator.

"Where are we going? Isn't the exit on the left?" She looked around, confused.

"Yes. But I need my dessert now and it's between your legs, Darlin'. So, I need you to be comfortable in a bed with your legs spread open for me."

"Alev!" she moaned, and I couldn't resist. As soon as we entered the empty elevator, I pressed my woman against the wall as gently as I could manage. My lips assaulted hers, and I lifted her body, pulling her leg up for my cock to rub against her clothed pussy. She wasn't a short woman, but still small in comparison to me.

My lips wandered down her curved neck as my hands found their aim, her already dripping pussy. I caressed her teasingly over her underwear, earning a sweet stream of moans from her.

"Can you come before we reach the 20th floor, Darlin'?" I purred in her ear, brushing my stubble against the soft skin of her neck.

Her hips buckled towards my touch, and she let out a moan of protest.

"Inside me, please."

"Soon," I chuckled.

"Teasing a pregnant woman is pure evilness," she grumbled, shaking her head and brushing her lips against mine.

"I will give you everything very soon, Beautiful," I whispered back and as the elevator's doors opened, I took her hand and ran down the hall, rushing to room number 2013. "Don't you have to check-in first?" she asked as we reached the door.

"I've taken care of everything online, Darlin'. I just need to put in a code to open the door," I explained, punching in the code in and taking my sweet witch directly to the bed.

In a matter of seconds, her panties were ripped off, on the floor and I dove between her legs feasting on her orgasm. As her body calmed down and she rode the aftershocks of her pleasure, I snuggled her in my arms, her head against my chest, right above my heart.

"Before I met you, I was so lost," I exhaled sharply, running my fingers down her hair. I wanted to tell her everything that was on my heart, things that I'd never told anyone about.

Nicole lifted her head and cupped my chin. Her eyes fixed on mine, filled with emotion and tenderness.

"My ex left me suddenly, but now I understand that it wasn't the worst part. It was the succubus' spell and the place it took me that hurt me deeply. An insane evil witch, Meghan, invaded our house not only once, but twice. The first time she tried to kill Egan as she looked for something in his office. The second time, she was even crueller; she

199

brought along a succubus from Hell, a demon, to our house. The succubus seduced all us males in an attempt to both distract and overpower us. Not only that, but she manipulated the men to harm their own mates, to even kill them. On me, the succubus' spell had an even deeper effect." I exhaled. Nicole's blue eyes looked even deeper as she listened to me in silence.

"The other males came back from the high and dark-erotic energy of her haze and found the light, the comfort and the love of their mates to heal them. In my case, all I had was emptiness, and not even Jen's healing magic could help me. Her spell took me to my deepest feelings of emptiness, to my darkness, my fear. A place in my soul in which there are no flames, only ashes. For months I couldn't come back from the spell completely, not until I had someone to come back to, a light to guide me through the darkness, not until I met you."

To my surprise, my words made not only tears, but deep sobs leave Nicole's chest.

"I'm so sorry for what happened to you, Alev. That succubus, you must have gone through hell," she breathed, looking away for a moment. Her heart was beating very fast as if her chest couldn't contain all the emotions.

"It's not your fault, Darlin'."

CHAPTER 33
Nicole

Breathing deeply, I tried to silence my tears. It wasn't directly my fault, but I was part of it. I didn't know what my sister did when she invaded the mansion and how badly she had hurt this clan. More tears streamed down my face since nothing could contain my sadness, my grief, my guilt.

My heart broke for my sister, for everything she had become. Meghan was so lost in her dark magic addiction that I hardly recognised her anymore. She used to be so good and giving, and now she was terrorizing people and using a sacred bond of love to hurt them.

My heart also broke for Alev. Even hearing about his suffering was enough to make my heart clench so tightly in my chest that I could only breathe through sobs. His pain was because of Meghan, because of Kadmus and I was only there only to add to his misery.

Shaking my head against Alev's warm chest, I inhaled deeply. He deserved so much better than I could give him. Holy Nyx, he deserved so much better than me!

"Alev, I wish I could be your girlfriend. I wish we could be together. But for reasons beyond my control and things I can't tell you now, I can't. Please forgive me and —

let me give you all I have now, the care, tenderness, desire; it's all yours, but only for now," I sobbed through my tears. That was the most sincere I could be, the most honest I had been with him since we met.

A flame of urgency lit in his eyes. Urgency and agony.

"Nicole. I can help you. I won't have you in harm's way. Never. I vowed to you that regardless of where our paths take us, I will always protect and look after you." He sounded candid and completely filled with determination. With a thumb on my chin, he gently lifted my face, making my moistened eyes meet his hazel-green ones.

"I wish it was true, but no one can help me," I sighed. I was lost, torn, and gone in an impossible situation. Anything I could choose or do now would end up hurting the people I loved.

"Darlin'," Alev exhaled sharply, pressing me against his chest, his protective hand roaming around my stomach, "You don't have to tell me anything. Whatever happens, whatever it takes, I will protect you, Dye–Darlin'," he concluded.

His words, his protectiveness and the loving, hot, dreamy way he was, only made me feel more guilty. I was either going crazy or it was the hormones' fault, for the fierce way he stood to protect me, brought me another sensation. Within all my sadness and guilt, I was horny as a cat in heat, as Lucky would say.

I needed him now.

Alev stood up to fetch me a bottle of water. Coming back to bed, he placed me on his lap and ran his fingers down my hair.

"Is there anything I can do to make you feel better?" he asked. I was such a mess, my face still covered with the stains of my tears.

"Take me, Alev, fuck me hard!" The words left my mouth without passing through the filter of rationality.

Alev's eyes opened wide before his face contorted into a naughty smile, which quickly became a chuckle filled with joy, carefree, and yet so appealingly masculine.

Lifting my little vintage dress, I stood on all fours and lifted my butt for him. I didn't want him to make warm love to me, but to take me hard and unreservedly as he did in the club.

"Fuck, Nicole!" he muttered under his breath, running his fingers down my butt. His lips dove down my inner thighs, wandering up slowly, teasingly, he was about to kiss me there and make me lose my mind when I stopped him.

"Alev, can you spank me? I'm a bad girl!"

I looked over my shoulder and saw him blink twice, then he chuckled.

"I will spank you until you come hard, Darlin'."

Placing a pillow under my arms and making sure I was comfortable, he took off his clothes, making both my mouth and my pussy gush. Adjusting himself behind me, he brushed the tip of his willy against my entrance, before smacking his dick on my butt cheek and making me release something between a moan and a gasp. I was looking forward to being wrecked by his delicious monster.

Next, Alev's fingers started teasing my folds as his other hand met the skin of my butt and the noise of a "smack" filled the room. It wasn't a hard slap, but the slight burn sent a jolt of pleasure through my bloodstream, making me moan loudly. A new wave of wetness dripped from my sex, and a grunt of approval left Alev.

"So wet, Darlin'!" He thrust his finger in and out of me fast before, spanking me once again.

"Harder, please!" My voice was desperate, almost begging him to really give it to me. This was the only way I could feel better, the only way I could breathe, erase part of my guilt. I needed this, and I needed him inside of me.

As if he could read my mind, Alev pounded into me with his member, filling me completely. A song of moans

203

left my lips as I pushed my butt back against him, wanting, craving for more.

The next deep thrust was accompanied by a delicious smack, and I could already feel the knot in the pit of my stomach untying.

"Spank me harder," I cried out.

Both of his hands crashed down onto my buttocks.

"Darlin', you are getting it wrong. You are not the one to call the shots, not in this bed." His words were followed by a deep and hard thrust and a resounding smack. Not as hard as I wanted, but it was enough to hurt so good and make my pussy clench around his dick, strangling it.

I almost leapt as he slapped my clit. Wetness dripping along my thighs. Throwing my head back, I moaned. I called. I begged.

"Alev!"

"Yes, Darlin'. I will give you everything!" He picked up his pace, fucking me with reckless abandon and making my whole body feel like exploding, combusting in all-consuming flames.

He gave me a hard and loud spank, pushing me down the edge. I was so close that I couldn't think straight anymore. My butt moved towards him, which earned me a couple of delicious spanks.

"Be a good girl now and come for me," he groaned, his voice gravelly, almost guttural. Oddly enough, it seemed to be all I needed to fall into an abyss of pleasure. Screams left my lips, my whole body tingling, sparking with pleasure, lust, magic.

"God!" I cried out, only afterward realising that I was leaving my religion and declaring my worship for this man. The man I couldn't love, but loved nevertheless — fiercely, immensely, absurdly.

Alev held me up, preventing me from falling onto the bed on my belly. His next thrusts were erratic, short and hard. Soon, I felt the delicious thrill of being filled with his warm seed. Laying on the bed, he wrapped me in his arms and covered my face with sweet kisses.

As soon as my breathing was normal again, he pecked my lips one last time before he left for the toilet. A white haze shone behind my closed eyes; I was still riding the aftershock of my violent climax. My heart felt a little lighter and my body exhausted, a tad sore and completely well-used.

Feeling his weight pushing the mattress down, my eyes blinked. He sat by my left side, a small bottle in his hand.

"I only found this cream. We can go out to buy ointment soon," he let me know, spreading the cool-feeling moisture across the aching skin of my butt.

"I don't need it, it's too much," I protested.

"No, Darlin'. There are no compromises. I will take good care of you."

My head nodded at his affirmation and, giving in to my tiredness, I closed my eyes and enjoyed his soothing touch.

"Let's rest a little," he said, after giving me some water.

My dragon snuggled me against his warm chest. Being in his arms was the best thing and made me feel much better than I deserved to. Yet, I refused not to enjoy every second of his touch, his warmth, and his love. I couldn't say the words, they would only bring us both more heartache, but I loved Alev more than I deemed possible.

After a few minutes, my body stirred with need. I couldn't sleep, since I was still too horny and needy. "Alev? Are you awake?"

"Yes," he replied.

"I need more. I need you inside me," I whispered, running my fingers down his scruffy beard, and kissing him over and over.

"Anytime and always, Beautiful." He gave me a mischievous smile, scooping me up in his arms.

"That's the main reason I booked this room. I know how much you love water," he said, desire clear in his eyes.

"The swimming pool?" I asked, looking around the private swimming pool. Alev nodded, confusing me. "But we have a swimming pool in the mansion."

"This is different. There are always people around the mansion and here we have complete privacy. So, I can have you all wet and do wicked things to you," he told me with a wink.

"Oh!" I gasped, already getting wetter for him.

Lucky

Leaving my room through the little flap door my dear Alev had made for me, I went for business. My paws moved as quietly as possible as I looked around, searching for signs. We had to find it before Kadmus lost his patience and hurt Meghan. Not that I especially liked her. Nicole was my witch; she was the only one I cared about — I kind of cared about our baby too. But I knew that Cols needed her sister back. Meghan was not only a sister to her, but the person who raised her like a mother would, her only family. Meghan was all Cols had before she was gifted with my amazing presence in her life. Sad, I know!

So, my high priority was to get into my spy role, find the treasure, give Kadmus what he wanted and rescue Meghan. That way, my girl would be free from the toxic old warlock. In the best-case scenario, we could also keep the dragon and the baby.

Approaching Egan's room, I looked around and my ears stirred up, trying to capture all the sounds. It seemed like the place was empty. Good! I *tip-pawed* around the bedroom, trying to pay attention to every detail in the way that only a highly intelligent feline could do.

What could the Golden Dragon's most precious treasures be? I had been wondering about it since I stepped my paws into this house for the first time. At first, I thought it could be a golden egg, but these guys didn't seem to lay eggs. It was just a stereotype, like the one that says that cats were pussies. Prejudice was indeed the bane of the world, my thought was accompanied by a dramatic meow I couldn't contain.

To my surprise, the very chubby and even more orange Bob-cat appeared from nowhere. He was definitely stalking me.

He came close, and I took a good look at him. Maybe he had lost some weight, and his fur wasn't looking so unruly. Was it a good fur day?

He rubbed his side against mine, waking my inner tigress. I knew what I wanted; I was a secure and confident female in total control of herself.

I let him lick my muzzle, and a purr escaped me.

"It seems to be your *Lucky day*, Orange Boy!" I meowed, fluttering my eyelashes and giving him a taste of my natural charm.

After all the kiss and play, I let him have his way with me. Another surprise, he wasn't half as bad at it as I imagined. He knew how to ride.

After we were done, his willy extended in the hurting way Bob-cats always do. So, jumping from his grip, I tail-whipped.

"Yes, that's only a one-night-stand, guy. Move on. I know you won't be able to get over me, but that's not my problem, is it?"

I was shocked when, instead of giving me a pleading look like males used to, the chubby bob-cat stirred his tail and walked past me as if he had something better to do.

"Snob! Damn, if he kept doing that, I would fall in love."

CHAPTER 34
Nicole

Being surrounded by both his arms and the water, made pleasure bolt through my veins. His lips caressed my nipple as his hands roamed between my waist and my hips.

"So good." I threw my head back and leaned further into his touch.

Suddenly, I felt something in my belly. Something tiny moved against my abdomen. It was different from when she fluttered.

My eyes popped open, and I pushed away from Alev's skilled lips.

"Alev! She kicked! She kicked!" I exclaimed, a huge smile on my face as a rogue tear left my eyes. I was lost in love with this little girl, even though I knew I couldn't be with her.

Alev's gaze moved from my little bump and my eyes as a smile even bigger than mine lit his handsome face.

"Can you feel it?" I asked, putting his hand on my lower stomach.

He seemed to concentrate on it for a moment and his eyes went gold, his pupils became slits.

"Yes, I can feel it!" he beamed, enveloping me in his arms and taking my lips with his, he kissed me between heavenly smiles.

Leaning down, he went underwater and kissed my lower stomach.

"My little princess, I can't do wicked things with your mum anymore. Not after that. Now I have other plans."

Mum? He referred to me as her mum, rather than only a surrogate. My heart expanded as if it had grown wings, only to shrink painfully. I couldn't stay with them; I couldn't be this little girl's mum and Alev's woman.

Alev wouldn't ever refer to me like that if he knew the truth about my mission in his house and about my sister. Goddess, he wouldn't even want me as a surrogate if he knew the truth!

I swallowed hard, trying to hold back my tears. What my sister did to him and his clan was horrible but not worse than what I was about to do.

Alev scooped me up in his arms and left the pool, taking me to the room and making me snap back from my thoughts.

"What are you doing?" I asked, looking at him, confused.

"Let's shop for baby clothes, get *our* princess something, everything. I know a witch shop nearby here. They have magical clothes, as Alma and Marion said. They bought most of their dragonling things there." He smiled, overexcited.

"It's not necessary. I... "

"Of course it is, Darlin'. Time is passing so fast, and I've been so lost between your legs, that I haven't started the preparations. We need a nursery, and everything for her," he told me, as he put his pants on. Going commando, are we? A little smile tilted up the corner of my lips.

210

"I made a few things for her myself: a little hat and shoes," I said in a small voice. I couldn't resist. I wanted her to have something from me when I was gone.

Actually, if I hadn't stopped myself, I would've spent hours making her little clothes while I dreamed about her sweet face. It wasn't good for my heart! I would only sink into pain once I had to leave her. Would Alev let me spend a few days with her after birth? I knew that if I asked now, he would tell me to stay *as much as I wanted.*

As much as I wanted would be forever. Yet, I was sure that if I asked after he got to know about my kinship with Meghan and my link with Kadmus, he would kick me out of his house immediately and with reason.

"I really want to see them, Darlin'," he pressed a kiss on my forehead.

After getting ready, we took a cab to the shop. Alev didn't want to make the raw skin of my butt even more sore by sitting on the motorcycle.

Arriving at the normal-looking shop, my gaze roamed the place. I knew well that like in every other witch shop, the human-looking shop was only a front. We would have to go through a little door to the bottom, a door only visible to those with magic in their blood, to get to the real witch story.

Making sure that there weren't any humans around, Alev and I crossed the wooden door, arriving at a huge and beautifully decorated store.

In one of the corners, we could see many potions, herbs and crystals in every colour and size. In the middle of the shop stood a very large tree with a trunk almost as big as a car. I stared, fascinated, at the purple and blue vines dancing around it, holding many bottles of exclusive and very expensive potions. Lights and even potion and spell books hang from the tree's top.

I'd heard about this kind of tree. It was called 'Fíniúnacha Cumhachtacha.' I could order anything from within the store and the vines would reach the object and bring it to me.

As soon as Alev saw the tiny clothes section, he strode towards it like a hyper pup-dog, taking me by the hand.

"The girls were right! They have so many things, many options!"

Picking up one of the floating baskets in the way, he filled it with pretty much one of each style.

"Look, those have some sort of magic and keep the baby warm, it's not so necessary for dragonlings, but we can get one or two just in case," he said, placing four tiny bodysuits in the basket and making me giggle. He was the sweetest. This Baby was so lucky to have him as her daddy.

"Darlin', those little trousers change colours when the baby is wet. Oh, the pacifier has calming effects, since it's bound by some soothing herbs," Alev mumbled, placing more and more items in the basket. My eyes wandered to a little blue dress, and I ran my fingers across it, imagining the baby wearing it. I couldn't stop picturing her smile, her giggles and blabbering, my sweet little kicker. A tear rolled down my face as I caressed my stomach.

Someone cleared their throat behind me and I turned around.

"May I help you?" the sales assistant asked, her undertone formal.

"I am just looking around." I gave her a little polite smile and was about to walk away and look at stuffed cats; Lucky would chastise me if I got one of those. She would surely say something like, 'Nicole, what am I to you? A joke?'

"Are you new to the region? What's your coven?" she asked, bringing me back from my musing. Some witches lived for the gossip, I swear. Besides that, seeing me accompanied by such a handsome Golden Dragon surely enticed her curiosity.

212

"I don't have a coven." My voice sounded much lower and weaker than intended. It was actually sad that in the twenty-first century, being a witch without a coven was still taboo.

"You must have been born into a coven and gone rogue, no? What was your coven?" she tried to hide her little frown, but I still could get a glimpse of it.

"The Purple Highlands in Ireland," I told her.

"Oh, I heard about your coven. The coven leader, Katarina Claire, died a horrible death a few years ago. Dark magic," the woman said with a sharp exhale before waking away. Weird woman!

My eyes popped open, and I gulped hard. I didn't know about what happened to Katarina. She wasn't a good person; she was awful, but I didn't wish such an end to her.

Oh, my holy Nyx! I hoped it wasn't Meghan's doing, but after some point, I didn't know what she had done or what she was capable of anymore. She was lost to the dark magic, addicted and possessed. That's why when I had her back, she would have to agree to go to rehab.

"Darlin', don't you want to take anything?" Alev asked as he walked towards me. Noticing how unsettled I was, he wrapped his arms around me. "Let's pick what you want and go back to the hotel. They can deliver the things to the warehouse close to the mansion later," he told me, and without thinking, I took the blue dress and a stuffed cat-toy and put them in the basket as Alev and I headed to the cashier.

"Please send everything to this address," Alev said, giving the cashier a little card. To my surprise, he took a bottle from the bottom of the basket, and when I saw it was a magical ointment to soothe pain, a smile formed on my lips.

Returning to the hotel, he massaged the red skin of my butt once again and covered me with kisses.

"Darlin', let's rest tonight. Tomorrow I have great plans for us. We will fly, and I want you to wear this for me," he murmured in my ears, placing a small piece of fabric in my hand. A gasp left my lips as I realised that it was a thong with a thread of pearls in the middle. Wait, those will be in my pussy?

"It will feel good, Darlin', massage and tease you and get you wet and ready for me, for when we get to our destination," he assured me.

"Oh my Goddess, Alev!" I gasped, making him chuckle.

The next day, we woke up late and had breakfast by the swimming pool before a very excited Alev took me upstairs to the rooftop. Was that a helicopter landing pad?

"Are we flying in a jet?" I asked, as my confused gaze roamed around.

"No, Darlin'. You will fly on my back, or as Horus likes to think, you will ride him. Wear this pendant, so you will be invisible to all eyes but Horus' and mine." Alev placed a necklace with some sort of rune pendant around my neck.

"Where are we going?" I asked, without taking my eyes from the beautiful milk-white rune.

"We are both looking forward to showing you our hoard," he said, wrapping his arms around me. His smile was somewhere between excited and naughty.

"Your hoard? I thought dragons were very possessive and territorial with their treasures, and they never let anyone go to their hoards," I told him, my eyes still wide, startled.

Alev caressed my face and ran his fingers down my belly. My shocked eyes fixed onto his hazel gaze.

"That is right, but my biggest treasure is here in my arms. Horus is jumping in my soul, excited to share all his shining toys with you. He knows that there is nothing there or in any treasure chest in the world that he could love more than what we have here right now." His words made me gasp as my heart both leaped and clenched. Even though all I wanted was him, his warm and scorching love, I wished he was talking about the baby only. No, Alev. I can't break your heart, because it would shatter my own heart and soul to pieces.

"After one loses almost everything, they realise what their most precious treasures are," he added.

Alev kissed my lips before taking off his shirt, giving it to me. Taking a few steps away, a translucent golden flame surrounded his body, and within seconds, Horus stood proudly in front of me in what I believed to be his full height. He was huge, even bigger than I imagined he could be. His golden scales looked so beautiful, shining as the sunlight caressed them. Maybe it was the first time someone ever referred to a dragon like that. But Goddess, he was so cute! Gorgeous!

Approaching me with huge strides, he closed the distance between us. The giant and sweet beast brushed his muzzle against my face before leaning down and both nuzzling and licking my belly.

My hands ran down his head, and I felt his rough and stone-like scales against my fingertips. They were so beautiful and hard as if made of gems.

Giggles left my lips; his caresses were ticklish. The giant dragon wrapped both our bags around his claws and leaned down. He released a soft sound I could never imagine coming from such a giant creature and motioned with his head for me to sit on his back.

I did as he wanted, holding firmly onto his back and letting the wind caress my face as he started flapping his enormous wings, taking to the skies.

My heart tugged painfully and my mind swirled at the thought that maybe what Lucky and I had been looking for was there in Alev's hoard.

CHAPTER 35
Alev

Horus was happier than ever with Nicole on his back. He was grinning like an odd gecko as he flew over the Balearic Sea towards the many surprises had prepared for Nicole. She seemed happy and comfortable on his back. We could both hear her giggles and almost feel her joy at being up in the sky.

Every now and then, my dragon would turn around to check on her and make sure she was alright. I, on the other hand, couldn't stop thinking about the pearls on her thong caressing her pussy, making her clit swollen and her dripping wet pussy as the smell of her arousal perfumed the air.

After a few hours of flying, Horus landed at a very special port in Sardinia. He let out a loud whimper as soon as Nicole got off his back. Nicole giggled, approached him and patted his head, making the giant lizard purr like a kitten.

Only after a few minutes did he allow me to shift back to my form. Nicole's gaze roamed up and down my naked body, making me laugh. She was the way I wanted: happy, safe and ready to take my cock. Yet, I wanted to give her something else before I got started with her.

Walking towards her, I wrapped her delicate frame in my arms and kissed her lips.

"How did you feel during the flight?"

"It was amazing! I loved every minute of it, especially the feel of the wind on my skin and the small droplets of water condensing within the clouds!" she beamed, a smile clear in her blue eyes. Lately, even though she looked worried, her eyes were gleaming more and more. The sadness and gloom in them were almost completely gone. I knew that our little princess was responsible for that, for making her mummy glow and look even more beautiful.

"Horus is whimpering in joy at hearing that. We were worried you wouldn't be very comfortable," I told her, brushing a lock of hair behind her ear.

"He is a great flyer, precise, strong, attentive — pretty sweet, really," Nicole gushed, and Horus melted into a puddle within me.

After I put my clothes back on, Nicole started looking around, her arched brows a sign of her confusion.

"Where are we? Is your hoard in a port?" she finally asked.

"We are in the south of Sardinia, and no, Darlin'. I have something else planned for us before we fly to my hoard. That said, the hoard is on a tiny Italian deserted island nearby," I explained.

Taking her hand in mine, I guided her towards my small yacht, the Naomi. Stopping in front of it, she looked between the boat and me. Besides the confusion in her eyes, I could see something burning in them, a blue flame.

"Who is Naomi?" she asked, making me chuckle as I wrapped my arms around her. *Aren't we jealous!?*

"It's named after my little sister, Darlin'." The boat was named after my youngest sister, my sweet little Nay.

As soon as she heard my words, her face turned to a cute shade of pink, and she tried to hide her face in my chest. I couldn't control my chuckles; letting her hide her pink cheeks, I scooped her up in my arms and carried her to the boat.

"Alev, you don't have to. I can walk," she stated.

"I want to have you in my arms, Nicole." My words made a sweet smile appear on her face. After I put her down, she looked around the boat.

This wasn't as private as my hoard, yet I had never brought anyone here before. It was where I came to whenever I needed some silence, to be alone and think deeply. The ocean gave me all the solitude I needed, and none of the other dragons would believe it if I were to share this more introspective side of myself with them.

The last time I came here was right after my break-up with Niki. Oddly enough, it seemed like years rather than months ago. My lips curled into a smile as I looked at her curious blue eyes. My life had taken so many important turns since then, it actually felt like my life had been renewed in Nicole's smiles, kisses, curves and in the gift of life she was carrying in her womb.

"It's beautiful. It looks old... I mean vintage, and perfectly cared for," she commented, running her hands across the wooden railing and looking around the cabin. It was a comfortable place to stay for a couple of days, with two bedrooms, a small kitchen and a dining area.

"It is old, Darlin'. It dates back to the 1800s, but I restored it around 1930," I explained, and she chuckled a little.

"Sometimes, I forget just how old you are." She shook her head, her chuckles growing into a melodic laugh.

"I will show you who is old when I pounce and thrust hard into you against every solid surface of this boat," I teased, taking her in my arms and claiming her lips. I had every intention of going through with that promise. "But for

219

now, let's get moving. We can stop somewhere with clear water and swim a little. I know a great place near the caves called Cala Goloritzé," I told her, cupping her face and brushing a dark lock of hair behind her ear.

A bright smile lit her face. "I love the idea! I can't wait to swim!"

I started the boat and showed Nicole how to drive it as we headed towards the deserted beach.

As soon as I stopped the boat in front of the white-sand paradise, Nicole ran out of the cabin, taking me by the hand. The excitement in her eyes made my heart leap with joy.

"This place is a dream! And we are the only ones here!" Nicole gasped, looking at the deep blue waters. There wasn't a soul around, just like I imagined, and a naughty smile surged to my lips; there were so many things I wanted to do with her naked and wet body there.

Pulling her shirt and bra off, I bared her beautiful swollen breasts for my hungry eyes as my hands wandered down her waist.

"What are you doing?" her voice wasn't louder than a whisper.

"Like you said, we are indeed alone, and I have every intention of taking advantage of that, Darlin'!" I grinned, pulling her shorts down and playing with the thread of pearls from her thong in such a way that I could tease her little clit, my fingers sliding on her smooth skin.

"Are you all nice and wet for Daddy?" I whispered in her ear, and she moaned in response, pressing her bare body against mine.

"For you, I am always a waterfall," she murmured back, earning a smile from me as my hands cupped her buttcheeks. Tugging her panties down, I leaned down and pressed a kiss on her pussy before standing up again.

MINE, the word echoed in my mind.

My head shook.

"We better swim now before I end up eating and fucking you for hours and the sun is gone."

Smiling, Nicole ran her hands across my chest and pulled my t-shirt up. Her greedy delicate hands undressed me completely in a matter of a minute. As soon as we were completely naked, I held her hand, and we jumped into the translucent blue waters together.

Giggling and smiling like an overjoyed child, she swam around me before diving deeper. My sea witch was kicking her feet remarkably fast against the water. She was *in* her element, literally.

Horus groaned within my soul. He was more than happy to see her completely naked and content.

Diving, I tried to reach her, but she was too fast, even for me and my extreme stamina. Horus, however, didn't want her that far away from us, and shifting abruptly, he moved his huge arms and kicked, reaching our woman. As she saw him, Nicole smiled and swam his way, wrapping her arms around his enormous neck and placing a bubbling kiss on his face. My dragon was a whimpering mess and wagging his tail like a puppy; he was a goner.

The way she swam and seemed so comfortable in her own skin here under the water was fucking sexy! I had to force Horus to control his erection; I didn't want to scare Nicole with a huge golden double penis.

Horus roared within my mind in protest.

"Horus, she isn't used to seeing a dragon's double penis, and you don't want to scare our treasure, do you?" I asked him, and in response, he gave me a grumpy and low roar of agreement.

With lots of care, he placed his retracted claw on her belly and whimpered even deeper, making her laugh. In need of oxygen, Horus headed up, taking Nicole with him. As we reached the surface, I forced the golden-headed lizard to shift back and crushed my lips on Nicole's, devouring her sweet-tasting mouth.

221

"You are so fast!" My voice carried amazement. My sweet witch was much more powerful than I imagined, simply remarkable.

"I have been fast in the water since I was little. Even though the sea in Ireland is so incredibly cold and the waters are darker, nothing compared to this place, I loved it so much!" she giggled.

I love you so much; the words didn't leave my throat. They shouldn't, not now. I would give her the time she needed. Because of her smiles and the look in her eyes, I knew well that there was love for me in them.

After swimming for two more hours, we went back up to the boat. My impatient hands grasped her as soon as we stepped foot on the wooden surface. With inhuman speed, I laid her down on the nearest mattress at the outside part of the boat and my head dipped between her legs.

"Alev, you shouldn't do that. I'm salty." A moan abruptly cut her off. My fingers dug in the soft skin of her butt as I pulled her closer, opening her further for me.

"I could eat this pussy coated in sugar or salt. I want you in any and every way," my voice was guttural, animalistic. Horus was on the surface and my irises were surely completely golden and parted by a long reptilian slit.

Mine, Mine, Mine. That was all I could think about as I kissed her and inhaled the sweet scent of her arousal.

After pressing a long kiss on her sensitive spot, I ran my tongue along her folds. Suddenly, I heard flapping wings, and a familiar smell set all my senses into a high state of alert, making me stand up with a jolt and wrap her in my arms.

Her face contorted with shock as she gazed at me.

"Nicole, you have to hide. The Scarlet Dragons are coming."

CHAPTER 36
Alev

How the hell did they find us? The boat was under a cloaking spell, so it was supposed to be untraceable.

As I guided Nicole to the cabin, I glanced at the sky and saw the three approaching red points. They surely had a spell or rune in place, concealing them from human eyes, but not from other magic creatures.

"Darlin', go to the bedroom downstairs and call Marion. She will teleport you to safety," I told her, pressing a quick kiss on her head.

"Alev, there are three of them. I can help…" she started.

"No, Nicole. Please, protect yourself and our little princess." My words sounded both like a plea and a command. I wouldn't have her taking any risks, especially not while carrying our child.

"Alev, please," she argued, and I shook my head.

"No. I will protect you this time. I won't lose you ever again!" I didn't know where these words came from, but they resonated within my soul with no conviction.

Nicole looked at me with startled eyes before nodding and heading to the safest place on the boat. After making sure she did what I asked, I headed to the upper deck of the boat, and a spurt of fire almost reached me. They were three big Scarlet Dragons, probably high-born and powerful ones. On top of that, they had many bionic enhancements, armaments that they had developed in their freaking labs to enhance their powers and abilities, as well as for protection. I knew that I would have to be at the top of my game to defeat them. Fortunately, I felt more powerful than ever now that I had the best reason possible to fight for — my family, my love.

Shifting to Horus' form, I gained the skies, flapping our wings and flying high in an attempt to drive the three red beasts away from Nicole and the baby. Horus moved faster than ever and the three of them followed us. My plan was working until Horus' wing crashed into something invisible. A stream of fire left Horus' nostrils, bringing the invisible Scarlet Dragon in front of us to sight.

Hell! *His bionic armour was able to make him invisible?*

As Horus lashed his tail at one of the red beasts approaching from behind, dodging the burst of flame from another one, he spewed flames at the now half-invisible Scarlet Dragon once again.

Flying fast in spiral movements around the half-invisible beast, Horus created a whirlwind of fire, enveloping him in flames. His lifeless body fell on the water with a loud splash. One down, three to go.

Roaring loudly, Horus was ready to attract the surviving beasts further away from my treasures, but to our despair, two of them flew towards the boat. They surely smelled the baby when they were near the boat.

Dodging a burst of fire, Horus released his flames at the two leaving dragons and rushed towards the boat. Arriving there before the Scarlet Dragons, Horus shielded the boat with his large body, spouting flames at our attackers.

Two Red Beasts spewed fire at us, which we dodged almost completely. As Horus breathed fire through the pain on his burnt wing, the third beast attacked from behind, both burning the wing in the already wounded spot and clawing at Horus's shoulder. Horus held back his whimper of pain as the beast broke through his flesh. His red claws were covered in metal: he was the freaking Wolverine version of a dragon. The third beast had even more bionic parts than the others, just like a cyborg from hell.

"We have to hold on, Horus! Keep fighting!" I told my dragon, and I knew he had no intention of stopping. He would give everything to protect our girls.

Turning around, Horus released his shoulder from the violent grip and covered his attacker in flames. Horus' tail whipped around, smashing the other beast before he had a chance to attack us. Yet, the third one dove and bit hard at Horus' already injured wing.

The combined flame of the two other beasts were about to reach Horus and finish him when he lashed out his tail insanely quickly, catching them on their necks. They recovered surprisingly quickly and were ready to attack again. It had to be something in their robotic enhancements, giving them stamina and healing them.

The fire erupted from my dragon — it didn't matter what the Scarlet Dragons had become, we would fight until the end.

Ignoring his wounds, Horus flew towards one of the beasts, firing at him with full power when a metallic bullet suddenly hit his other wing, causing him to fall onto his half-broken wing.

Nicole

225

Breathing slowly, I tried to calm myself down as panic built up in my chest. I tried to call Marion, but my phone had no signal here in the middle of the sea.

"Horus is strong," I repeated to my panicking self, only hoping that he would be strong enough to defeat the three red monsters.

A quivering exhale left my clenching chest. Staying here instead of being there and helping him was torture. I had to do something. I had to help him.

My hand roamed across my swollen stomach.

"You will be alright, my sweet baby. You and your dad will be fine," I cooed with a sigh.

I wasn't afraid for myself, but for Alev and the baby. Besides that, a disturbing thought wouldn't leave my mind; *was Kadmus the one to send these dragons here?* I knew his patience was running short.

Azula, the Spirit Dragon, fluttered within my soul, bringing me a bit of reassurance. He was close to me, just like every time I was either afraid or in danger. I didn't even have to call for him or summon him; it seemed like he could hear the frantic beating of my heart.

Suddenly, I felt a piercing pain in my heart and my vision went black for an instant as something in my very soul stirred.

"Alev, he is in danger," I muttered. "Azula, we have to do something!" I told him as I rushed upstairs.

"Please, Azula, protect Alev and the baby. And if I'm hurt, don't try to tend to me, take all my life energy to the baby to keep me alive until she is born. Remember: save her and Alev, they are what matters most."

As a rare spirit of a Golden Water Dragon, Azula was able to transfer the life energy present in every single molecule of water, even the water in my cells. So, he would be able to do as I asked and use my life energy to protect my baby in case the worst happened while I fought for the man I loved.

Azula roared within my soul, infuriated by my words.

"Please, Azula! Do it for me!" I begged as I couldn't have it any other way. This deep fear freezing the blood within my veins showed me what mattered most.

As soon as I left the cabin, I saw Horus struggling while three Scarlet Dragons attacked him at the same time. They weren't only simple Scarlet Dragons; they had mechanical parts incorporated to their bodies, making them look like metallic monsters.

Fire spread across the boat, consuming everything in its way and leaving behind only ashes and destruction. Breathing deeply, I raised my hands slowly, calling for the seawater to rise and extinguish the fire.

I didn't even need to look at Horus, since the pang of pain in my heart was enough to know that my gentle dragon was in danger.

Two thick spurts of water left my palms, and I attacked the monster that was about to lash onto Horus' back with his metallic spiked tail while he was too distracted fighting the two other red beasts.

Azula roared within me. He could feel the certainty vibrating in my heart and he would do what I asked, even though he hated the idea. He would give everything to save and protect Alev and my baby girl.

CHAPTER 37

Alev

"No! Horus, right behind you!" I heard Nicole's desperate yell. When Horus was about to turn and face the red monster attacking him from behind, another burst of flame was about to reach him. Before Horus could react, the golden spirit form of a dragon moved gracefully through the air. Shielding Horus with his plasmatic form, the Spirit Dragon spat not fire but a powerful gush of water on the Scarlet Dragon, smothering his fire in a matter of seconds.

The Spirit Dragon connected to Nicole's soul just saved Horus and me. Horus' eyes opened wide in surprise since neither of us had ever seen a Golden Water Dragon before, in any form. They were legendary.

Nicole was so powerful and indeed special to be connected to such an incredible dragon.

Nicole! Horus glanced at her. She was smart and skilled and had already erected a firm barrier of water in front of her. But it didn't matter, nothing mattered! She shouldn't be out here, putting herself and our baby in danger. Horus roared his agreement, advancing to the red beast closer to her and whipping him hard with his golden tail. Using his broken wing, my dragon hit the almost completely bionic

Scarlet Dragon, making the cyborg lose balance. Our fire and fighting-spirit revived by having Nicole near this danger. We wouldn't let anything touch her.

The Spirit Dragon moved fast, splashing a violent jet of water at the red beast approaching me. Even in the middle of the chaos, Horus and I noticed that the Spirit Dragon's water gleamed in a shade of gold, looking otherworldly.

Nicole moved her hands frantically, raising the sea water to contain the fire that started to devour the wooden structure of the boat.

The Spirit Dragon and Horus exchanged a single glance and seemed like they both knew what to do. As the Spirit surrounded one of the red beasts with its glowing waters, Horus moved closer to Nicole, shielding her with his large body while she worked incessantly to stop the flames consuming the ship.

Without moving away from our treasures, Horus released a surge of fire at the cyborg. From the corner of his eye, my dragon saw another metallic bullet coming towards him and about to reach his chest when a lash of water pushed it away.

"Alev! Horus!" Nicole yelled, raising more tendrils of water from behind Horus' huge Golden frame.

The jets of water emerging from her moved precisely and gracefully, preventing all flames from reaching Horus.

With firm threads of water, she managed to immobilise the attacking Scarlet Dragon, allowing Horus to fire at him with full power and reduce him to ashes.

Nicole let out frantic pants. I could hear her quick heartbeat and smell the adrenaline in her blood. She was fighting with all she had, exhausting herself. This fight had to be over soon. I couldn't risk hers and the baby's lives for a moment longer.

An enraged roar filled the air, and the other Scarlet Dragon fired against Horus. My dragon tried to dodge, yet he was too wounded to move fast enough. The fire was

229

about to reach his wing when Nicole made the sea rise in an enormous wave, smothering the fire and smashing into the Scarlet Dragon. It fell.

Horus glanced at her, pushed through the water as Nicole fell onto her butt. She looked pale and exhausted, but her eyes had an intense gleam — love, bravery, fire.

Looking at the other side, Horus saw the Spirit Dragon trying to contain the cyborg. Yet the robotic red beast was too strong, and he was advancing towards us. The other Scarlet Dragon stood up fast, rushing towards us too.

"Azula!" Nicole's yell echoed like a lash, and in a blink, the Spirit Dragon was shielding Horus from the two red reptiles.

"Horus, I can hold the normal Scarlet Dragon as you and Azula attack the cyborg," Nicole said between pants for air as potent torrents of water left her hands, shielding Horus' broken wing, making it possible for him to move properly.

No! I couldn't leave her unprotected. To my surprise, she jumped to the side and ran towards the Scarlet Dragon, raising her both hands and sea waves. Nicole's waters enveloped the dragon. He was struggling to move.

Still keeping an eye on her, I did what she said. Moving in sync as if we had done it countless times before, Horus and the Spirit Dragon released both water and fire, managing to penetrate the cyborg metallic structure. We were about to break through his reptilian skin and cause some actual damage when the roar of the other dragon echoed around. Nicole was about to lose her grasp on him. She was now on her knees, using one of her hands as support and using a single hand to control the waters that kept the dragon still.

Horus dove closer to her, blowing enormous flames on the dragon. The aggressive attack made him shift back to his human form and fall unconscious on the ground.

The cyborg was once again advancing. And once again, Azula and Horus attacked in perfect synchrony, this time, successfully breaking through the cyborg's metallic armour. To my surprise, our summoned fire and water didn't convert the cyborg into ashes, but rather, made him fade away as a dark toxic smoke.

Shifting back to my form, I ran towards Nicole and wrapped her in my arms. I scanned her thoroughly, checking for wounds.

Azula's translucent golden form was right behind Nicole, protecting her and making sure she was alright. An exhale of relief left my heavy chest; in short, I was glad she had such a powerful spirit to guard her. By some sort of instinct and a strong gut feeling, Horus and I trusted Azula completely. I could almost feel in my soul how much this Dragon Spirit loved and worshipped Nicole, and that wasn't common. The summoner witch and the spirit animal were normally close, but those two had a rather special link. Instead of jealousy that another dragon, spirit or not, was that close to Nicole, brought Horus some sort of pride and happiness. Weird, given dragons are normally very territorial and possessive of their treasures, especially towards other dragons.

Why did Azula feel so familiar? Why did seeing him bring both Horus and I some sense of peace?

"Alev, your arm," Nicole's words brought me back from my thoughts. Her little hand motioned to my dislocated shoulder, her eyes filled with worry. Sitting her on the ground carefully, I knocked my dislocated shoulder back into place.

"It's okay. Don't worry, Darlin'. Are you hurt?" I asked, cupping her face gently and looking at her exhausted blue eyes.

"No, but…" The deep groan of pain released by the surviving Scarlet Dragon cut her words off. Taking my Darlin' in my arms, I walked closer to him.

231

The semi-conscious man glanced at us, blood running down the burn wound on his stomach and leg.

"Wait. Azula, please, help him," Nicole asked, and the Spirit Dragon wrapped my wounds with his unworldly water, bringing my injured body instant relief.

"Water can be both violent like a tsunami, a lash, and soft like a healing touch. Especially spirit water," my water witch told me as she ran her fingers down my bleeding shoulder. For some unknown reason, her soft touch seems to heal me further and even made a pleasant tingle sparkle on my skin.

The wounded Scarlet Dragon groaned again, attracting my attention. I had questions to ask, and I had to do it fast before this man lost consciousness completely or ended up dying.

"Did you know we were here? Were you following us?" I asked, my still draconian golden eyes fixed on him.

"No. I didn't — I didn't. It was a coincidence, I swear. We weren't chasing Golden Dragons this time," he stuttered, his voice no louder than a whisper.

"It can't be a coincidence!" Nicole said under her breath, a shadow of worry clear in her blue eyes.

"Our King knows your hideout is close, somewhere in the south of Europe. Our people are around. We have new bases in this region. But not the four of us; we were only flying around…" he spoke with difficulty.

They were close, way too close to Marbella. First in Portugal, and then, now, here.

"How did you manage to see through the cloaking spell concealing the boat?" I asked, worry spread through my mind like flames in the wild. If they could find this boat, soon they would be able to find the clan's mansion as well.

"I, I… We were just travelling. We didn't know that there were Golden Dragons here. We were just able to see the boat when we were very close because of the bionic incorporation in the boss' eyes," he murmured, motioning with his head to the ashes of the man on his right side. "Spare me," he asked, fear burning in his orange eyes.

My head shook, and a roar left Horus. Only a few minutes ago, he and his companions used all the dirty tricks and moves to kill me, and now he was asking for mercy.

I couldn't let him live, not when he knew Nicole was carrying my child. It would make her and the baby Scarlet Dragon's targets as well.

"Can we spare him?" my sweet witch asked, her voice almost inaudible. She was too gentle to watch someone die.

My face contorted into a frown of exasperation as I swallowed hard. I wasn't a cold-blooded killer, and I didn't take any joy in that, yet I couldn't leave this Scarlet Dragon alive. I promised I would protect Nicole with whatever it took. And if she wanted to follow the Surrogacy Contract and leave me after the baby was born, to make that possible, I couldn't allow the Scarlet Dragons to know about her. These monsters would surely use her as a leverage, hurt or kill her to get to me and my clan.

Nicole

The Scarlet Dragon looked at me through his hooded eyes, fear clear in them. I knew this look well since I was very familiar with fear and saw it so many times in the mirror.

"Can we spare him?" I thought out loud, my heart heaving in my chest.

"I have to kill him, Nicole. Otherwise, he will tell the others he saw me. Worse than anything, they will know about you and our child," Alev explained. The word "our" made my heart stop for a moment.

I took a lungful of air, my mind racing with a spiral of thoughts. "We can find another way, a forgetting spell and spare his life," I suggested.

"It's war, Nicole. It's not over, and it won't ever be over," he said, his voice laced with sad resignation. He had been through so much and pretty much everything he knew in his life was either war or the fighting for survival. I could relate to the survival struggle. That was what my life had always been like as well.

"We need peace. Everyone does. Let's wipe his mind and spare his life. I can't… I don't want another death on me." I sobbed.

I'd already caused the death of my mother and if I didn't find a solution, I would soon have Meghan's death on my hands, too. Despite my heart being torn, something was clear: I wouldn't harm the Golden Dragon clan.

Azula exchanged a look with me, and I was sure I could see a smile surging on his translucent muzzle. Looking at me once more, he let out a sweet whimper and disappeared. His work was done. He saved Alev. He saved my heart.

"His death is not on you, Darlin'," Alev reassured me, giving me a look of sympathy.

A heavy sigh left my chest, and I nodded. I understood his point of view, but wished we could find a better way. Couldn't we just find a solution, a way to save everyone I cared about?

"We can't do it," he said, holding my hand before a blast of fire left his mouth and nostrils, and the Scarlet Dragon turned to ashes.

A gasp parted my lips. I had never attacked anyone before. Actually, that was the first time I'd both fought and seen anyone dying in front of me. I knew it was necessary, yet it still felt disturbing.

"Are you sure you are feeling okay, Darlin'?" Alev asked, his golden eyes scanning my face slowly, carefully.

"I'm fine, but you are still hurt," I told him, looking at his wounds. Azula did a great job with the bleeding and the bigger burn wounds, but Alev was still injured. My body was unharmed, yet my heart was still beating like a drum in the rhythm of my lingering fear.

"I have many healing runes and potions here," he said, taking a box from the wooden drawer and drinking a purple concoction. To my relief, in a matter of minutes, the cut on his forehead started healing.

Alev took my slightly trembling body in his arms and rocked me back and forth, comforting me. I was tired and dizzy, still stuck in the aftermath of my terror.

As I closed my eyes and sighed, the moment of dread replayed in my mind. When I saw those dragons attacking Horus, my heart stopped for a moment, and something stirred within my soul. It felt like a memory, like a dream, and all I knew was that I couldn't see him suffering. I couldn't see him coming to harm.

No! I couldn't have anything happening to him. This love and connection was much stronger than I could ever imagine. It filled every corner of my soul. Without a single doubt, I would give my life for his.

My teeth grazed on my bottom lip. At that point, I didn't want to know what the Golden Dragon's main treasure was anymore. I was pretty much closing my eyes to it, refusing to see the truth. Else, I knew Kadmus could find a way to compel me to tell him everything.

My heart was warm at the light of the deepest certainty: Alev was my most precious treasure.

This immense love and all-consuming fire was bigger than me, and I loved him despite myself. All the answers were in front of my eyes, and I knew what the best thing I could do for him was.

"Let's go to my hoard. There, you can stay safe and rest, Darlin'," he said gently, helping me to lay down on the sofa. My head was heavy and my body so mushy that I ended up falling asleep as soon as my head met the cushion.

After a deep and dreamless slumber, I woke up to the warmth of his embrace. When I opened my eyes, everything around me was golden and beautiful as if I was inside a treasure chest.

Azula whimpered within my soul, and a sense of familiarity washed over me. We were in Alev's hoard.

CHAPTER 38
Nicole

Stirring quietly, I took a lingering look at Alev's shoulder. It was healing quickly and well; Azul had done a great job with his healing spirit-waters. He used to heal me when I was little, when other kids *accidentally* bumped into me or dropped potions on me at school.

"How are you feeling, Darlin'?" Alev's deep and sexy sleepy voice made goosebumps rise all over my neck and shoulders. Clearly I was alright and recovered from the exhaustion and dizziness.

"I am fine. How about you?" I asked, unable to resist covering his face with kisses. He was so handsome, and a pang of fear lingered in my heart. Seeing him in danger had broken my heart, but seeing him now had revived it, giving my soul a new light — clearer, bright and eternal like golden fire. Alev said he would always protect me, but I, too, would do anything to protect him.

"I am fine; drink some water, and I will get us some food," he said, placing a kiss on my lips whilst giving me a bottle of water.

Blinking twice, I looked around the bedroom. We weren't in a cave as I'd imagined, but in a fancy golden bedroom. Gold and gems covered the walls, and there were jewels on the shelves. My lips opened with a gasp as I realised that the bed itself was made of what looked like pure gold.

Lifting my head slightly, I saw a mirror. Wait, why did it look so familiar? My gaze wandered, and I didn't recognize only the mirror, but also the chandelier and some other objects. More than that, they were calling me, as if they wanted to tell me something.

I shook my head and clenched my eyes shut for an instant. Nothing made any sense. I was still a little sleepy and confused, yet I made up my mind: I wouldn't look for any treasure or steal anything.

"I thought your hoard would be in a cave," I said, still confused.

Alev's chuckle was deep and sexy. "No. Every dragon has their own kind of hoard. This place is a small cottage with a sea view. I've heard that Egan's hoard is in a cave, though. He is old and likes to keep it classical."

"I like this better than a cave," I smiled. Now, all I wanted was a warm shower, to feel the water run down my body and recharge my energy.

"This place is much safer than the boat, Darlin'. It's under invisibility, and many cloaking spells, cast by powerful wizards and warlocks alike. No one can hurt us here," he reassured me before standing and leaving the room. I stood slowly and headed to the equally bejewelled bathroom where a fancy and big golden bathtub stood in the centre. *Great!* I would wash my hair in the shower and then have a relaxing bath.

As I laid my exhausted body in the bathtub, the warm water relaxed my muscles and made my little girl flutter and kick.

I caressed my belly and giggled. "Do you like water just like me, sweet Angel? I am sure your dad will take you to the beach and the swimming pool," I told her. Soon, my words became a lullaby, every word filled with my love for her. Funnily enough, my little lullaby drove myself to sleep, and I woke up to Alev's sweet kiss on my lips.

"I have to join you, Darlin'. Dinner will have to wait. You can't imagine how beautiful you look naked and surrounded by gold," Alev's voice was husky and his eyes had a gold gleam. Horus was on the surface and he wanted to play. My hands wrapped around Alev's neck and I parted my lips for his ravenous tongue. I also wanted to play with them both, to feel the flames of desire and pleasure consume my body.

Taking off his shorts, he entered the bathtub and settled between my legs. "I have to continue from where I left off. Since you are now clean, I will have to dirty you all over again, Darlin'." He flashed me a naughty smile before he raised my hips enough for his lips to attach to my slick folds. His thumb flicked my clit energetically as his tongue entered my pussy, thrusting quickly and deliciously into me.

"Alev, please," I pushed my hips onto him, my hands twining with his dark curls.

The vibration of his chuckle made my pussy flutter. "I will tease you, my sweet bad girl!" he winked, licking his lips. Before I could protest, he cocooned me in his arms and took me to the bed, and instead of joining me, he walked away with a raging erection.

"Alev, what are you doing? Come back here, please," my words came out with a couple of moans. I needed him, his willy, and all the magic he could spar in my feverish body.

In a matter of excruciating minutes, he was back with a sweet yet mischievous grin on his face and something in his hand. He sat beside me, and to my relief, he thrust a finger deep into my starving pussy, making me squirm in delight.

"So greedy, Darlin'!" Alev chuckled. Straddling my hips, he hovered over me carefully. His lips brushed against mine. "This little pussy can't wait, can she?" He shook his head.

"No, and neither can I. Please give me your wi-..." I mumbled.

"Tell me what you want, Darlin', and I will give you everything," he smiled, taking my hand in his free one.

"Everything?" I asked absently, and he nodded. "I want you inside me," I replied, biting the inner part of my lips to contain a moan like a moron.

"My finger is inside of you," he teased, arching his dark brow and swirling his finger in a slow motion.

"I want more. I want your pe... penis, please." The words came out as a cry as I arched my aching body. I needed him deep inside me.

Alev chucked, pulling his finger out of me. To my frustration, instead of impaling me with his huge willy, he took my hand in his and kissed the back of it.

"I have something else for my naughty Darlin'," he said, showing me the ring in his hand. My heart stopped for a moment; it wasn't any ring but a *Claddagh* ring. This was very special: a traditional Irish ring that represented love, loyalty, and friendship. Ultimately, it was a token of love. I looked at the small jewel, and this one was gorgeous. Besides the classic look, it had two hands holding a crowned heart in the middle, surrounded by tiny pearls, and a bigger pearl made up the heart itself.

"Alev, I..." I stuttered, my heart filled with both love and grief.

"It's a symbol of my loyalty and care, Nicole. This ring means I will always protect you, care for you, come what may. It's something beyond sex and a romantic relationship," he explained, cupping my face softly and wiping the tears I hadn't noticed were falling.

My head nodded of its own accord whilst he placed the ring on my finger and filled me with his dick at the same time.

"You are giving me all I wanted, the best gift ever, Darlin'. So, I want to give you everything too, my care, my loyalty, my vow to always protect you. Oh, and a powerful orgasm." He gave me a naughty grin as he covered my lips with his.

Alev

My sweet witch, I want you forever. My tongue swirled into her mouth, and I sucked her plump lips as I pushed harder into her. She was indeed a bad girl and liked it rough. Of course, I would be careful not to harm her and her precious belly.

Something burned within me ever since I saw those Scarlet Draconian-demons flying towards her, a feeling beyond passion and love. It was some sort of recognition, and I was starting to believe Horus; he claimed she was ours, our mate, our soul.

Regardless of anything, I was sure that she was mine, and that word echoed in my mind and soul over and over.

Kissing her lips, I thrust harder into her, my hand playing with the swollen nub within her folds.

"You feel so good, Darlin'," I hummed as she ran her fingernails across my back gently.

"Faster, please," she cried out, pushing her hips towards me, her inner walls strangling my cock — she was close.

"Naughty, Baby!" I chuckled, smacking the side of her butt and earning a sweet moan from her. I stopped teasing, gave her what we both wanted, and pumped deeper and faster into her delicious pussy.

She looked at me, her semi-closed eyes filled with desire and pure fire. Beautiful. Perfect. MINE.

Caressing her lips with my thumb and looking at her eyes, I thrust faster. I could feel the tug on my balls, telling me I was close as well.

I was about to lose control, lose myself in her, and come hard. My sweet Dyekhadee. Mine. Mine. "Mine!" the word left my throat in a throaty groan. As soon as I realised that I had said it out loud, my entire body stilled.

Nicole's eyes popped open, and she gulped hard. "I.." she gasped, breathing hard.

CHAPTER 39
Nicole

"Nicole, I…" Alev's eyes popped open, too, and the shock in his eyes mirrored my own.

"I am yours for now, Alev. Make love to me, Honey. Make every cell of my body know that I am indeed yours… for now," I replied, kissing his lips and pouring every ounce of my love into it.

He kissed me back and kept pounding into me in a passionate rhythm; his fast and deep strokes sent hot jolts of electricity throughout my system. His hands, playing with my nipple and clit, pushed me over the edge into delirious pleasure.

In my naïve fantasy, I thought we could let this flame burn only now. I thought I could leave him after the baby was born, leaving my heart behind and that he would eventually forget the passion between us.

Yet what we had wasn't only a flame. What we had was wild-fire, uncontainable, insatiable, infinite. A claim was forever, and so was that feeling. If I kept feeding the fire with my heart, my words and our pleasure, in the end, my beloved Alev and I would be only ashes. That would be our undoing.

What could I do when I couldn't stay away? Everything in me, my heart, body and soul, called and craved him. I was completely lost in love not only with him but with the baby as well. That meant I had to do the right thing for them.

Closing my eyes, I focused on the pleasure and the love to let go of the pain and fear for a while. I wanted him. I wanted to give him everything I could, for now. All the pleasure and the love.

My hips moved towards him, and I clenched his huge willy with my inner walls.

"Harder," I moaned before welcoming his tongue into my mouth. Within a few minutes, we both melted together in an infinite hot sea of ecstasy.

After eating the instant noodles he prepared, and taking a short nap, I remained in the warmth of his arms for a while.

"Let's go home?" I asked him. I had to redirect and resume my research, and find out what Kadmus wanted to do with the dragons' most coveted treasure, and what kind of harm he could cause. That was all I could think about now.

"Sure, Darlin'. I am sorry that our trip was cut short by the attack," Alev exhaled sharply, frustration clear in his voice.

Turning around, I kissed his lips. "It's not your fault. All that matters is that we had a great time, and I loved swimming in Sardinia," I told him, running my fingers through his soft dark hair.

"I don't think Horus can fly now, not safely, and I won't put you and the baby in any kind of danger, but we can use a teleporting rune to get back to the mansion. Horus is roaring in my mind as he wants to know if you liked our hoard and the shining objects he collected." Alev caressed my lower stomach gently.

"I loved it. He has a great taste!" I smiled, kissing him.

244

After getting dressed, we used the rune to get back to the mansion. As soon as we got to the living room, I saw a distressed-looking Lucky, striding downstairs.

"Nicole, come with me. We have a situation. Sorry, Lev, it's a girls' thing!" Lucky said, rushing to the living room.

Alev and I chuckled at Lucky, earning both of us her burning judgemental stare.

"Does it have something to do with Burbus?" I asked as I followed Lucky upstairs.

"Frankly, Nicole, it's disappointing to know that you think so low of me! Why do you even consider that my main concern would be an orange-furred dude?" Lucky meowed in annoyance. As we entered her new room, Lucky jumped on the shelf and motioned to my slightly glowing purse. "We have bigger issues here. Kadmus' mirror is gleaming non-stop. I am pretty sure the big and bad wizard isn't happy."

A sigh parted my lips, and my heart clenched. I was back to the cold and raw reality, to Kadmus and his demands. Opening the purse, I rubbed my fingers against the mirror a couple of times, and his frowning face appeared on it.

"Nicole! You finally answered me. Never do that again! Never make me wait, and pay attention to the mirror; you must be at my beck and call. Otherwise, you know well how Meghan will pay for your lack of care. You don't want to hurt your sister again, do you? She is in her current predicament because of you." His cold voice carried a threat, and it made me swallow deep. How I dreaded these calls!

"I won't do it again. I'm sorry Kadmus," I replied.

For a long time, I'd blamed myself completely and thought that Meghan's suffering and her association with Kadmus were both my fault. Out of naivety, I allowed Kadmus to gaslight and manipulate me.

A sigh left my lips. I'd come to understand that it wasn't my fault, at least not directly. My sister made her own choices, like I had just made mine. There was always a way, an alternative, not to harm people.

So, what Kadmus said wasn't exactly true. I never asked Meghan to practise dark magic and lose herself, yet I felt terrible for her. Fear and sadness crept up in my chest, devouring my heart because, in the end, my sister only started doing this to give me a better life and get us out of our coven.

"Good. I won't be this generous next time. Do you have any news? Have you found out what the Golden Dragon's most precious treasure is?"

A long sigh left my lips. "Not yet. But I'm close. I've found some clues. I'm certain that I will find it sooner rather than later"

"Yes, you will find it soon. You don't want anything bad happening to your dear sister, do you?"

My gaze lowered and my heart dropped as his threats always made my blood curdle. They were always filled with power and darkness.

"No. I don't," I said sadly, my voice weak. I felt completely powerless, subjected to his whims and blackmailing. I had to fight back, reclaim my power and myself. I couldn't fall prey to his manipulation games again, and if I had any chance to protect all those I loved, I had to keep my mind clear and my heart at peace, or at least as much peace as I could.

"If you came here and agreed with the alternative solution, your life would be easier, young witch. You are the one bringing chaos upon yourself. You are the one putting Meghan in danger." His lips twisted in something between a grin and a smirk.

I knew well what his "alternative solution" meant. He wanted me to bond my soul and my powers to him and become his lover. In other words, he wanted to make me his

246

toy, keeping me at his mercy forever. Kadmus had made it clear many times that he wanted everything from me: soul, body and even my heart.

Not even at the peak of my desperation could I bring myself to do it. Sometimes, I wondered why couldn't I give my heart for the sake of saving my sister's life? When I was willing to give my life, my honesty and my womb.

Now, I couldn't give it even if I wanted to, seeing that my heart didn't belong to me anymore. It was Alev's. More times than I cared to count, I found myself thinking that I couldn't ever give my heart to Kadmus because it had always belonged to Alev, even before I met him. It was a crazy thought, and I knew it. Yet, it felt so right.

"Pay your debt, Nicole. I won't wait much longer to get my payment, be it the dragon's treasure or everything you have and everything you are," he warned before his image disappeared from the mirror. Now, all I could see was my reflection, my sad face, the worry and the raw pain in my eyes.

A heavy sigh left me as my heart shrank painfully. I hated the idea of betraying the man I loved and his family. This was much more than a clan, but a real family. They were loving, warm, good people and didn't deserve to be harmed, not even in the slightest bit.

My hand moved to my bump of its own accord, and I caressed the little Angel growing inside me.

"Forgive me, sweet baby," I whispered.

A few tears rolled down my face as I looked at the painting on the wall. It depicted dozens of Golden Dragons flying free in the sky, surrounding a tall castle within the mountains. That was a token of old times, of all that they'd lost, their dukedom, their lives, their people.

What would the dragons do when they realised it wasn't ever about money? I'd entered both the Surrogacy Agency and their house with the sole goal of stealing their most precious treasure from them. Kadmus had a contact in the

Surrogacy Agency, someone who made it easy for him to make the agency contact me, even though I wasn't in any of their files or even listed in the covens' population in the recent census.

I didn't know how he found out about Alev's intention to hire a surrogate. Maybe his contact in the agency had informed him.

In the warlock community, Kadmus was a powerful and highly respected member, someone beyond any reproach. They didn't know the real Kadmus, the cruel and power-craving man who used dark magic to get whatever he wanted, ruining many lives in his pursuits.

Laying my head on the pillow, despite Lucky's meow of protest, I let a few tears flow down my cheeks.

Meghan had met Kadmus when she was very young and eager to leave our coven, the harassment and mistreatment behind. She had practised her magic for years and developed her talent into power. But she wanted more. She craved more power and the high it brought, just like a junkie. I didn't know her goal was to kill our mean coven leader Katarina. Meghan always said that Katarina was responsible for our misery, the source of our sorrows. I never understood why, though.

At some point while secretly practising some forbidden spells in the depths of the forest, my sister was visited by Kadmus. As far as I know, he offered her what she wanted, more power and a way out of the coven.

What she didn't know was that it would come with a price, and he got her addicted to dark magic, making her lose herself. From that moment on, Kadmus owned my sister, and he owned me too, because he knew that I would do anything, including sacrifice my future, my heart and my happiness to save Meghan.

Lucky lay by my side and placed her paw on my belly gently. "I trust that you will make the right choice, Cols. You are my witch and I raised you well!"

Only this silly, cheeky cat could make me smile after a call from Kadmus.

Now things had changed again; they took another turn as Meghan wasn't the only person I loved any longer. I had to protect the baby and Alev as well.

Sighing deeply, I wiped away my tears and stood up slowly.

"As soon as Alev goes to work tomorrow, we go to the library, Lucky. Let's look for answers and find out what Kadmus wants with the dragons and what he can do with their most precious treasure."

I knew well that a man like him wasn't after riches since he already had it. He wanted power, even more power than he already had. That was what it all was about, his thirst for power but not something any rune, talisman or spell could bring, but surely, much more than that.

Before our little trip, I had researched the witch-net, and even looked at some books in the small library they had downstairs, but I couldn't find anything.

"You know that reading is hard for me, Cols. I am dyslexic," Lucky meowed, making me roll my eyes. I knew those were excuses, and she wanted me to do all the reading. "Fine, I will help."

The next morning, with a cup of tea in my hand, I met a visibly sleepy and irritated Lucky in front of the door of the library.

"Do you mind opening the door, Nicole? I have short paws, remember? I am no morning cat!" she complained. Shaking my head and chuckling, I opened the door for lady Lucky, and we started the hours of research, reading all the witchery and even the history books and all the encyclopaedias we could find.

"Nothing. No, no, no," Lucky mumbled as she flipped the pages with her paws.

"It's the last book. If we don't find an answer here, I don't know where else to look," I sighed, covering my face with both hands.

"I know, but there is no point looking for it here, Cols. Maybe you could try to reach out to someone from your former coven and ask," Lucky suggested, and I shook my head. The people of my coven didn't like me at all because they believed I was the cursed fruit of a crime. They wouldn't help me; they never even helped me when I was a little kid needing food and clothes. Why would they do it now?

"I will look for it on the witch-net again," I told her as we headed upstairs, and I let my tired body fall onto the mattress, exhaling deeply.

"Hey, we didn't read all the books." Lucky's words attracted my gaze to her. She was beside my old chest and I knew exactly what she meant: my mum's grimoire, her old spellbook.

"I doubt we will be able to find much there," I told Lucky as I stood up and took the book in my hands, starting to read it. My fingertips caressed the pages containing Mum's handwriting. It was beautiful.

"You never know, Nicole. You are powerful, your sister is powerful, so it means that your mum had some sway as well. She must have known things," Lucky said, casually jumping on the edge of the bed behind me and reading the book from over my shoulder.

I gulped hard after reaching the end of the written part of my mum's book and coming across the blank pages. Mum didn't have time to finish writing before dying and thirty percent of her grimoire consisted of blank pages. No answers here.

Running my fingers across the pages, I sighed. At least I could see my mum's handwriting again and feel a bit closer to her. I was about to put the book down when a little spark of light left my fingers. As I brushed my fingers against the page once again, more sparks left my digit, and words appeared on the blank page.

"It's some kind of cloaking spell that you activated by your touch!" Lucky exclaimed.

In a matter of seconds, the text was complete, and I could read it. It wasn't a spell but rather a little message.

To my sweet daughters,
I am suspicious that our coven leader, Katarina, is dealing
with dark magic, and I fear for my future. So, I am studying
her movements and the theories behind dark magic and
laying everything I know on these pages. I hope it can help
you girls in case I am not around anymore to protect you.
Shed your light towards the darkness and let your instincts
and heart illuminate your path, my girls. Dark magic is
strong, but so are goodness and love.
Have faith in yourselves, my Rainbow and my Sunshine.
With all my love,
Your mother.

"Oh my Nyx! Mum was afraid of Katarina! How? She couldn't possibly have killed my mother, right? Mum died out of a broken heart," I murmured, shock tensing the muscles of my neck. But above anything, a light shone in my heart. It was so good to read something Mum wrote to us, even if it was only a little note.

Tears rolled down my cheeks, and a smile surged on my lips. I could hardly remember a thing about my mother, and sometimes, I feared she hated me because of what happened to her, since I was the fruit of abuse and violence.

"She loved you, Cols," Lucky replied to my unspoken question, rubbing her neck on my head affectionately.

Why was Lucky being that touchy and sweet? Was she okay? It didn't matter now. The only thing I could feel was sweetness and happiness at my mum's words, at feeling loved by her.

"Let's see if what you wrote can help me, Mum," I uttered as I read the next pages of the book carefully.

"What is it? The Prophecy of the Gem?" Lucky asked after a good half an hour of reading.

"I think that's the answer. It's here, Lucky!" I replied, my lips curving into a smile of relief.

Looking up and placing my hand on my swollen stomach, I said, "Thank you, Mum!"

CHAPTER 40
Nicole

I read it out loud:

*"If a dark sorcerer—wizard, witch, warlock or
necromancer—enchants someone's most precious gem with
shadows and blood,
the soul no more volition will hold.
Holding their most coveted treasure in their palm is a
parallel to holding their hearts.
Their will is bent and their spirit void;
and great evilness can't be avoided.
Under the sorcerer's control, will the soul forever trapped
be.
The willingness of their hearts gone; nothing can set them
free.*

A gasp formed on my lips, and Lucky squealed, "Holy bloody Nyx!"

If Kadmus owned the Golden Dragons' most precious treasure, he would forever control them, taking their free will, making them his puppets. He surely wanted the Golden Dragon's powers, or to use them as weapons. It would surely be the end of this beautiful clan.

No! Kadmus wouldn't put his dirty hands on it! Hell, I would tell him anything.

"What will you do, Cols?" Lucky asked.

"I can't find out what the dragons' treasure is. I know that if I have the knowledge somewhere in my mind, Kadmus can find a way to spell me and take the information he needs from my memory. If the Golden clan move away from this house, Kadmus won't know where their new hideout is, Lucky. He can only find out if I remain here; he has Meghan's, and consequently, my blood. If he uses a dark magic blood tracking hex, no concealing or protection spell will help the dragons. He can always find me, so my presence puts a tracking device on their backs. I will buy time, lie to Kadmus until the baby is born and when it happens, I will leave the clan and tell the dragons to move to a safer place, and do everything according to the contract. That's the only way to protect them," I told her.

My hand inadvertently roamed down to my belly, and I swallowed hard. My heart shattered into a million pieces, and I wanted to cry until I fell asleep and could forget the heartbreak my actions were going to cause. I was about to leave my heart behind, but it was the only way.

"Cols! This is a horrible idea! We can't leave our baby behind. Besides that, I know you love her daddy dragon. You can't leave him either. You know I am not into these sentimental shenanigans, but you can't do it! It will tear your heart and soul," Lucky told me.

"My feelings don't matter! If it's the only way to keep them safe, it doesn't matter. Kadmus won't be able to trace the dragons using Meghan's blood. The baby isn't a direct relative and the fact that she is a hybrid also makes her very hard to trace. So, they will be safe as long as I am away," I told Lucky.

254

"I don't want to leave our baby and..." Lucky started.

"I know, and you don't have to. You love this clan and Burbus, even though you deny it with your nine lives." My words made Lucky growl and give me her ultimate burning look. "I want to ask you something, Lucky. Please stay behind and look after the baby, protect and love her for me. You will be happier and safer here, without having to run away from Kadmus," I told her, running my fingers across her furry head.

"Are you nuts, witch? I am your familiar, we are connected, and I am not leaving you. You can't survive without me. You would do everything wrong and you would be so sad," she told me.

"Our familiar bond can be broken, Lucky. You know that. I will be sad, but you will be safer and my baby girl will have part of my love through you," I asked her as my eyes cascaded with the tears I couldn't hold back, "Please, Lucky!"

My tearing eyes looked at her in a plea. I'd made up my mind; that was the right thing, what had to be done for all of them, even though it meant ripping my beating heart out of my chest. It was the only way to protect them. The dragons wouldn't be able to defeat Kadmus and the last thing I wanted was to throw them into a battle and have them risk their lives. They had already lost enough.

"Holy Nyx, Cols! I hate this so much. That's worse than cheap milk and dry cat food, but I will do it for our baby." Her meow carried annoyance. Giving Lucky a sad smile, I ran my fingers across her head and back, and to my surprise, she purred.

"Hey, don't hold this purr against me! I have been feeling a bit funky lately!" she sighed, and I nodded.

Now that my decision had been made, I had to find another way to save Meghan, a way that wouldn't harm Alev, the baby, and their clan.

Lucky and I ended up falling asleep, cuddling together, only to wake up to Alev's deep and sexy voice.

"Darlin', it's already dinnertime, and I brought Lady Lucky some of her favourite milk and the wet food she likes."

"Lev! Aren't you a dear!" Lucky meowed, and as soon as she realised she was cuddling with me and her head lay on my shoulder, she jumped away. "What's happening to me? Since when am I the cuddling kind? Daddy, can you please call a doctor?" she asked Alev, her green eyes wide open.

Alev and I chuckled at her shock.

"I am sure you are fine. That's the effect Nicole has on people and ca… familiars like you. It's only natural to want to hug her," Alev said with a heart-melting smile.

He offered me his hand, and I stood up, leaving my startled cat alone in bed.

"How are Lucky's girl's issues doing?" Alev asked as we headed down the stairs.

"I think she is in love with Burbus, but she still denies it," I told him, giggling a little.

"The orange guy has his charms! Maybe we will have kittens running around the house soon," he chuckled, and my heart clenched at the image of Lucky and her furry babies running around the garden. I wished it would actually happen, and Lucky would find some happiness, safety and comfort, but I knew I wouldn't be around to witness it and share her joy with her.

As we reached the dining room, I was surprised to see almost the whole clan there, Alma, Egan, their twins, and even Marion, Adrian, and their new baby girl.

"Now that the whole family is here, we can eat. I am starving!" Adrian declared, earning a small frown from his mate.

Marion had her baby wrapped in her arms in some sort of sling. The little one was peacefully sleeping in her mum's arms, not bothered with the noise and chattering. A sad smile surged on my face, but I breathed deeply and pulled myself together swiftly.

"Nicole, I am so glad you and the baby are okay! Alev told me that you were attacked," Alma said, holding my hand gently.

"It was scary, but we are fine, though, I think Alev should have a healer to take a look at his shoulder and wing," I told her, and Alev shook his head, pulling out a chair for me to sit on.

"I am fine, Darlin'," he reassured me.

"Mallory and Daniel went to visit her sister." As I looked at the two empty seats in front of me, Alma replied to my unspoken question. Her intuition was remarkable; she was a powerful witch.

"I am happy to see people again. I loved every second of my nesting time and every single moment with my baby, but I need adult company," Marion sighed after she took a forkful of Egan's delicious paella.

"I was with you the whole time, Babe, and I am an adult!" Adrian declared, and Marion chuckled at him.

"You don't count, Baby. We are like one. I need other adults. Besides, with all the baby talk and daddy jokes, lately you've been quite…" she started and Adrian raised his brows in indignation.

"I've been what?" he asked, narrowing his eyes at his mate.

"She needed some grown-up girl time. I am sure that's what she's talking about," Alma rescued Marion, and I had to contain my chuckles when I saw Marion discretely mouth the word thank you to the redheaded witch.

"Exactly, Baby," Marion told her mate, running her hands down his shoulder and smiling.

"The important thing is that we are together as a family, safe and sound," Egan added with a smile as he fed one of the twins some kind of green soup. Chuckles, chatter, and love filled the air as we ate. They accepted me and treated me as one of their own rather than a simple surrogate or a *gold or spell-digger*. For the first time in my life, I felt as if I was part of something bigger: a clan, a family. The dragons were a loving and kind family, and I would protect them until my last breath.

After dinner, we all headed to the living room while Alma and Alev brought coffee, Marion's favourite tea and dessert there.

"I've made Alma's favourite: *crema catalana.* She used to crave it while she was expecting the twins," Egan told me, handing me a bowl with the dessert. He was surprisingly down-to-earth for a noble and clan leader in this position.

"Thank you," I smiled, trying the creamy dessert and letting out an inadvertent moan that made them all laugh. I could feel my cheeks heat a little; surely they were turning pink.

My sweet Alev moved me to his lap and wrapped me in his protective embrace as if he could save me from my own embarrassment.

"Don't worry, Nicole. That's exactly the right reaction to *crema catalana,*" Alma giggled, placing a reassuring hand on my shoulder.

"Yes! That's true!" Marion added with a smile. Her little girl had just woken up and was smiling at her, her tiny green eyes so full of life and joy, "Do you want to hold her, Nicole?" Marion asked and I nodded, unable to resist little Lorelai's cuteness.

As soon as the baby was in my arms, Adrian let out a little growl, and Marion elbowed him slightly. "Adrian!

Don't be a cave-dragon! Nicole is part of our clan. She won't harm our child!"

Alev's arms were around me in no time, and he narrowed his green-hazel eyes at an apologetic-looking Adrian.

Alma laughed at their exchange, "Behave, guys, no one will harm your precious females or babies!"

These men were so sweet and protective of their families; they worshipped them completely. It was heart-melting!

"I am sorry, Baby. I am sorry, Nicole," Adrian said, and I nodded, looking down at the little sweetheart that wrapped her tiny hand around my finger. I smiled at her and placed a soft kiss on the top of her head, making her coo.

"You are a natural," Alev beamed, making my heart clench in anguish and swelling at the same time.

"You have to stop this kind of behaviour, Adrian!" I heard Marion complain with her mate and glanced back at them.

"I know, Babe. In my defence, it wasn't me, it was my dragon! You know how touchy we are when it's about our most precious treasures," Adrian said, looking between his baby daughter and Marion.

Realisation hit me hard, and my heart dropped in my chest. How could I have been so blind? I didn't want to see the truth, but now I couldn't deny it anymore. It was clear: the dragons' most precious treasure was their family, more precisely, their mates and children.

The whirlwind of thoughts and worries made my stomach churn, and my blood froze in my veins. I was getting dizzy, and cold sweat was forming on my hairline.

No! I couldn't have found it out, but now it was too late.

That was the gem Kadmus was looking for. Yet, because he was an evil man who surely couldn't understand and feel love, he was looking for something material, an object rather than what the treasure really was: people, love.

"Darlin', are you alright?" Alev asked, running his fingers down my cheek as Marion took baby Lorelei in her arms.

Inhaling deeply a few times, I tried to compose myself, but the bad feeling in my stomach was only intensifying.

"Sorry, Marion… I am okay. I just have to… to go to the bathroom!" I told them half-absently. Standing up as fast as I could, I quickly made my way to the closest lavatory.

Breathing deeply, I knelt in front of the toilet and emptied my stomach's contents into it. My over-stressed body was quivering slightly, shaken by all the happenings and findings from the last twenty-four hours: the attack, Alev's words, my mum's note on Katarina, Kadmus' real intentions and the treasures. Everything together made dread creep into my mind and body.

I pressed my back against the pleasantly cold surface of the wall and sighed. My thoughts couldn't stop whilst my mind was working dizzyingly fast. The revelation about the treasure meant that the most precious treasure of Duke Egan was Alma and their twins. So, if Kadmus put his dirty hands on them and cast a dark spell, he would control this whole clan and destroy this sweet family.

"Never!" I muttered under my breath. He wouldn't do it! I wouldn't allow him. However, the sole fact that now I knew the truth put the dragons in danger. I had to do something about it, but I still didn't know what.

CHAPTER 41
Nicole

"Darlin', are you alright?" I heard Alev's voice coming from the other side of the door.

"Yes, it's just my stomach. I will be out in a few minutes," I replied, standing up slowly and heading to the sink. My gaze met the reflection of my pale face and my red eyes in the mirror.

Breathing deeply, I clenched my hands into tight fists. I would find a way to protect this clan. After washing my face, I opened the door of the lavatory and moved straight into Alev's arms.

"Let's go upstairs for you to rest," he told me, cupping my face gently and placing a soft kiss on my cheek. I only held him tighter in response, not wanting our embrace to end. Not soon. Not ever. Alev took me in his arms and headed to his room, where he caressed my hair and held my hand until I managed to fall asleep.

My head was hazy as I opened my eyes. He was there in front of me, his tanned back naked and a sheet covering his lower body.

"I am afraid, Vasilis," I said.

261

"What's wrong, Dyekhadee?" he asked, turning around and cupping my chin gently.

"I came across your father in the hall yesterday. I am afraid he would find out about us and set us apart. I am afraid that we won't be able to be together." Tears slid down my cheeks, and he held me firmly in his arms, giving me the sweet warmth that only a dragon-shifter could.

"Nothing and no one will set us apart, my Love. I will always find my way back to you, no matter what it takes." Looking intently into my eyes, he kissed me.

"I will find my way back to you, too. It doesn't matter how long it takes. You are my life and my soul, my Dragon Prince," I promised, my breath fanning his lips.

I woke up to the fast beating of my heart. For the first time, I could remember something about the unknown man of my dreams, Vasilis, appearance. His warm golden eyes were a copy of Alev's when Horus was on the surface. A sigh crossed my lips. Was it only a dream, or was my subconscious trying to tell me something? Was the dream a metaphor of my soul that craved not to leave Alev? Despite dreaming about Vasilis since I was young, way before I met Alev, I still believed that it could be the way of my soul to tell me about the great love that would burn and possess me completely. A love that I would have to let go.

My eyes met Alev's sleeping face, and I whispered under my breath, "Everything for you, my Love."

The next two weeks passed quickly as I tried to both enjoy every second with Alev and sew as many clothes for my baby girl as I could. I wanted to leave as many tokens of my love for her as possible.

I was working on a tiny blue cardigan when a piercing pain radiated from my head to my spine. The cardigan fell from my hands as my vision went completely black for a moment.

"Cols, wake up!" Lucky called as she gently hit my face with her tail over and over. Once I opened my eyes, I looked at her grey furry face and gasped for air a few times. "What happened?" Worry laced her voice.

It wasn't only a blackout, but I could feel heavy and thick darkness creeping down my spine.

"Kadmus," I replied, knowing that it was his doing. He was angry and impatient, and I had to report to him before he hit me again and ended up hurting my baby.

Closing my eyes, I tried to feel her and make sure she wasn't affected by Kadmus.

"I will protect you, my sweet baby," I told my little girl as my fingers ran around my swollen stomach. She fluttered inside me, and a sigh of relief trembled through my lips. My baby was moving, which was a great sign; she was alright.

Kadmus was using Meghan's blood and his dark magic to reach me. Since we were closely related, dark spells using her blood that were directed at me could be very harmful to my health.

"The mirror is shining, Cols. That horrible wizard is calling," Lucky told me as she jumped down from my sewing table and walked towards my gleaming purse.

Standing up slowly, I took the mirror and brushed it a few times, making Kadmus' face appear. His image made icy fear roam down my spine, and I swallowed hard. I'd never seen him like that before. His dark brows raised in anger, his grey hair oddly dishevelled, and dark shadows were around his eyes.

"Nicole, it seems you don't care about your sister anymore. At least her blood is useful to spell you and attract your attention. Next time, I won't be that nice, and it will actually hurt you, do you understand?" he asked, a frown on his face.

"I understand," my voice came out quieter than a whisper. I was still trying to steady my breath.

"I need an answer and I won't wait any longer. You either tell me about the dragons' treasures or give your soul and magic to me," Kadmus demanded, his voice angry and cold.

"Kadmus, please, give me a little time. I still don't know about the treasure. Lucky and I are looking for it," I said, trying to keep myself calm.

"You are lying, Nicole! Now that I have your blood in my hands, I can feel it," he hissed, raising his bloody hand. Meghan's screams in the background made my heart fall and tears slid down my face. My whole body was trembling. Nothing would keep me calm now.

"I am not lying. I swear. Please, Kadmus, just a few more days! We are getting very close."

"If you don't give me what I want in two days, I will find the dragons' mansion, go after you and the Dragon clan, find the treasure myself and make you completely mine!" he spat before his image disappeared from the mirror.

Dragging myself to the bed, I let my aching and tired body fall to the mattress. I knew it would happen sooner or later he would lose his patience. Yet, I couldn't predict that he would hurt me this way and come here.

"He can't take your soul and magic without your consent, Cols. You know how the magic union spells work. For him to bind your spirit and magic to his for eternity, you would have to agree and perform the ceremony," Lucky told me as she lay by my right side. I nodded half-absently, knowing that she had a point. Besides, I knew that if Kadmus came here, the dragons would put up a fight, and he would likely ruin his own plan and never be able to control the Golden Clan and use the dragons as weapons to feed his thirst for power and whatever dark agenda he had.

"It might be a bluff, but he seems desperate, and he went to the extent of spelling Meghan and my blood. I can't risk this clan's safety, Lucky." I sobbed into my pillow.

As a trusted member of the warlock community and a powerful noble, it wouldn't be hard for Kadmus to find out where the clan's mansion was located. Warlocks didn't know the monster he was since he hid his true colours very well.

"Something has changed; the old evil warlock looked desperate. Maybe that's why he is speeding up the timeline." Lucky looked into space, lost in thought.

"I think so too." I sighed, curling up into a ball in an attempt to warm up my cold and quivering body. A new batch of desperate tears trickled down my face. I was afraid for Meghan and for myself. I was terrified for this clan, Alev, and my baby girl.

"You have to tell the dragons about Kadmus. You don't have to tell them the whole truth if you can't. But they have to know that Kadmus is coming for them and for you," Lucky said.

"I wish I could tell them about Kadmus." A sigh heaved in my chest. If only I could tell them everything. Alev would hate me, but at least they would be safer. "You know I can't tell anyone about Kadmus, Lucky. He made sure of it when he made me take a blood oath; if I say anything, I will bleed to death and the baby will die with me."

"Shit! I know that. Well, well, things have changed now that I can speak, Cols. Kadmus could never predict that a feline lady would save the day, right?" Lucky let out a proud meow as she licked her paws almost ceremonially.

CHAPTER 42
Nicole

Tilting my face up, I looked at my cat.

"It might work. I don't know to what extent the blood oath impacts you since we have the familiar bond."

"Right, there is that too. You know I hate the idea of breaking our familiar bond. We could try that for me to spill the beans, but with you *that* pregnant, it could hurt you and our dragon-baby. So, that's a no. But I could try to tell my dear Lev about Kadmus and see how it goes," Lucky told me, and I nodded. That was the best thing we could do for now.

"This afternoon, when Alev is back from work, we will try," I told her, and she meowed before yawning.

"Deal, but now it's time for my beauty nap. Please be a dear and rub my back. I know this is odd coming from me, but I have been feeling cuddly lately. Maybe it has something to do with my star sign. Who knows?" she meowed again, placing her head on my belly and stretching out her slim body.

Had Lucky gained some weight lately? Maybe she had. She always ate more when she was tense, and because of me, my poor feline had been exceptionally stressed and worried in the last few months.

As soon as I managed to stop crying, sleep claimed my exhausted body, and I woke up to Lucky's meow.

"Cols, it's time."

I nodded and knew what she meant; I could hear Alev's approaching steps as well. Rubbing the sleep from my eyes, I stood up quickly. We had no time to lose.

As soon as Alev knocked and entered the room, I went towards him.

"Are you alright, Darlin'?" he asked, concern clear in his eyes. Did I look pale or something?

"I… Lucky has to tell you something," I muttered, swallowing the nervous lump that formed in my throat. Taking his hand in mine, I guided him to the expectant cat on the bed.

"Hello, Lev. How are you?" Lucky said nervously. Alev looked between the two of us, his forehead creasing with confusion.

"Are you alright, Lady Lucky?" he asked, and she nodded.

"I am okay. I have to tell you something important about a…" Lucky's words were cut by a deep cough, and a splash of blood left her mouth as she fell to her side.

"Lucky!" I screamed, panic rising fast and spreading through my body and soul. Rushing towards her, I knelt by her side. My heart was beating so fast that my mind went hazy. My trembling hand wrapped around Lucky's cold paw while a torrent of tears left my eyes as I sobbed senselessly.

"She is breathing, Darlin'. She will be okay," Alev reassured me, wrapping an arm around me and placing his right hand on Lucky's side.

Burying my face in his chest, I inhaled a few times deeply and let his warmth wash over my battered soul. Now that I was a bit calmer, I could feel that she was okay in my

267

magic and in the familiar-witch bond we shared. She was affected by the blood oath and Kadmus' dark magic but not seriously hurt.

Looking at her through my wet eyelashes, I felt the icy grip of guilt spread through my heart. My poor Lucky! This mess almost cost her life! I had to find another way to help the clan, and alert them.

"We should call a healer or…" A meow interrupted my words.

"I am alright, Cols. I just need some warm milk and head-rubs. By the way, can you ask Burbus to come by? It's not because I want him, you know, but in my medical condition, it seems like the right call," she said, standing on her four paws again and shaking her body slowly.

"I will bring the orange cat here!" Alev chuckled, rubbing Lucky's head and earning a purr from her before he left the room.

Lucky must have been completely out of her mind lately to react like that.

"Lucky, have you and Burbus mated?" I asked, as a thought occurred to me.

"Of course not! It was only a one-night stand. You see, I am a free feline lady and I stand for one-night stands. It's called female emancipation. I know, I know, I am a role model! Why are you asking?" she asked, licking her paws slowly.

"Could it be that you are carrying?" I raised my eyebrows in confusion.

"Well, we didn't use protection." She shrugged, and I shook my head. There was no such a thing as cat-condoms. "It was only a one-time thing, and I don't feel pregnant. I feel peachy!" she meowed, and I nodded, not sure if she actually had a point.

Soon, Alev was back with Burbus, and without a meow or even a judging-cat look, he lay by Lucky's right side and licked her ear slowly.

Alev took both my hands in his, leading me out of the room.

"Let's leave the two love kittens alone and have our own privacy as well. What happened to Lucky? Was that a spell?" Alev asked, and I gulped nervously. He was a smart man and noticed how sudden Lucky's reaction was.

"Yes. She was trying to say something important, Alev. Something that neither of us can say," I said, my gaze roaming down for a moment.

Alev tilted my chin up, and with his familiar optimism, he gave me a small smile.

"We will find a way. Meanwhile, I will keep you both safe, Darlin'."

I wish it was that easy and he could actually protect me. Yet I wasn't naïve. I knew how complicated our situation was. Being used to solving my issues on my own and dealing with the darkness that Kadmus' brought to Meghan's and my life, I knew that I had reached the bottom of the pit, and there was little or no salvation for me. Kadmus might come in two days, bringing his powerful allies with him and leaving only darkness and death behind.

May the Goddess help us!

My heart clenched in my chest, and I caressed my lips against his. So much love and regret pumped from my heart. Alev was an extraordinary man. He still had so much hope and kindness in him, even after all he had suffered. He went through a lot during the Dragon Wars that cost him his people, his home and his family, besides being left by his ex and being under the spell of the succubus Meghan had brought to this house under Kadmus' orders. He had a heart of gold, much more precious than any treasure.

Heading to his room, I spent the entire night in his arms, making love to him and letting this love feed my heart and give me the strength to do what I had to do next.

The next morning, I went to Lucky's room as soon as
Alev left for work. My *familiar* and I had a lot to do today.

"Lucky? Are you okay?" I asked as I shook my head at
the sight of a happy Burbus leaving the room and wagging
his tail.

"I am alright and ready to find a way to help this clan.
Let's get to the job!" Lucky jumped off the bed
energetically. It seemed like her romantic night had
renewed her stamina.

Opening my mum's spell book, I said in my mind as I
flicked through the pages, *"Mum, please guide me, give me
some clarity and show me a way."*

Feeling a gentle touch in my heart, I let my fingers act
of their own accord and opened the book on a random
page.

"The Chant of Clairvoyance. How to talk to your
Goddess and be able to hear Nyx's voice," I read it out
loud.

"Let's do it!" Lucky meowed. Following the
instructions from my mum's grimoire, Lucky and I made a
circle with my old crystals. We lit a spell candle in the
centre of it, sitting together in front of it.

Looking at Lucky, I smiled while she nodded, placing
her paw on top of my hand. Having Lucky do the spells
with me always made them more effective. She enhanced
my magic even more than a standard familiar could, maybe
because we had always been very close. Beyond a familiar-
witch connection, there was love and friendship bonding us
because Lucky was family.

Lucky and I both closed our eyes and focused on our
shared magic. I could feel our connection pulsating in my
heart and fluttering with a soft blue and yellow vibration.

As soon as I felt empowered by our bond, I chanted the spell words.

"Holy Nyx, make my eyes see with clarity, open my ears and the mazes of my soul. Have your words echoing through me, showing me where to go."

With my eyes closed and my mind completely focused, I meditated for what it felt like hours, yet I couldn't hear a word from Nyx. My tired eyes opened on their own, and I breathed deeply. A gasp left me as the candle's flame faded and the crystals shifted slightly. I didn't understand why it happened when the spell clearly hadn't worked. Glancing at Lucky, I sighed in confusion as she just opened her green eyes as well.

"I didn't hear or see anything."

Her next words widened my eyes in surprise. "But I did, Cols. Nyx talked to me, and I know what we should do."

CHAPTER 43
Nicole

"What did she say?" I asked, still shocked by Lucky's revelation.

"She has a deep, although gentle voice and made my fur stand up. I even had goosebumps. It was magical, Cols!" she meowed, and I gave her an impatient look, urging her to get to the point. "There is a place in Greece, on the island of Naxos, where we will be safer from Kadmus. Both his blood spells and his grasp on you would be much weaker," she added, and I released a long exhale of relief.

"We could talk the dragons into moving there too. A safe place is what we all need. We all should move to this safe place soon," I told her. A smile formed on my lips as a spark of hope shone in my heart. I would worry about what to do with Meghan later, but at that place, Alev and I could have a chance of being together, free of Kadmus and the other threats to his clan. Well, that would only be possible if he could forgive me for my lies and the way I had entered his life.

"About that, Cols, I don't think the dragons could join us there. You see, the place the Goddess showed me in the vision is a priestesses' temple for Nyx. It's only for the daughters of Nyx: witches, and familiars such as myself. The dragons wouldn't be accepted there." Her words broke my heart in a single strike, and I nodded, pushing away my frustration while holding back my tears.

"I have to head there, and the dragons have to find a new hideout immediately. If I stay with them, wherever they go or move to, Kadmus will be able to locate them using Meghan's blood to track me," I said.

"I will go with you. I won't leave you and our baby; besides, as long as our familiar-witch bond still exists and we share magic, Kadmus might be able to track me using Meghan's blood, too. The magic runs in the blood. What will you tell Alev, Cols?"

A deep sigh left me as I covered my face with both hands. I knew what I had to do, and it made my heart shrink in my chest.

Standing up, I started packing. Lucky and I had to leave before the forty-eight hours Kadmus gave me ran out.

"We have to leave everything behind, at least for now. That's the only way to prevent Kadmus from hurting this clan," I told Lucky.

"Can you be without him? You are so deeply in love, Cols. It's shameful for me to say, but you fell like a puppy dog for him. No cat would lose their minds that much. This is surely a *doggy* thing."

"I don't know, but it doesn't matter now. I will give the baby to Alev once she is born, as it was first agreed upon. We can break our familiar-witch bond, and you will be able to stay with the baby, and alert the clan about Kadmus when I leave forever. That way, Kadmus won't be able to find the clan through me or spell me to get the answers he is looking for. Being around this clan would only put them all in danger," I told her, placing a hand on my aching heart and the other one on my belly. The baby was kicking; she could surely feel my despair.

"Cols! It's our baby! You love her so much too!" Lucky meowed.

"It doesn't matter what I feel. I will do whatever it takes to protect all of them," I replied as my fingers ran down my belly in soothing movements.

"I was thinking about it over and over and wondering if we can stay. Can't the dragons protect us?" Lucky asked.

She loved this place, and even though she denied it with her nine feline lives, she was in love with the orange bobcat. If only we could stay, but I wasn't so naïve to believe that the Golden Clan could defeat Kadmus. I didn't know how powerful Kadmus was, not exactly. But I was sure he was mighty, relentless and had many powerful allies also well-versed in dark magic. The last thing I wanted to do was to gamble on the dragons' lives and safety.

"No. Kadmus is too powerful, and he has equally powerful allies. Meghan mentioned something about his alliance with a Lycan Prince once. He is deadly, Lucky. The best thing I can do for this clan, this family, is drive Kadmus away from them. If the dragons move away from this house and I am gone, Kadmus won't know where their new hideout is and won't be able to track them through me."

Taking a big purple crystal from the chest of my mum's belongings, I recorded the message I wanted to. Telling them everything in person would only make them ask the questions I wasn't able to answer.

Sitting on the bed, I placed the crystal in front of me, and chanting the spell, I activated its magic; it would record me like a camera. However, unlike a camera, I could choose who could open the message.

"Dear Golden Clan, you are in danger, and you have to move away from this mansion within the next couple of hours. I can't tell you any more about it since I have been bound by magic, but you can't tell a soul about your new hideout. Don't trust anyone, not even the Warlock Society.

274

An unknown threat is after you and your treasures, so please protect yourselves." Wiping my tears, I continued, "Alev, I am so sorry for everything. I have to go away, and it breaks my heart. Please forget about me and find the happiness you deserve. I was never worthy of you, and you are the most beautiful and incredible person I've ever met. You are bright like the sun, the sweetest of the flames, gentle and powerful. I pray to the Goddess that your life will be filled with miracles and light. Please, be safe and have a great life in the new hideout."

I couldn't tell him how much I loved him. It would only hurt more, so I chanted the reverse spell and finished my message. My half-numb body fell on the mattress, and I let a few more tears fall before getting up to resume packing.

"That's sad! I will need therapy to recover from that; just saying." Lucky let out a strangled meow and shook her head. "What will you do? Run away while Alev is working? He will go nuts, and he won't ever let go of you and the baby. He will look for and find you, Cols," Lucky told me as she jumped on the bed.

She was right, and I couldn't have that happening, else everything would be ruined, and all the sacrifices to protect the clan would be in vain. A shiver danced down my spine as a horrible idea surged to mind. Yet, I didn't have another option; it had to be done. "That's true. I will have to prevent him from coming after me. I will have to lie to him. While the baby is still in my belly, Alev must think she is no more, and when she is born, I will find the clan and give her to Alev," I said, biting my lips at the sting of the words in my heart. How I hated the idea of breaking his heart. It would shatter my own soul to pieces, but I didn't have a choice. Telling him about Kadmus wasn't possible, and if he believed I was still carrying his little princess, he would chase me to the ends of the world.

Looking among mum's things, I found the potion I was looking for and drank it in a single gulp. It was done, and now, we just had to call Alev.

"Cols, I know how hard it is. I can call him for you. Give me your phone," Lucky meowed, and I did as she asked. Within a few minutes, and definitely much faster than I expected, Alev burst the door of the room open and took me in his arms. He lay me on the bed and wrapped his muscular arms around me as his hand rested on my swollen stomach. The potion was working, and no one would be able to hear the baby's heartbeat or feel her magic and energy coming from my womb for the next six hours.

"Darlin', how are you feeling?" Sadness and sympathy shone in his hazel-green eyes. I couldn't look him in the eyes else my heart would break completely, and I would let go of any rational thinking and give up on the plan.

"I can't feel her anymore, Alev. The baby is no more," I cried between sobs. The lies left a bitter taste in my mouth and raw guilt crawled up my guts, making me want to puke.

Alev covered the top of my head with soft kisses, and I felt his tears wetting my hair. I held him tightly and uttered into the silence of my broken soul. *If there was another way, I would do it. I would take any hit and sacrifice myself before having to break your heart. Yet that was the only way out I could see. Soon, the lies will be over and you will have your little princess in your arms, my Love. I will be gone, and so will be all the danger and evil in your life. Only the best part of me and my eternal love shall stay with you in the form of the sweet little soul that is growing within my body.*

"I talked to Alma and Marion. Alma is coming to see you and use the Great Spirit Dragon to give you some healing energy. Marion asked her doctor friend to come to check on you and… we just have to wait a little," he told me, his voice filled with deep sadness and grief.

276

"There is nothing to wait for! We all know I had a miscarriage. The baby is gone. I want to leave," I said under my breath, sinking my face into his warm chest for the last time.

"Leave?" he asked, tilting my head in an attempt to make me look at him, but my face remained firmly sunk in his chest.

"Leave this house and go back to Ireland, to my life. I can't go through that again, Alev," I sobbed as I repeated in my mind that it was the only way, and I had to do that.

"I can.. I can't imagine how hard it is for you, how you feel. But I beg you to wait, to at least consider staying here in the mansion with me. Once you feel better, we can think about trying again, having a baby, bringing the child's soul into this world. We can do that together; we will be cautious. It will be different this time. I'll quit work and be by your side all the time, holding you, loving you. Loving you both," he said gently.

Oh, Nyx! Why did he have to be so sweet? He was putting his own sadness aside to tend to my wounds, reassure me, even though this baby was his dream, even though he already loved her before she was conceived.

"Alev, I can't. I can't try it again. I can't stay! It's too much for me to be away from my life, sick and in pain, for longer. The money and the contract benefits aren't worth it," I sobbed, the words cutting my heart like a blade. I hated all those words; I hated the moment and the situation, and I loved that man so much.

"What?" he asked, sounding confused.

"I was in it for the money and the potions and power the contract would give me. You know that; it's a contract. But now I see that the business transaction isn't worth it. It's nothing personal, but I have to fend for myself and Lucky." Azula's spirit cried within my soul at my words. This plan and the separation were hurting him as much as it hurt me.

277

"Nicole, are you sure you want to talk about it now? Don't you want to rest and clear your head first? I know that what you feel and what we have goes way beyond the contract. I know you…" he started.

Leaving the sweet heaven of his warm embrace, I pushed away from him. Cursing myself and my words, I stood up and glanced at him for a few seconds as the biggest lie I'd ever told left my lips.

"You are wrong. You are way too naïve for a centuries-old dragon. Alev, I don't love you." Putting more distance between us, I took my belongings in my hands, leaving behind what I couldn't carry, and headed to meet Lucky in the living room like we planned.

Alev came after me. He looked pale, his eyes were red and swollen, his expression was of pure consternation and brokenness. Breathing deeply, I pushed myself to do what I had to and went down the stairs without looking back.

"Nicole, you can't leave like this. You need medical treatment, to rest, and…" he continued, following me to the living room. After everything I had said and done, he still cared about me. His love was deep like mine. It was deep, tragic, and fated to become ashes and tears.

"Alev, I have only one thing to ask you, and I need you to promise, swear, that you will do it. Please," I begged, turning to steal a last glance at him.

"Yes, I swear."

"There is a pink crystal in Lucky's former room. There is a message for the clan there. Listen to it now.; it's very important," I said between sniffs.

"I will listen to it. Nicole, when you have time to think clearly, if you want to come back, you will be welcome to do so," he told me.

"I won't come back. Stay safe, Alev. You have a beautiful clan and a family here, and I wish you all the best. Take care," I said before gazing at Lucky as we left the house together.

While I was with Alev, she got some money and runes for us to fly to Greece safely and then come back to give the baby to Alev. I was a liar and a thief.

I ended up hurting everyone I love, or letting them down. My mother, when I was born, then Meghan, the dragons, and Alev. Maybe I was indeed cursed as the kids in my coven claimed. Meghan tried to protect me from their mean words and bullying, but she could never do it completely; after all, I had ears.

Lucky and I got a cab and headed to the airport, taking the next flight to Greece. Hopefully, we would be at Nyx Temple on the island of Naxos before Kadmus' forty-eight hours were over or he noticed that I had left.

I cried during the entire three-hour flight. My heart and soul shattered, yet it was the only way to keep my baby, her father, and their clan safe. My love for them was more vast than the sea. I would do anything for them.

CHAPTER 44
Alev

A deep sob left me as I covered my face with both hands. Horus was whimpering and screaming in my soul. Being left by my ex-girlfriend, Niki, was nothing in comparison to what was happening. Nicole was my heart, my fire, my life.

I'd just lost her and our precious princess, my dream, my family, my daughter. Letting my tears fall and sulking in my pain, I almost crashed into Alma's petite frame.

"Oh Gods! Alev, are you okay? Is Nicole okay? Is she in the room?" Alma asked, running her hand down my arm soothingly.

"She left. She had a miscarriage like Lucky told me. I couldn't feel the baby, hear her little heart beating, and smell her amber scent. They are both gone." I sobbed like a lost child, completely shattered.

Alma hugged me tightly and ran her hands down my arms, over and over. I felt the reassuring Spirit Fire flow from her fingertips to my chest, calming Horus and me. It lessened my pain and grief a little.

Our sweet Dragon Duchess hugged me until I controlled my tears. As we parted the embrace, she gazed into my eyes, her green eyes filled with doubt.

"Alev, it makes no sense. She should have been resting now." Alma sighed, her face contorted with confusion and sadness. Even though her first instinct was not to trust Nicole, Alma ended up getting attached to her.

"I know. But she looked stressed out as if she would suffocate if she stayed in this mansion any longer. She said that the contract and the money weren't worth it anymore," I said sadly, recalling her words and the pain they brought me.

"That makes even less sense; Alev, something is definitely off. Even a blind mouse can see that the girl is completely in love with you!" Alma explained, looking thoughtful. "Has something weird happened lately? Something does not add up at all."

Exhaling sharply, I recalled the very odd thing that happened to Lucky yesterday and told Alma about it.

"It seems like they wanted to tell you something but couldn't. The reaction Lucky had could be the effect of a blood oath, a strong one, maybe even sealed with dark magic," Alma thought out loud. Her words only brought me fear and unease. They might be in danger.

I was so focused on Lucky's health that I didn't question Nicole about what they had to say and why they couldn't do it. Then, I was too lost in her curves and her love to question anything, to be able to think straight.

"There is something else, Alma. I have to go upstairs. Nicole said that she left a crystal for me and made me swear to look at it immediately."

"Oh Gods! Let's take a look at this crystal and see what we can find out."

We both headed to Lucky's room, and I brushed the crystal with my fingers the way Nicole said I should. The crystal got warmer and shone before projecting her image.

She looked pale, dishevelled, and her eyes held a deep sadness that mirrored my own. She told the clan that we should move before directing her words to me.

"Alev, I am so sorry for everything. I have to go away, and it breaks my heart. Please forget about me and find the happiness you deserve. I was never worthy of you, and you are the most beautiful and incredible person I've ever met. You are bright like the sun, the sweetest of the flames, gentle, and powerful. I pray to the Goddess that your life will be filled with miracles and light. Please, be safe and have a great life in the new hideout." Her words made me sad and angry in equal measure.

"She loves you." Alma sighed, sympathy clear in her gaze.

"She left, Alma. She can't say she wishes me the best, drop these words of care, have her eyes filled with love, and leave me!" My words thundered across the room as Horus roared and whimpered within my soul.

"I know. Alev, I don't even know what you feel. If Egan left me, I would torch his hot ass! We will find her. That woman loves you, and you love her. And love, my friend, is damn worth fighting for! But now we have to take her warning seriously and move out of this house immediately. I will talk to Egan and tell everyone to start packing. I am pretty sure my wonderful husband has always had a plan B and another hideout ready for us in case things ever went south. We have to get ready and rush out of here," she said, giving me a quick hug before leaving the room to arrange everything.

Covering my face with my hands, I let a scream burst from my throat. Seeing Nicole's face in the projection of the crystal, and the undeniable love in her eyes, I understood that she didn't leave because she didn't love me or only wanted money as she had put it. I would fight for her and get her back. Above all, I would help her and Lucky.

What was the link between the blood oath Lucky was under, Nicole's warning, and their departure? My mind swirled with aggravating thoughts: how didn't I realise that Nicole and Lucky were in danger before?

My hands clenched into fists, and my insides burned with anger and helplessness. The fact that she left and her warning for us to leave this house must be related. I wondered if the tension and fear she must have been through were responsible for her miscarriage. My chest shrank with immense pain as I thought about my little princess. She was gone and her mum was nowhere to be found.

"Fuck! I should have held her in my arms, kept her in my embrace and protected her rather than let her go!" I berated myself as warm tears of grief and regret leaked from my eyes.

For quite some time, I had known Nicole was hiding something and decided to give her time and space to open up. Yet I didn't imagine she was in such deep trouble, let alone that it was related to a threat that would force us to move from Marbella.

As I left the room that still held her lingering smell, Horus protested with a loud roar. I knew what he meant. If we left this house, his mate, our mate, wouldn't be able to find her way back to us. He firmly believed she would come back, that she would always come back to us.

"We should move now with the rest of the clan and make sure they are all safe in the new hideout. Then we will return to this mansion," I told Horus, successfully soothing my hurt beast.

Meeting the others in the living room, I welcomed Egan's hug.

"Alma told me everything. First, we will ensure our safety, and then we will find your woman."

"I am so sorry, Alev," consoled Marion, and Adrian gave me a look of sympathy as he firmly wrapped his arms

283

around his mate and infant daughter. Mallory and Daniel were still away visiting her sister, so we had to move their belongings to the new hideout.

"Let's go. I will first teleport Alma and the three babies and then come back for the rest of you and the things," Marion said with a sigh.

I was the last one Marion teleported to our provisional hideout, a penthouse in Malta. I didn't want to leave the house that held so many memories, where her giggles still echoed along with her lingering smell.

Arriving at the penthouse, I joined Egan to make sure that the entire clan was settled before heading to my lonely and plain new room. I had brought a few objects, memories, tokens of lost times, photos of my long-gone family, and the small pink chair that used to belong to my little sister Naomi.

Laying on the bed, I fell asleep immediately and was pulled into a dream. It was a dream about her, the brunette in a long-flowing tunic. My beloved, my Darlin'.

I was walking through the dim-lit halls of a palace that looked like a maze. Rage was still burning within my blood. Why did my father have to be like that? Once again, he was imposing his desires on everyone, regardless of other's choices and even their own lives. I could see the fire from the window. He had burned the coven to ashes and imprisoned the survivors because Alice, the coven leader, had resisted his lustful possession.

My legs strode faster, my mind lost in thought when I crashed into something. Looking down, I saw a young brunette. Her scared eyes were beautiful and alive, like two flames. She was a witch and surely had just escaped from the Dungeon.

"You can't be here! If they find you, you will be killed," I told her, wrapping a hand around her cold arm and pulling her with me to the room nearby.

284

"You are a dragon! Take your hands off me!" she yelled, her fear replaced by fierceness as she tried to push me away.

"I am only trying to help you. The last thing we need tonight is more death of innocents," I told her, and in a surprising move, she tried to launch at me.

"Who said I am innocent? I am dangerous and very powerful. I will turn you into the greenest frog in existence!" she declared as I easily avoided her attack and immobilised her arms.

"I can see how powerful you are. Oh, daughter of Nyx!" I chuckled, earning a frown from the beautiful witch. Those eyes, that fire, there was something absolutely magnetic about the woman.

"You won't eat me, dragon!" she declared, narrowing her eyes. Even in her anger, there was something gentle and sweet about her, and I couldn't do anything but chuckle at her words.

"My dragon doesn't eat witches; the meat isn't that nutritious!" I joked and her lips curled up in a snarl. "Please, stay silent. I just want to help you, but if they find you here, you will either be killed immediately or sent to the Dungeon," I reasoned.

"If you want to help me, set me free. I can't stay in this castle!" she exclaimed, and I nodded.

"I will try, but not tonight. Tonight, all the guards are on high alert. I will hide you in my room, and if anyone asks, I will tell them you are my lover," I told her and she pushed me away.

"I won't sleep with you, dragon!"

I had to contain my chuckles. The woman was amusing. Who else would be that brave after being captured and easily manhandled?

"I didn't imply that. But I have to hide you somewhere safe and have a cover story in case someone asks why there is a witch in my room."

She stayed silent for some time before a threat came from her beautiful lips. "Fine. But if you try anything, I will bite you."

I nodded, and as quietly as possible, I led her to my ample quarters. My father, the tyrant Golden King, would take a long time to come to my rooms, hopefully long enough for me to help the young witch run away.

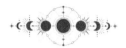

Everything went blank for a moment before the images started appearing again. She was looking through the window. The sun kissed her skin, and the sea breeze lifted her hair gently. She was a sight to behold. The smile on my face contorted into a little frown as I felt the worry radiating from her.

"Do you think all the witches are dead? Did your father kill them all?" she asked, without turning around to look at me.

"Yes, Eos. I am so sorry, but I think so. He killed your aunt Alice and her entire coven, only you survived," I said, taking a step closer to the sad beauty.

She turned around, small, and crystalline tears sliding down her flushed cheeks.

"I survived because of you, Vasilis. You will always have my eternal gratitude, but I have to leave now. Aunt Alice didn't accept your father's orders and give herself to him, because she needed her freedom, and so do I. We witches are like cats; we are born free, and without that, our magic fades away while our souls shrink."

I had been hiding Eos in my quarters for the last four weeks, and we had grown close. She wasn't my concubine like everyone believed, but rather someone I looked forward to seeing and talking to after a long day of training and studying to be my father's successor and the next King of the Golden Dragons.

I took her hands in mine, reassuring her.

"I know, Eos. It is what makes you so brave and powerful, and I never want to take that from you. My father seems to accept and even laugh about the fact that I have a witch lover, meaning you could stay and be safe here. Yet, I wouldn't ask you for that. I want your happiness, your freedom, and I wouldn't ever dream of having any part of you and your light shrinking. You are perfect the way you are, complete, brave, free like a cat." I smiled at her, and to my surprise, she wrapped her arms around me.

"Vasilis, you haven't asked me to stay, and that shows that my suspicions were right," she said with a sweet smile.

"What do you mean?" I asked, raising my brows.

"It means that I love you, and you love me too." She placed her hand on my chest, calming my racing heart. "Can you feel it? It's like an eternal flame. I want to stay with you."

"What about your freedom, Eos? I don't want to deprive you of anything." I brushed a stray lock of her hair behind her ear and pressed a chaste kiss on her forehead.

"I can exercise my freedom in my choice to stay with you. Love feels like a higher level of freedom, one that makes two able to fly together. I would be even freer than a cat, like a loving bird in your arms." My sweet witch giggled, throwing herself into my arms and filling my heart with an unknown level of joy. Eos wasn't only fire; she was light, brightness, and happiness. She was like the sun to me.

I spun her in my arms, and her giggles filled my ears and my soul. When I stopped, she melted into my embrace and our lips met in a sweet and hot kiss. To my surprise, my sweet witch broke our embrace and took a few steps back. Looking intently into my eyes, she let her tunic fall from her shoulders, revealing her smooth and completely bare skin. I

287

couldn't stop looking at her. Unlike the sun, her light was gentle on the eyes and sweet to the soul. Without being able to wait, I took her in my arms and lay her on my bed, covering her body with mine.

"You are right, my sweet witch; I do love you," I purred, kissing her once again. She tasted like a delicious ripe fruit.

I woke up suddenly, my forehead drenched with sweat. That was an odd dream. I'd dreamt about that woman so many times and even recognised her as Nicole. Why, then had I called her Eos, and why had she called me Vasilis in the dream? I was out of my mind and needed both a cold shower to calm down my raging erection and a glass of whiskey to silence my broken heart, at least for a moment.

"I will find you, Nicole," I murmured to myself, and Horus whimpered his agreement.

CHAPTER 45
Nicole

Arriving in Athens, I bought a heating pad to make sure the little dragonling in my womb would be warm and healthy since we couldn't sleep in Alev's warm embrace anymore. Afterwards, Lucky and I took a boat to Naxos island and arrived at Nyx's temple.

My gaze roamed the tall pillars of the ancient temple, a place I hadn't known about until Lucky's vision, yet it felt very familiar.

The old temple stood in front of the sea, and there I would have the sanctuary I needed, surrounded by my Goddess Nyx and the sweet sound of the waves crashing onto the shore.

Closing my eyes for an instant, I inhaled the sea breeze and took a few steps forward. My tears were still falling, and my heart was still completely shattered. Time would eventually make the tears stop, but I knew that nothing would fix my broken heart and soul.

I exchanged a look with Lucky, and she rubbed against my leg as we both crossed the temple hall. Once again, it was only my sassy feline and me fending for ourselves.

Things were like they'd always been since my sister lost herself to the highs of power and forbidden magic.

"May the Goddess give me strength," I said under my breath.

With each step, the tingles radiating from my feet to the centre of my forehead grew more intense. The energy and magic of the place were so strong that I could feel them reverberate in my bones. I also could feel the baby kicking again. A sigh of relief parted my lips, and I caressed my lower stomach. My little girl was fine.

This temple was calling for something in my soul, except the calling coming from the sea behind it was even stronger. Oddly enough, it felt like I had been here before, walked across this hall and even swam in these waters.

"Welcome to the temple, young witch and feline familiar. I am Alicia, the second priestess," an old woman in a dark blue tunic said as she approached us.

"I'm Nicole, and my familiar is called Lucky. We need the Goddess' protection. Can we stay here?" I asked, fidgeting with my shirt as my other hand rested on my belly almost protectively.

"Of course. All daughters of Nyx are welcome here. I will show you to your room," she said, taking my hand in hers. Her soft and warm touch brought me a spark of peace, and I followed her upstairs. "I hope you find the strength and clarity you need here in our temple. We were expecting you, so the room is ready," she told me, opening the door to a small but comfortable room with a sea view.

"Did the Goddess tell you that we were coming?" Lucky asked the priestess; she had been remarkably quiet on the way here. I knew that it was because she missed Burbus, Alev, and the clan. Her heart was broken as well.

Priestess Alicia smiled at Lucky, not seeming the least surprised that my cat could talk.

"Yes. The Goddess talked to me this morning. Nicole, you are still to be reunited with an essential missing part of

290

yourself. Once you are whole, listen to your deepest heart and connect to the roots of your magic, and you will be able to hear the Goddess as well. For now, rest while I ask someone to bring you some food, water and herbal tea with the best Greek honey." Priestess Alicia gave us a small smile before she left the room. Her words echoed in my soul. I felt exactly how she had described me, torn, incomplete, broken.

"No four-poster bed, but this place will do," Lucky said as she looked around. "The Goddess is good, and I already feel safe here. No toxic men like Kadmus can touch us in the home and heart of a powerful kickass woman like Nyx! I only wish they accepted orange male cats and dragons too. But nothing is perfect, right? Now I am down for a nap. I will try to sleep off my sadness, and you, my witch, should do the same. If you keep crying, no elemental water magic will save your butt, and you will end up with severe dehydration," she added, lying on the bed and yawning.

Placing our luggage on the dresser, I also lay on the bed, and without even noticing, I fell into a deep sleep.

I entered the ample room, my long blue tunic dragging on the floor. My eyes met Vasilis', and a nervous smile formed on my face. I could feel the anticipation building in my stomach.

"Vasilis, I did something crazy with the help of the women from your cousin's harem. Good crazy, I hope," I told him, chewing on the inner part of my lips.

Letting my tunic fall from my shoulders, I exposed my breasts and the golden ornaments decorating my nipples.

"The women told me that it was an old tradition for Golden Dragon royal brides to pierce their nipples with gold and the colours of her mate's family," I told Vasilis.

Vasilis' eyes fixed on my bejewelled chest. He was looking at me as if I were the Goddess herself. His golden eyes were pure lust, love, and adoration.

291

He ran his fingers across the delicate jewel; first, the two rings hanging on my nipples, then the golden thread in between them. It carried a golden pendant with an emerald and some kind of emblem in its centre, a dragon, a crown, and, to my astonishment, a fish.

The gorgeous man went down to his knees, wrapping his muscular arms around my hips and pulling me closer to him.

"No one has done it in the last couple of centuries. It's a great honour for me, Eos, to have you wearing these jewels. You look more beautiful than the sun and the moon."

Wait, why did Vasilis call me Eos? I was completely lost until I realised it was a dream and something I couldn't control. The woman in Vasilis' arms was both me, Nicole, and Eos. Inexplicably, I could feel everything Eos felt, and in the mysterious way of dreams, I was her. I was his Eos.

Eos giggled, going to her knees as well and kissing her man with urgency, love, and need.

"Azula is fluttering around my soul. He is even making water bubbles! I didn't know it was possible! You make us both impossibly happy, Agapiti," he told her between kisses.

That word, Agapiti, I knew it somehow, even though I wasn't sure where I remembered it from. It meant beloved.

"The women also said that Golden Dragons like to see their beloved covered with gold, silk, and jewels, but the piercing of one's body was even a step further, some sort of vow of eternal love. That's what I feel for you, my Prince. Now our love is imprinted in my body, not only in one but in two ways."

"Yes, in each nipple," he agreed, his eyes once again roaming to the sensual jewels.

Eos giggled, throwing her head back. I could feel her joy in my heart as if it were my own. Vasilis' eyes were entranced by the golden rings hanging from her nipples.

292

"That's not what I mean, my Love. I have a second surprise: I'm pregnant!" she smiled.

"It's a miracle, a gift from the Gods! I didn't know our love could have fruits, Agapiti mou Eos.*"

"Maybe our love is a source of miracles!" Eos' smile was radiant, and streams of tears ran down her face as she giggled.

Vasilis also looked like he was in the seventh heaven, crying, and chuckling. Then he finally captured her lips with his.

"Maybe now my father won't be a danger to you anymore, Agapiti," he said, looking into her eyes, his gaze filled with hope. Yet Eos didn't share his hope. She sighed, and I could feel her fear make my body colder.

"The Golden King won't ever accept having a half-breed grandkid. Especially not a half-witch child. You know what happened when he found out I wasn't your whore but that we were in love. He tried to make you get rid of me and threatened me many times. I am afraid for this baby, for you and myself, my Love. I can't die, I can't lose you both, I can't lose myself and this love."

Waking up with a start, I sat up and placed a hand on my belly.

"The magic of this place evokes powerful dreams, Nicole. You will have time to think about your dreams and memories to fully understand them," the priestess told me as she covered my chilly body with a wool blanket. "Go back to sleep and get yourself ready to listen to the Goddess in everything. She is the night, the moon, the sky. She is both life and death. I can see you are sad, and the stain of tears has marked your face, but trust me, you are here because it's the place you are supposed to be. You have to find yourself, dear girl," Priestess Alicia added with a smile before my eyes closed again, and I drifted back to sleep.

CHAPTER 46
Kadmus

After opening a portal, I arrived at the dragons' hideout. Locating the place wasn't hard at all. As a trustworthy member of the Warlock Society, I had my connections, and no one would hesitate to tell me anything, anything I asked for.

Nicolai followed me like a shadow. The sneaky Lycan Prince depended on me the same way I depended on him to achieve our mutual goals, and our time was running short.

"Where are they? I can't smell anything," Nicolai hissed.

"They left," I growled.

"We need to attack my rivals soon. You told me we could use the witch and the dragons' powers, and now we have nothing! We have no time, Kadmus! If we don't act, we will lose the upper hand. *You* have to fix this!" the entitled piece-of-shit Lycan nagged. If I didn't need him, I would have hit him with a bolt of lightning by now.

"I will find a way. Go and take care of your part of the deal!" I told him, and shaking his head, he left the house and slammed the door behind him.

"Animal!" I spat. Nicolai and I had to act fast in order to overtake the Lycan King's throne. At first, I believed I had enough power for the enterprise, but quickly realising who my enemies were, I understood that I needed extra time. I needed Nicole and the Golden Dragons under my control!

Walking across the living room, I clenched my hands into fists. I couldn't feel their magic; they were indeed gone. My little bitch disobeyed my orders and told the dragons to leave. I suspected something like it when she didn't answer my call this morning.

A wisp of smoke left my clenched fists as anger radiated through me.

"Nicole, you will pay for your disobedience. I will find you and subdue you. You are mine, and it's high time you accept your fate." I sent my threat into the wind, knowing it would reach her and strike fear into her soul, making her tremble as she should. I was tired of her defiance, and this little act of rebellion would cost her a lot.

Nicole, Nicole... a frown and a smirk found their way to my lips. She was enraging and amusing! A rare creature that I had to possess; not many could resist the seduction of darkness, but she sure was strong.

Striding around the house, I looked for clues as to where they could have gone. She cared about these dragons, and I knew that the sunlight that insisted on remaining in her could end up ruining my plans for now.

Unlike her sister, the younger witch was always impossible to control. Dark magic and power didn't seduce her as they normally did to outcasts like her. Darkness could never touch her. Even with her soul crushed and her hopes dead, she still held a raw fire in her soul.

I had my suspicions of why; that dragon within her soul whispered in her mind and made her see further and think higher. As soon as I stripped her of him and took everything from her, she would crumble at my feet and give me what I wanted.

I couldn't kill Meghan as I needed that harpy's blood to locate Nicole and constantly remind her how close I was. Yet, I could always torture Meghan, make her scream, and pay for all of their sins. It wouldn't be enough though, since the Lycan Prince and I had no time to lose! I needed more power, and I needed it now.

Taking the vial with Meghan's blood from my bag, I opened it and covered my hands with the crimson fluid, chanting the dark spell under my breath.

"I call you through your blood; through your life,
and the magic I now hold.
Feel my rage plaguing your veins.
All your hope it shall drain.
Dark blood cursed within her veins,
do now as I please; tell me where she is."

"Nicole!" A scream of rage broke through my lungs as I realised I couldn't reach her. I could hardly feel her.

Nicole

I woke up to the sunlight entering the circular window and the soothing sound of the waves. The temple made me feel a little better and closer to myself and my dreams.

"Thank you, Nyx," I said under my breath, looking up.

"Yes, I slept like a baby. Maybe it was because I dreamt about babies. I almost feel like someone who didn't have her heart broken," Lucky sighed. She missed Burbus, Alev and the clan a lot, too.

I couldn't remember the details of my dreams, only the sweet feeling of love. Vasilis was there once again, and I

297

could still feel his love on my skin, making my heart flutter and healing my soul a little. He felt good and warm. He felt like… Alev.

Shaking my head, I stood up and headed to the small adjoining bathroom, where I got ready for the new day. I had to be strong and take care of myself well for the next few months. It was the best thing I could do for my baby, a way to love and nurture her.

As I walked back to the room, I came across Priestess Alicia again. She smiled at me and placed a tray of food on the shelf.

"The priestesses have already eaten, so I brought you something," she said and motioned to the toast with tomatoes and basil on top, and the cup of tea. "Now all you need is a little love, magic, and fresh tomatoes."

"Thank you, Alicia… oh, sorry. Priestess Alicia." I cast my gaze down. The woman was the second priestess in the temple; I had to treat her with due reverence.

"You can call me Alicia or Alice. A soul has many names, dear Nicole." She gave me a small smile and left. Something about her and her words felt so familiar. It was so odd, but coming to this place felt like coming home to a certain extent.

I looked at Lucky, who was busy enjoying her dry food and milk, meowing like a little kitten. She could tell me whatever she wanted, but I was quite sure she was expecting. A sigh left me as the icy feeling of guilt made my heart shrink. Lucky should be in the mansion with Burbus now instead of here with me.

After eating, I looked out of the window. I closed my eyes and let the sea breeze caress my skin and give me some comfort. The waves resonated in my ears, filling my whole being. They were calling me; it wasn't a simple call but a pull, flowing from my veins to my Water Elemental magic. Opening my eyes, I saw a thread of water leaving my fingertips. I had to go; I had to be close to the sea.

298

My legs took my absent and almost hypnotised body out of the temple, and only as I reached the beach did I realise that a confused-looking Lucky was following me.

"Cols? Are you possessed or something?" she asked, her eyes wide.

"Maybe I am. I am possessed by this call, this pull, the infinity of the sea before us. Can you feel it?" I asked.

"You know I am allergic to water. Well, except the water that comes from our shared magic." Lucky meowed. I shook my head at her, knowing well that she wasn't allergic to anything. It was only her excuse not to shower every time she got herself covered with mud.

Azula fluttered within my soul and I knew Lucky could feel him too as she released a shocked meow.

"I think my allergy is gone. I am healed, and we have to go; we have to go, now!" she urged me, walking to the water and wetting her paws. My heart beat faster than ever, and I felt a whisper flow from the top of my head to my feet.

I took a lungful of air, letting my tears fall down my cheeks, and my water powers leaked from my fingertips. Priestess Alicia's words came back to me.

"Get ready to listen to the Goddess in everything." The Goddess was there. I could feel her, Nyx and Azula were both trying to show me the way. More than that, something deep inside my heart and soul wanted to find a way back home.

Azula wrapped me in his gentle spirit of both fire and water as Lucky opened the way for us, walking across the sea. To my surprise, the waters parted for her to pass and only came together again after I had followed her.

Closing my eyes for a moment, I allowed myself to feel, and I noticed that my fingers had been working on their own accord; I was the one parting the waters without realising it, only following my instincts, the pull, and my destiny.

"It's here, Nicole," Lucky said, and I nodded. Even without being aware of it, my hands seemed to know what to do, and moving them in a circle, they created a hollow water ball, surrounding Lucky. She raised her tail to show me she was okay. It was her feline version of thumbs up.

Azula enveloped me in his ethereal embrace, and the three of us dove into the water, reaching deep. My eyes blinked over and over as I studied the unknown yet familiar wonder surging before us.

CHAPTER 47
Nicole

Azula, bubble-Lucky, and I landed on the seabed. The site washed me with peace and warmed my heart. I gasped as a spiral of water suddenly came out of the blue and surrounded my legs. The gently swirling water attached itself to my skin like a flowing skirt, giving my movements more fluidity as if the water and I could almost be one.

An unexpected smile formed on my lips, and my wide eyes looked at the high copper-coloured gates. Two tall and bulky men guarded them. My lips opened in a gasp, and I choked on seawater as I looked below their exposed chests. From their waist up, they looked like human men, but to my surprise, they had a lush teal-coloured fishtail instead of legs.

Lucky and I exchanged a surprised look before she shamelessly licked her mouth. Fish was one of her favourite meals.

The two men, or rather Mermen, drifted towards us. Their jaws were tight with suspicion, and everything about them looked rigid, military-like.

"Who are you? Why do you request entrance to our kingdom? What kind of fish do you have in that bubble?" One of them asked, looking between Lucky and me.

"What? Lucky isn't a fish. I didn't request anything," I replied, confused. I didn't even know how I could understand them or even communicate under the water. Nothing made any sense.

"Filus, she resembles the Queen," the other Merman said quietly, staring at me and my shocked face.

"I don't trust anyone without a fin or scales," Filus told his colleague, shaking his head. "You and your fish are coming with us. You have a lot to explain, *tailless* female!" he said, wrapping his hand around my arm. Strangely, Azula was quite calm and didn't do anything about it, which was enough for me to know that these mermen guards didn't pose a threat.

His grip on my arm was firm, but it didn't hurt. To my amazement, as Filus held me, his colleague opened the doors to a beautiful and colourful world. Jellyfish of all colours and shapes danced in a circle, moving so delicately as if made of water itself. Many fish and a few merpeople swam around colourful stone buildings decorated with shells and pearls. Some of them were even luminous, making the place radiate in a prism of colours.

"So beautiful," I hummed. I was enthralled to such an extent that being pulled by guards didn't bother me. My gaze roamed across the merpeople, men and women wearing jewels and stones around their necks and long hair, and moving around by their colourful translucent tails. A beautiful purple-haired mermaid swam in front of me.

My eyes followed the beam of sunlight coming from the surface and passing through the water, reflecting directly on the bright pearl she had on her wrist. The light seemed attracted to it. Looking around, I noticed that each merperson was followed by their own ray of light, and these beams reflected on the wrists. My lips opened in a gasp when I took a better look at the purple-haired woman's wrist and realised it wasn't a bracelet, but part of her.

"Holy Nyx!" I exclaimed as we came close to an enormous castle. The base scintillated with tiny radiant stones and orange, red, and pink coral. My gaze lifted to the top, and it looked like some sort of glass or even a crystal. Beams of light coming from the surface danced around it. Sometimes it looked pink, others purple or blue.

"Here we are!" The guard said as he took me into the castle's large hall.

We crossed a few empty rooms, and the few merfolk we came across gaped at Lucky and me as if we were some kind of freak show. Azula roared at them, releasing a jet of water bubbles and successfully making them look away.

A small smile formed on my lips; the sweet Spirit Dragon was always looking after me.

As soon as we stopped in front of a tall door made of blue crystals, the guard leading the way stared at Lucky and spoke.

"What kind of fish is that? Is it a weirdo from the deep sea, the abyssal zone? My cousin went there once, and he swore he saw a mermaid with five boobs, at least."

"Lucky isn't a fish," I replied, looking at Lucky's huge frown. She seemed very offended by the guard's question.

"I will take the intruders to see one of the High Guardians," another merman said as he swam towards us. In a swift move, he wrapped his hand around my wrist. He gaped at it and frowned. The two guards bowed to him before leaving in a rush.

"We are not intruders," I told him, letting him gently pull me across another hall. Strangely, I didn't worry about him or where he was taking me. The place made me feel at peace. Bubble-Lucky and Azula were following me. Lucky seemed quite startled by pretty much everything we saw, while the Spirit Dragon simply glided around as if he owned the place.

"Harperon, I've heard about our unexpected visitors. I can take it from here," a melodious, sweet, yet powerful female voice said, making the guard turn around and pull me with him. It made me a little dizzy.

"Your Majesty." He bowed to her. As soon as I recovered from my dizziness and blinked twice, I took a good look at Her Majesty.

"How? How was that possible?" I gasped, and my heart almost stopped as I looked at the woman in front of me.

Alev

After Alma and her babies settled down in their new nursery, we met in her newly established spell room.

We were still trying to find Nicole to make sure she and Lucky were safe. I had already contacted the Surrogacy Agency. They didn't know anything about Nicole's whereabouts and had even looked for her in her small loft in Dublin without any success. The person responsible for the surrogacy process was so vexed about Nicole's disappearance that she wanted to compensate me for any losses and damages.

Fuck! I didn't want any money, any words, anything but my Darlin' back. I would kiss her lips, love her hard, spank her naughty ass for leaving me rather than asking for help, and then fuck her even harder again.

"Alev," Alma hugged me as soon as I entered the room. Yet, not even the Great Golden Fire flowing within her could bring me any peace now.

With a deep sigh, she took the objects she needed from the wooden shelf.

304

"Alev, as you know, making spells that don't have anything to do with the Golden Fire isn't my forte, but I will try anyway. We have excellent runes, which gives us a much better chance," she told me as she set a circle of salt on the floor. Alma placed a rune, a map, and the blue scarf Nicole left behind in the centre of it. She hadn't even taken all her things when she left.

"This is Laguz, the rune of water and love. I think that's pretty much the most related thing to you and Nicole I can think of," Alma explained, showing me the blue rune and I nodded. I was half-determined and half-numb, my heart still trying to process all the pain and loss.

"Alev, I believe in my soul and in my fire that you both will find a way," Alma reassured me, placing her small hand on mine, and once again, I only nodded.

Alma sat in the centre of the circle of salt and took the rune in one hand and Nicole's scarf in the other.

"Nicole, let the wind, let the water, and let the fire of this immense desire and love find you. Show me where you are," she chanted under her breath, closing her eyes.

Beams of Spirit Fire left Alma's fingertips, slowly intertwining with the blue energy flowing from the rune. My eyes opened wide, and hope built in my chest as the golden blue thread of magic surrounded the map. Except it remained there, on the edge, for painfully long minutes, not going anywhere while Alma chanted the words over and over.

Alma opened her eyes and sighed, wiping her drenched forehead with her hands. She looked exhausted and even pale. Before I could help her, the door of the spell room slammed open and Egan burst into the room, taking his wife in his arms.

"Little Ruby, I felt your exhaustion and desperation. It's time for you to rest in my arms, recover your breath and your fire," Egan told Alma, cupping her face gently.

Alma smiled at Egan and kissed him before turning her head to look at me.

"I didn't find her. The spell worked, but I didn't find Nicole or the Spirit Dragon she can summon. Something overpowering must be blocking it. However, there was one thing I could feel through Azula's soul, and that was that she was safe, Alev. We will find her. Don't lose hope," Alma reassured me.

Egan gave me a look of sympathy, patting my shoulder.

"We won't give up, Alev. Your chosen mate will be back where she belongs!" Egan added before scooping his Alma into his arms and leaving the room.

Exhaling deeply, I headed to Marion's room to ask her to teleport me to Marbella. I didn't care about the risks. I had to go back to the mansion in Marbella and be there in case Nicole returned. It was the only place she could find me.

Horus roared in contentment. He, too, hoped and believed with all his fire and soul that our Darlin' would come back.

Acknowledgment

I would like to thank my husband, the love of my life, for all his patience, affection, and help during this long process.

Many thanks to my brilliant editors: Kemely Parfrey, Zita Low, Matthew Spades, and Renae Ballantyne for helping and reassuring me. They had to deal with a short deadline and an anxious writer, yet they weren't anything but solicitous, and delivered excellent work on polishing the manuscript.

Thanks to the outstanding and loving ladies that have been with me through this journey. I couldn't have made it without you, Arielle Lavecchia, Nichole, Kemy, Myranda, Hali, Julia, Caro, Pri, Ljilj and Emily. Behind — or better said, beside — every woman making her dreams come true (aka a panicking writer) is a great team of supporting women. Especially to Arielle and Hali, who, with great sensibility, played a fundamental role in the improvement of this book-baby. They both were a great source of inspiration.

I also would like to thank Kemy for helping me write the "About the Author" section.

I am not thanking my bunny rabbit, since she still hasn't accepted the fact that she isn't an editor and insisted on changing the manuscript a few times. Get over it, Mel!

ABOUT THE AUTHOR

T. R. Durant is a young author very dedicated to her craft, with over ten completed books. This daring novelist is now transitioning into the world of self-publishing.

Our lawyer-turned-author, whose passion for character profiles of the stories she grew up reading and creating, drove her to study psychology. She has always believed in love and magic and used to lose herself in the verses and rhythm of poetry.

Having lived in eight different countries, she is currently based in Europe, and you will always find her on https://linktr.ee/trdurant.

.

Printed in Great Britain
by Amazon

15289463R00181